USELESS
COWBOY

Center Point
Large Print

**This Large Print Book carries the
Seal of Approval of N.A.V.H.**

ALAN LeMAY

USELESS COWBOY

CENTER POINT PUBLISHING
THORNDIKE, MAINE

This Center Point Large Print edition
is published in the year 2002 by arrangement with
Golden West Literary Agency.

The text of this Large Print edition is unabridged.
In other aspects, this book may vary from the original
edition. Printed in Thailand. Set in 16-point
Times New Roman type by Bill Coskrey.

ISBN 1-58547-104-6

Library of Congress Cataloging-in-Publication Data

LeMay, Alan, 1899-1964.
    Useless cowboy / Alan LeMay.-- Center Point large print ed.
    p. cm.
    ISBN 1-58547-104-6 (lib. bdg. : alk. paper)
    1. Large type books. I. Title.

PS3523.E513 U84 2002
813'.54--dc21

                                        2001042130

❧ 1 ❧

A t least once in the life of nearly every man the world quietly hauls off and goes lunatic—not in a general hell-for-breakfast stampede, but in a personal, single-action sort of way that is bewildering. Things happen to him without cause or sense, and people's actions become those of crazy people; and this may go on without let-up for a long time. It is as if the law of gravity failed, and left a fellow walking about the ceiling, unable to get down. And everybody looks at him as if he were nuts.

What has probably happened is that some simple bit of misinformation has thrown the victim out of step. A single missing fact is enough to start it off. But before the thing is over, what with one thing leading to another, a man can lose his mind, or his life, or get himself talked about.

Melody Jones and his side-rider, George Fury, had not expected to wind up in Payneville. They had meant to ride to Hot Creek, down near the Mexican border; but some miscalculation in crossing the Red Cloud plains had got them into a wrong pass through the Wolf Ears, causing a miss of nearly one hundred dusty miles.

Consequently, as they rounded the shoulder of some mountain—it later turned out to be Big Bone Ledge— they were rocked in their saddles by the sight of a size-able town immediately below. It stood out clearly in the hot bright light, a straggling disorder upon vast ragged plains. Its roofs of grey weathered shakes shone like metal in the hard smash of the sun.

To the best of their belief, they were a full two days' ride from any place where a town could possibly be.

Old George Fury looked surprised. The town was big enough to hold several hundred people, and it gave George a creepy sense of insecurity to see it appear out of nowhere. He put his hand over his eyes and rubbed them a little, but when he looked again it was still there, shimmering dustily in the sun.

Melody didn't look any special way. At twenty-two he was lanky and relaxed, and looked four years younger than his age. He was very seldom surprised, for he never expected any one particular thing, but took unexplained events as they came.

"I should judge she's a cow town," Melody said. "I can tell by the corrals."

George Fury snorted. Corrals or not, the town could not possibly have been anything else. "You plumb astound me," he said.

Melody shrugged. "Them things is easy for me."

George Fury knew himself to be over fifty years old, but had quit counting, not liking to think about this. He was spare and rope-necked, with a mustache something like a dead mouse, and gimlety eyes, sun-faded to an indiscriminate eye-color. One shoulder was higher than the other, and he sat crookedly in his saddle, limping as he rode.

"It beats hell out of me how she come here," George Fury said, staring at the town.

"I mind one night I rode into Salice," Melody said, "and it was right where I thunk it was, and all, only some way I come into it from the east, instead of from the west. Feller don't live that can figger them things through."

George Fury turned in the saddle with great deliberation. "For God sakes, shut up," he said. He studied his partner slowly, with a sort of resignation. Melody's face was smooth leather from perpetual wind and sun, varied with sleet, frost-bite, and blowing sand; it was lopped over by a bronco mop of sandy hair, which he barbered himself, because of some bad experiences with original-minded cowboys who had kindly cut it for him. His idly wandering eyes were slit-squinted from the desert glare, but in the shade were uncommonly mild, and brightly blue, as if lighted by an unjustified inner hope.

"And don't start in with that Gar' damn singing again, neither," George Fury added. "I don't aim to stand for it."

Melody could not carry a tune, so of course liked to sing, but he did not get his name from this. His real name was Melvin, and this had got changed to Melody at Javelina, Texas, where the Rio Grande draws the wandering border with Mexico. The Mexican people could not pronounce Melvin, seemingly; by the time they were through batting it around it was nearer Melody than anything else. Jones did not object; the north-trail cowboys could not pronounce Javelina, either. They called it Musk Hog.

George Fury snorted again, and pushed his shaggy pony down the twist of the trail toward the town which he did not yet know was Payneville.

Payneville was a crossing town. A wagon route west from Diamond Forks to California crossed the river here, and trail herds of cattle, pushing north to the railroad, forded the same shallows. The river was the Poisonberry, hell-dry in summer and a howling flood in the spring. An early trader had named it the Strawberry, because he wished he had some, but later wagoners watched their Conestogas tumble end over end in the spring rise, and changed the name. Nobody ever sang any songs about moonlight on the silvery Poisonberry, rolling on, ever on, to Syrup Creek.

Up on Payneville's Boot Hill there is still a sandstone slab marking the grave of this town's founder, and carved upon it, perhaps by an enemy, are his alleged last words: "Thank God I am a Payne . . ."

As they drew closer, riding between the bones of vanished buffalo, Payneville looked dustier, and more ramshackle. They entered the town through a drift of ruined huts, stared at by mestizo children; and turned at a slow plod into Court Street. Melody was riding more watchfully now, made alert, in spite of himself, by George Fury's nervousness.

He consciously stiffened his face. Melody Jones had a secret ambition to earn the title of "Unsmiling Jones," and command immediate respect wherever he appeared. Whenever he rode into a new cow camp he remembered this for an hour or two, and preserved as rigid an expression as he could.

George Fury glanced sideways at him. "What in hell's the matter with you? You got your snoozle snubbed up like you was going to bawl."

Melody modified his expression somewhat, as well as he could.

He also had an idea that he ought to ride into a town

"looking neither to right nor left," but he only thought he did his. His restless eyes were everywhere, self-conscious in the strange surroundings. He gave no notice to the dust that floated up from the trampled street, gritty in the corners of their mouths, and powdering their eyelashes white, but he took note of a thousand other things. After the long winds of the plains and hills Melody could hear every human movement in two blocks of street.

Melody had originally started out from Two Lance, Montana, at fourteen or fifteen, on the occasion of his father being rolled on by a cow in Montana's rustlers' war; but the wandering cow-trails he had followed had been pretty shy of people. Nearly everything he knew about people he had learned from horses and cows, and that was his trouble. Every mortal soul was a personal uncertainty; unaccustomed eyes bothered him like flies. George Fury was looking for the first saloon, and to see what the scat houses looked like, but Melody's eyes took in all details equally, whether they had any meaning or not.

He estimated the amount of jerky hanging up in a Mexican outdoor beanery, and his cattle-counting eye told him there were forty-seven strips about a yard long. He saw a camp-robber jay steal some frijoles from a sleeping Mexican. Just beyond the beanery stood the first bar, which was beginning to moult its silver-grey clapboards—the oldest building in town. But the builder had misjudged the future center of town, and now found himself at the foot of the street; so that this was naturally called the First Chance on one side of its sign, and Last Chance on the other.

George Fury, who sometimes took four days to pass a given saloon, would not get any farther, just yet. He turned his pony to the hitch rail and swung down rustily; and Melody Jones was freeing himself from the saddle, on which he seemed to have melted and stuck, when a girl came on to the street.

Melody didn't see where she came from; as he looked up she was there. He couldn't see her face, because she was walking away from him, down the unmended boardwalk, but he forgot George Fury, and lost interest in the First Chance Bar. Melody hadn't seen a white girl in nearly seven months.

"Now what?" George grunted.

"Huh?" A casual wind-devil kicked a twirl of dust into Melody's face; he dug at his eyes with buckskin knuckles, and sat there like a fool.

"Froze to thet hull?"

"Who, me?" Melody sounded vague and senseless. "Well, I—I—I feel kind of like a can tomaters."

"You *look* something like a can tomaters," George criticized.

"Never you mind," Melody said. "I'm going on down to the store."

George Fury looked at Melody queerly, and started to say something. He knew that Melody had no money in his pants; all they had between them was a few dollars George had managed to keep hold of. It was in his mind to holler after Melody, and give him a buck. But he smothered this idea, and went into the First Chance, rolling creakily on his run-over high heels.

Melody pushed his dopy pony on up the street,

through the soft dust. He was following the girl along with an innocent detachment that would have killed George Fury. He was like a dog who goes walking with a stranger, never looking directly at his companion, never getting near, but drawing a sort of undemanding comfort from the vague association of time and place.

Besides watching the girl, he saw that the boards of the Occidental's sign were splitting in the sun, and that an Apache Indian, asleep full length on the walk before the Grand Eastern Hotel, was drawing flies. The few shaggy ponies along the hitch-rails were saddled with center-fire and three-quarters rigs, hung with rawhide reatas, so he knew he was among the dally-men again. This touched him with a faint contempt a cowman commonly feels for any way of riding but his own. Melody was a double-rig, tie-fast man.

Far down the street a dog fight was going on. It kept up, with more dogs joining in all the time, until a razor-back hog came out from under the boardwalk and chased the dogs away.

The girl went into the Lost Dutchman Saloon.

The wind went out of Melody, so definitely that his pony took advantage of him and stopped. Melody sat where he was for a moment or two before he started it again.

"Got a right to get thirsty, ain't she?" he explained her to himself. "Why in hell shouldn't she get thirsty? Nuts."

He angled across the dust to the General Store, and tossed his reins loose across the rack. The pony's name was Harry Henshaw, according to Melody, and he had been with Melody long enough to learn that he had better stand, lest a worse thing happen next. Harry Henshaw toed in a little on the nigh side, and didn't look like much; and because of this he was the only pony, out of the scores Melody had owned, that nobody had bothered to get away from Melody.

As Melody went up the steps to the store's broad gallery he was wary and watchful again. Two men, a big one and a little one, loafed on the gallery, just outside the door. Both wore low-strapped forty-fives, the same as Melody himself, except that Melody's was in the thigh pocket of his ragged shot-gun chaps. They wore the easy clothes of cowmen, but that did not necessarily prove what they were.

Melody stiffened his face. The shorter man met his eyes briefly, an impersonal, cool flick of pinched pupils. The other didn't look at him at all, so Melody was able to study him better—a man long-geared but compact, with an expressionless face of deep-carved jack pine. His eyes were awake but lazy, like the flat side of a knife.

While Melody looked at him, the man's eyes changed, then the whole face. The eyes sharpened to a quick focus, not on Melody, but across the street; and it was as if the sleepy knife had turned point first and sung past Melody's ear.

Melody turned slowly on his high heel, feet apart to clear his long-shanked spur, and followed the man's eyes, It was like Melody thought. The girl had come out of the Lost Dutchman. Not thirsty after all. Looking for somebody.

The man by the door was whistling through his teeth, a stanza of "Chizzum Trail." It might have been the part about the night stampede, or the last of the Old Two-Bars; but Melody knew better. Unhurriedly, but with no trace of thought at all, Melody took two long, strolling steps, and knocked the stranger down.

He used the heel of his right hand, without closing his fist; he had understood that wallop for a long time. The heel of a hand, swung full-arm, packs nearly the same weight as a fist; but afterward, you get credit for downing your man with a slap of the open hand. A good thing to have said of you, especially if the other man wasn't looking, as now.

The stranger's hat flew off, and his head spun sideways, slamming against the board front with a boom that shook the store. Inside the wall some tinware fell down, quicker to fall than the man who was struck. After the tinware's first crash some more of it fell more slowly, so that the occasional clatter of a pie tin or a bread pan kept sounding at irregular intervals for some time.

The man himself half buckled at the knees, his face a blank amazement. He slid sideways against the wall, and came down sitting on his hat.

Melody stood watching the fellow shake his head and feel out the workings of his jaw, and Melody had never been worse dumbfounded in his life. The astonishment of the man he had hit was nothing, alongside his own. Melody was estimating now the exact distance, in thousandths of a second, between the stranger's hand, slackly palm up on the floor of the gallery, and the black butt of the stranger's gun, already half out of its leather by its own weight. It was no better than three inches away, or possibly three and a half. The hand didn't look like a cowman's hand—more like a bunch of bananas, really, but that is just the kind that knows its business, very often. Melody was beginning to sweat a little now.

Up from the wooden face the stranger's eyes were looking at Melody like a couple of cactus buds. Melody stooped and got a grip on the gun arm with both hands, his head canted to bounce off a possible crusher from the stranger's left. The arm was tense and ridged, made of wagon tires, or something. Melody pretended to help the other up, half hauling him to his feet, but keeping him off balance; and he began to talk as fast as he could, which was a kind of a loping drawl.

"Well, now," Melody said, "that's sure too bad. How come that? Your foot slip, you reckon?" He hoped afterward that he had sounded gruff and hard, but he remembered pretty clearly that he had stumbled along in a sort of a thin bleat.

In the brief seconds while he had the fellow out of action, he was able to snatch a glance at the shorter man. This other one had jumped away from the wall, to be out of the line of fire. He was talking now, quick and low, through a tight throat, with lips that hardly moved.

"Don't, Ira—easy, Ira—look out, Ira—"

But while he talked to Ira he was looking at Melody Jones; and the astounded fixity of his eyes was nothing like anybody had favored Jones with before.

Melody's eyes snapped back to the man he was holding on to for the love of life, and they looked into each other's faces at a distance of five inches and a half. At this range Melody noticed for the first time that the man was cross-eyed.

"Okay," this Ira was saying. "Okay, okay." When he spoke he smelled of niggerhead eating-tobacco, with a suggestion of sloe gin eye-opener taken hours before. The tone was thick and faintly breathless, surprisingly small. In the crossed eyes was the same weird look of surprise that Melody had seen in the eyes of the shorter man.

In the brief silence one more tin pan fell on the floor inside the store, settling noisily on its circular rim—kawowmp, kawowmp, dithery-dithery, until it revolved to rest.

"I didn't say nothing, or nothing," Ira said now, without any expression.

Suddenly Melody Jones realized he had hold of a man who was in fear of his life.

Melody eased back, relaxing slowly. Before he let go altogether he let his right hand fall on the butt of his own forty-five, in the forward pocket of his chaps, as if just to rest his hand. A fast man could still have got him handily, but probably wouldn't try.

Looking steadily at each other the two edged apart with casual, furtive shufflings, circling a little, Ira toward the gallery steps. As the inches between them increased, the man called Ira no longer appeared cross-eyed; he looked competent again.

"I'll stand a drink," he said.

Slow thinking saved Melody, then. In a moment he would have said, "Whut? Whut did you say?"

But as the seconds ticked away, and still nothing in Melody's head found its way into words, time and tension were too much for the other man.

"No offense," he said, with the dust heavy in his

throat. "Any time. Any time at all . . ."

Melody surprised himself again. "Keep the slack out o' your rope, from here in," he said, his voice flat. "And don't whistle no tunes at other men's girls."

Anger jumped into the stranger's eyes, like a flash of gunpowder, scaring the living daylights out of Melody again. For one short moment he thought that the incredible miracle which had saved his life was about to run out.

What he did then was pure instinct. He let his hand slide from his gun grip so idly that it expressed contempt; and he turned on his heel, slowly, toward the door of the store, putting his back to the enemies he had made. The muscles of his back tightened, expecting the possible blast that would tear out his spine. But it didn't come.

Over the door he saw the crude board sign that had been there long before slow prosperity built the wooden awning above it:

PAYNEVILLE
GEN'L STORE
Peter Abajian

"So that's where I am . . ." He walked into the cool shadows within. His shoulders rose stiffly as he pulled down his vest—a cowhide vest with more than twenty cattle brands burned on it, showing where-all he had been.

Deep back in the dim interior the little proprietor put up his hands. Peter Abajian was behind a counter, and flanked by hangings of blue jeans, stable forks, dried stock-fish, sheepskin coats, and Navajo saddle blankets. His round cheeks, always apparently blown full of wind, shone like billiard balls. His buffalo-horn mustache quivered, and his eyes were like agates.

Melody looked at him curiously. He had never seen people act like these people acted. His eyes left the storekeeper to run along the canned-goods shelves. He hadn't told the man to put his hands down, but after a moment the corner of his eye caught their wary motion as they descended. Melody jerked his head around, and the hands flew up again.

He tried this several times more, experimentally making sure that he was the one who controlled this thing. He stole a look at the street, and saw that it was empty.

"One can tomaters," Melody said.

Peter Abajian set it out, and stood watching Melody unhappily. Melody was thinking. He knew he didn't have any money. What blistered Melody was that he had saved his money for nearly three years, planning one magnificent bust some day, and he had built up nearly seventy-six dollars. And then he had lost it—not in a card game, not in any particular way—just plainly lost it, out of his pocket or something, some place. He and George Fury had argued many a mile over who had seen it last, and what happened to it. All they knew about it was that it was gone.

Now, after a month of bean diet, Melody was asking himself if canned goods were worth getting in trouble for. He decided that they were. At worst, the cooking at the jail ought to compare favorably to George Fury's. "One can peaches," Melody went on, "one can pork beans, one can pears, one can plum pudding, and another can tomaters."

"Yes, sir!" Peter Abajian moved with alacrity now, but kept his hands fluttering in view. "All in a nice gunny seck, maybe?"

"Eat 'em here."

Sitting on the counter, eating his cool wet canned goods, Melody Jones tried to fit himself into a world that was like a dream.

A slouching cowboy with a saddened, sandy mustache came in and pawed around in a box of harness buckles near the door. He kept sneaking glances at Melody over his shoulder. Then he realized that Melody was staring at him. He turned suddenly confused, and pottered out of there.

Two more cowboys and a man in a black suit came to the edge of the door and peered in at Melody, trying to look accidental, and missing eleven miles. When Melody Jones looked at them they went away.

"What the hell goes on here?" Melody said aloud.

The storekeeper's hands started up again, but he stopped them. He smiled at Melody in a sickly way, without meeting his eye.

It was time to face the issue. Melody supposed he ought to glare at the storekeeper, but he couldn't make it. He studied the side of his boot as he said, "How much?" The words came out in a thin squeak, so that he had to try again; but he managed to get a good harsh growl the second time.

"Nothing!" The little storekeeper said instantly, even eagerly. "It's a pleasure. Nothing at all."

"Whut?"

"It's free," Peter Abajian said quickly. "All free to a

nice gentleman like you."

Slowly, but with no real change of expression, Melody sat down on the counter again. He was trying to tell himself that it was true, that there was bound to come a time in each man's life when at last he got appreciated. People who know you too well always think back to when you was a kid. They kind of pass your kid reputation along from hand to hand, like when some old horse on a ranch is known all his life as the Colt. . . . It took new strangers to see you like you really was. Unsmiling Jones. . . .

Then Melody saw the girl again.

She walked along the gallery of the store from the steps at the end. She passed the door very slowly, looking in as she passed. There was something both tense and lazy, very proud, in her straight-kneed step, impossible to forget. He could see that there were straw-dull finger-curls, loose and carelessly kept, down the sides of her face. But against the eye-knocking white blaze of the street her face was in shadow. He couldn't see it at all.

When she had walked past slowly, and did not come back, Melody drank some juice of the canned pears from the ragged edge of the can, but his rolled eyes held sideways on the door as he drank, like a spooky bronc's.

"Dunno but maybe I might settle here," he said aloud; and the storekeeper made a bubbling noise in his throat.

❧ 2 ❧

After putting Melody out of his mind, George Fury rolled stiffly, hoop-legged, into the First Chance Bar.

Inside the door he came to a stop with a waspish dignity, and gave the conventional hitch to his breeches, while his eyes accustomed themselves to the shade. What he saw was the usual barroom, with a stuffed squirrel at one end of the back bar and a stuffed owl at the other end; and the bar itself so battered and scraped down that it had a sway-backed look. The oak foot-rail was worn half through.

After he had blinked, duck-like, for a minute or two, George turned his attention to the only two customers already at the bar—a couple of workless cowhands by their look, propped near the door. George looked them over with leisure.

Then he addressed himself to the nearer, putting on an expression intended to be friendly but remote. It was the shape and build of George Fury's face that made this seldom-used expression look different, from in front, than he intended. Instead of looking genial, but reserved, George looked vapid but insolent. But George never knew this; and it partly accounted for the awkwardness which always came between George and strangers.

"Where am I?" George asked.

The two cowmen looked at George Fury; then, with considerable deliberation, they looked at each other, their faces unreadable as sourdough bricks. Presently both looked at the bartender, who washed glasses in a bucket and minded his own business. And finally they turned to George again.

"This yere's Payneville," said the man addressed, with constraint.

George Fury took a deep breath, and his Adam's apple

jumped. "Painful," he snapped. "*What's* painful?"

"This yere is," the other said.

George looked both men over with angry care. The guns they wore looked well-oiled, their holsters well-soaped and well-used. He was aching for trouble, made irritable by the dust in his throat and the strangeness here. But George Fury had a poor opinion of his gunplay. Rheumatism in his fingers had made it as inept as Melody's own.

So he only walked past them now, but slowly, stiff-legged, like a bristling dog. "O-o-oh," he said half to himself, but in a tone of sarcastic insult. "Painful, is it?"

"Right—Payneville!"

George Fury snorted like a jumped buck, but he knew he had said enough. He took up a stand well down the bar.

"Forty-rod," he told the bartender. "From the bar'l with the snake-haid in it."

The bartender set out bottle and glass with the relaxed impersonality of practice. "How long," he spoke to George Fury courteously, "how long you been in Payne?"

George choked explosively in the middle of his first gulp. He slapped his glass down on the bar with such a ringing crack that the whisky jumped clean clear of the rim, then sloshed back in again.

When George lost his temper his dialect changed, slipping back to the far hills of his youth. "Naow, yew looky yare!" he spluttered, his voice up an octave. "Ga-a-ar' dammit! If yew fellers cain't answer a civilus question civilus, yew anyways daon't need to git new! I don't aim to stand fer it!"

The bartender looked at him tiredly. He was used to men with sun-sore nerves, drunken at that. He shrugged and went back to his glasses.

George was enraged, not mollified. "And daon't yew go sneakin' off when I'm speakin' to yew!" he shouted. "Ga-a-ar' dammit! I otter snatch yew out o' thet! I otter bewst this yare cheap stagger-mill inter the raoad!"

Except for George's voice, quiet fell. It was an interesting quiet, loaded and primed. George would have noticed that silence in an instant, and understood it, if it had been created by anyone but himself.

"I've seen taowns an' taowns, all the way from Medicine Boaw to Tewsday," George shouted, "an' I never see no sech dump as this dump yare, an' no sech stinky salewn!"

George noticed, then. The bartender's towel was motionless, and his eyes were on George with a sort of ironic pity. The other customers were watching him too, as expressionless as disused glass eyes. The quiet had come to full cock. George Fury let his voice trail off, and took a slow glance over his shoulder.

A pale, heavy man, six feet tall in Comanche moccasins, had come forward from a back table. He stood looking at George with small eyes without eyebrows, from a distance of about a foot.

George Fury turned back to the bar, looking much smaller, and his hollering stopped. He drank his drink slowly, with decorum, and poured himself another. Presently people began to move again. George heard the creak of a floor board behind him as the big man wheeled back to his table. George stayed where he was.

The back of his neck, crisscrossed with deep weather-scorings above his neckerchief, was turkey red. But he was too stubborn to be blasted out of there by any disfavor short of force.

And now as he stood there George Fury became aware that some new public affliction was building itself. Men were trickling into the First Chance by twos and threes. A dozen had wandered in; the bar was well filled. These men were cowmen, passing through or on the loaf, with a sprinkling of plains-bred townsmen who looked about the same. And all these newcomers were interested in George Fury. Low-toned informations ran along the bar, to everyone but George. Men looked him over, studying him with a strange candor he had never seen.

And there was no hostility in all this now. Instead there was a smirking complacency, broken with a disconcerting snickering worse than a plague of fleas. George sneaked a quick examination of his clothes, but couldn't find anything wrong. He craned his neck to see himself in the bit of cracked bar mirror, and between the banked bottles he discovered only that he was purple in the face.

Somebody slapped him hard on the shoulder, and a voice said, "Howdy, Roscoe!"

George Fury turned his head slowly, his eyes alive with death; but the other had moved on. Another newcomer edged toward George along the bar.

"Did you ever find out," he asked George confidentially, "just where the hell you are?"

Once more George Fury choked on his drink, and rang the glass upon the bar. He whirled upon the stranger.

"I'll tell yew one thing, my owl-nosed friend!" he

lashed out. "I ain't in pain!"

A grumble of laughter, rising to a roar, swept the bar-room. George Fury looked astounded. He had realized he had a keen wit, of course, very funny, but not this funny. As the laughter held up his anger died. He stuck his tongue in his cheek, winking largely, and the laughter increased.

George himself began to laugh with the others, and as he laughed they howled. He slapped his thigh with a rope-horny paw, and they laughed fit to collapse in the sawdust. This overwhelming hilarity went on nearly a minute.

Gradually it came to George that they weren't laughing with him after all. His own stiffening laughter died sickly. He stood looking around him in bewilder-ment, stonily brave, yet pathetic, too. In that moment George Fury was an old man, a man who had aged immeasurably in the last half hour.

He did not believe yet that he was insane. Tough-ening years of saddle-leather stood by him now, and saved him from that. He knew, therefore, that this town was crazy. . . .

He spoke to them once more, when the laughter finally ebbed. "What air yew whistle-britched poop-heads laughing at?"

Another howl went up from this. Purple again, glaring glassily, George went stamping out.

At the door he turned impressively for one parting crack, and was instantly called back to the bar to pay for his drinks. Unstrung, he rang a silver dollar on the bar and got out of there, while that insane, unaccountable laughter still rang, beating him about the ears as he fled.

He could not believe what he saw then. Outside, where his pony should have stood, was empty hitch-rail.

Men properly hang for laying hands on another man's horse. Now at last George Fury's gun whipped out. The door of the First Chance was full of people watching him. George let out the rebel long yell, and fired on them point blank.

They ducked back, laughing still, without counteraction or resentment. George Fury's bullets went no place, as far as he could tell. No window broke, and no wood splintered. He might as well have fired straight up.

Perhaps he would have gone in after them then. Perhaps he would have killed three or four of them while his lead lasted, and got himself shot down, and later hanged if he lived. But now Melody Jones was coming along the walk at his long-legged canter—the only man in the West who could spring at an easy stroll.

Jones was hollering at him. George Fury pulled himself together and waited for reinforcements.

☙ 3 ☙

Tch, tch," said Melody Jones. "Drunk so soon. This here's disgraceful."

"Them bastards stole my cayuse," George Fury said. "Ga-a-ar dammit! I aim to clar the town, and give 'er a fresh start, an' she needs it!"

"Nobody stole your moth-et old hide," Melody told him. "I taken and stuck him in the livery corral. Time, too. The old goat ain't seen hay for so long, he spooked at it. Some night you're going to ask him to balance you out of this dump on his top. I want to see your face when you find him so empty he's flat in the road like a sack. In town, you gotta keep stuffin' a hoss. Or he comes unstuffed," Melody said.

"Talk! Talk! Talk!" George wailed. "You git that cayuse back here, and smart quick! Yours, too. We're leavin'!"

"Why?"

"Because this dump is full o' crazy fellers!"

Melody pulled a splinter off a post and picked his teeth with it. He looked unimpressed. "They do somethin'?"

George Fury started to tell Melody what the crazy fellers done. He opened his mouth two or three times, but shut it again. "Ain't fittin'," he mumbled.

"Trouble with you," Melody said impartially, "you don't make no impression on people. Strangers, I mean. Get to know you, a feller realizes you mean well. But that comes slow. You better otter just kind of lay low at first, and let new folks get used to you more gradual."

"Just what," George Fury said in a quivering deep monotone, "just what do you mean by that?"

"Well, for one thing, take that silly lookin' grin you got, when you go in a new place."

"Where's that c'rral?" old George rasped, his mustache trembling. He started striding headlong down the street, lurching on his high heels.

Melody fell in beside him. "You go in some dump," Melody enlarged, "where nobody don't know you, and you pike all around with that half-rump grin; and next maybe you ask some dumb fool question a Comanche papoose could of answer for hisself, like, 'Whut time is she naow?' or, 'Where am I at, anyways?'—and naturally they don't fall flat on their face, or nothin'. *You* otter know that by now."

George Fury gave a low whimper in his throat.

"You got to walk in a new place kind of—unsmiling," Melody said. He hadn't meant to say that. It slipped out on him. He reddened a little. "Like me," he pushed ahead with it. "I ain't said two words in this dump, but already I got a certain standing."

George Fury slowed up, then. He said queerly, "Unsmiling. . . . Unsmiling, you said?"

Melody Jones flinched a little at the sound of that word out loud. "I can walk in any place," he said with mild defiance, "around a dump like this, and clear my own place at the bar. Until they get to know me," he added accidentally. "Before they even know me," he corrected himself.

"Come with me," George Fury said with lethal softness. The dialect was gone now. He had come to a full stop, and now turned Melody back with a grip that held like an eagle's bite. "Come with me," he said again.

Once more George Fury was entering the First Chance—Last Chance, from the way they had now come—an act he would have sworn could never happen in this life or the next. And this time Melody Jones was walking in, a little in front of him.

A little smile was on George Fury's face. He no longer cared what happened to himself. "Unsmiling Jones," he whispered.

Unsmilingly Jones walked slowly into the Last Chance

Bar. His thumbs lay lightly along the upper edge of his belt—the "gunfighter's hook," he had heard. More than ever he was trying to look neither to right nor left, so that his always restless eyes darted here and there in light, quick-glancing strokes. He moved so stiffly in his utter self-consciousness that his heels hardly sounded on the worn boards, even in the sudden stillness. You could hear his left spur ring faintly, though, a tiny, thin bell. . . .

Suddenly George Fury was looking very strange. Not in any way he had looked before. The old weathered face drew taut.

The crowd in the bar had fallen quiet for Melody Jones. They gave back as he walked, making room. They made a broad place for him at the bar.

George Fury came to the empty space beside Melody. But George was not looking at him. His shoulder was turned toward Melody a little, and his eyes were active across all those other faces.

The bartender was whipping out a special long-necked bottle, and his hand was unsteady as he poured. He said, very low, "Your pleasure, gents—" and tossed out a clean glass for George Fury.

"No, thanks," George Fury said, hardly hearing it himself.

Two or three who had drawn back from the bar eased forward now, resuming their places. Melody turned sharply on them—showing off for George Fury—and they fell back again.

Melody swayed over to speak confidentially in George Fury's ear. "Get that sheep look off your old swizzle, will you? You're all right s'long's you're with me. See, now?"

George Fury said, "Come out of here." Melody Jones had never heard him speak so flat and low. "Turn your back, if you have to. But don't tetch no gun. . . ."

Melody looked at George for a little bit; then he slowly drank the deep drink the bartender had poured. "Best liquor I ever et," he said. "Where you get that?"

"I make it," the bartender said, speaking like a child. "Listen—we didn't mean nothing—just the boys having a little fun with Roscoe, here—like you might yourself—"

"Sure," Melody said vaguely. "You don't want nothing?" he said to George.

"Pay and come on," George Fury said. "Now!" As Melody looked at George Fury's face he saw a faint damp sheen, like river-bottom dew, across Fury's forehead. Melody gave in.

"How much?"

"House. On the house. Any time," the bartender said. His words had that strangeness you sometimes hear when a voice does not properly fit the face from which it comes.

Melody looked at him oddly, then turned to follow George, swaggering slowly, his hands in the gunfighter's hook. George Fury let Melody pass, then backed out stiffly, his eyes watchful all over the bar.

"You see," Melody Jones said when they were alone on the boardwalk. "You see?" He looked sidelong at George Fury.

George was looking at Melody with glazed eyes. He was shaking with a minute harsh tremor, like the shifting of sand. "We got to get out of here," he said hoarsely.

"Whut?"

"We fetched up in a loonitical asylum, that's what we done!"

"How's that again?"

"I've knowed fellers that sprung a brain," George Fury said. "But this is the first time I ever see a whole town go high-leppin' crazy like one man!"

"Now George," Melody said uncertainly, "you know *that* cain't be. Ain't no way for how come—is there?"

George tapped Melody's breast-bone with his forefinger. "Loco weed! You've see it crazy up a hoss. Now you've see it crazy up a town!"

Melody thought that over, but he was looking at George queerly now. "They wouldn't eat it," he decided. "Not everybody in town."

"Maybe it got in the flour. Maybe it got threshed right in wholesale."

Melody scratched his chin. "What color?"

"Huh?"

"You figurin' on the white loco, or the blue loco?"

George angered. "Don't you go sassing me," he snapped. "I don't aim to stand fer it! What color! What do I keer what color?" The steam went out of him as quickly as it had risen. His voice was almost plaintive, it sounded so weary and far away. "I want my cayuse," he said. "Gimme my cayuse, with my saddle on him, and two rods head go. That's all I ask of God!"

Melody looked at George steadily for a long time, but finally he said, "Well then, goodbye, George."

George eased to a stop, leaning back on his high heels

as a man leans against a post. He couldn't believe Melody. He said, "You ain't comin'?"

"Uh uh."

"Melody," George said, "you realize I've side-rode you and looked out for you like—like a uncle—for mighty near forty thousand mile?"

Melody's long mild patience crinkled then. "Yeah," he said, "and I realize I topped upwards of forty thousand broncs, while you was settin' behind forty thousand different stoves. Your pony's in the corral behind the Grand Eastern Hotel!"

He pointed to a sign a little farther on, advertising the Denver corral. It spanned the narrow alley between the Crazy Horse Bar and the Grand Eastern.

"I ain't askin' you to come," George said in a dead voice. "I'm just sayin' you're a damn fool, that's all."

"Nobody asked nobody nothin', George."

A whispered warning, hissing and frantic, burst almost under George Fury's elbow.

"Señor—no tu bayas! No tu bayas, señor!" A brown mestizo boy, very Mexican, but very Indian too, was calling out to Melody under his breath from the narrow slit between the Grand Eastern and the saddlery. "Don' go to the corral! Don' look at me! Somebody with rifle, he's wait in the hay barn. He's for kill you, you go there!"

George Fury turned relaxed and cool. He shot an ironic glance of "I told you," at Melody; then turned his back casually on the opening from which the brown boy spoke. His stiff gnarled fingers were perfectly steady as he began to roll a cigarette.

"Who, son?" he said from the side of his mouth.

"What hay barn?"

"At the corral," came the thin scared whisper from between the buildings. "Don' know who. You come—I show you. . . ."

George Fury's eyes flicked left and right along the street as he licked shut his cigarette. Then he unhurriedly faded backwards into the narrow opening. Once out of sight of the street, he turned and went with the mestizo boy, shaking his gun loose in its holster.

Melody Jones hesitated, fidgeted, then followed.

Behind the Grand Eastern a ragged wreckage of rusty tin cans spoiled the shelving slope to the Poisonberry River; but beyond, looking past the cluttered kitchen-gallery of the hotel, they had a fair view of the public corral. Its fence, made of heavy, cracked cottonwood poles, stood eight feet tall; but through it they could see their ponies, and half a dozen more. The horses were eating hay off the ground; they kept tossing the hay with a throw of their heads, to shake the dust out of it.

And behind the corral stood the barn, small and ram-shackle, of curling boards. Some buckboards stood half way into its open front, and a strew of low-grade hay dribbled out of the loft above.

"There," whispered the Mexican boy. "Up where the hay live. This near corner—where the loose board is from at. . . ."

They saw it then—a small, unexplained projection, sticking out of an aperture where a loose plank had been swung aside. It might have been the head of a snake, or a man's thumb. But it wasn't. It was the muzzle of a buffalo gun, sighted on the front gate of the corral.

"Okay, son," George Fury said. He sounded very matter-of-fact, now that honest trouble had begun. He hunted in his pockets for something to give the boy, but when he turned the boy had disappeared.

George sidled past Melody and led the way to the street. They didn't have much to say to each other for a little while. Out on the board sidewalk of Court Street they leaned against the front of the saddlery, slow-moving, but edgily alert. George slowly lit his cigarette without looking at it. His eyes were all up and down the empty, sun-blazing street. Melody got out his tobacco sack, then stood for some time holding it in his hand. Finally he put it away again without making a smoke. He had forgotten what he started to do.

"You have any trouble with anybody," George asked Melody, "the whilst you was down the street?"

"Well—no—no," Melody considered. "Not what you'd call a bother, as bothers go."

"Melody, this ain't no time to be holdin' something back!"

"Well," Melody admitted, "I did kind of slap a feller. Just with my open hand."

"You kind of slapped a feller," George repeated, his tone slow and thick. "What did *he* do?"

"He set down."

"You slapped him, and he set. . . . Melody, how come you done this thing?"

Melody was willing to answer, but he didn't know. "Just to larn him, I reckon," he shrugged it off.

George Fury drew a long sigh. "We'll try to make it to the foot of the street," he told Melody. "If'n so be it we git thar, we'll cut back and circle, and wade the crick, and try at coming onto the corral from behind. We got to have them ponies, Melody, some kind of way. That saddle alone set me forty-seven dullers. . . ."

"All right, George."

Slowly, careful to give no sign of haste, George and Melody wheeled away from the Grand Eastern, back the way they had come.

And now Melody saw the girl again. She was coming quickly along the street with a nervous, reaching stride; and she was walking straight toward Melody, as straight as a surveyor's sight. Because her eyes were narrowed against the sun, he didn't know at first that her attention was fixed upon his face.

He saw that she was not a dance hall girl, nor even a girl of the town, for her face was tanned golden by the reflected light of alkali; so that her hair looked lighter than her face. It seemed to him that she was lovely; not pretty, maybe, but desirable and sweet, like bread and molasses, or a filly foal.

Suddenly he realized it was time to get out of her way. She was walking at him as directly as if he were a door, or an invisible man. Melody made a faint uncertain wobble to the left, then to the right, and stood rooted in the middle of the walk; for the girl smiled at him now, and still came straight toward him.

"Darling," she said to Melody. Her voice was clear, and strong enough to be heard by some of the shadowy men who were watching now from a dozen doorways. "Darling!"

She put her arms about his neck, pulling his head

down; and kissed him squarely.

Melody's hands held her gingerly, cupped lightly upon her back, and he was upset to find that she was shaking. As her arms slackened about his neck he saw that her eyes were grey, with blue shadows under them that didn't seem to belong there; and she was looking from one of his eyes to the other with a question approaching panic. The one thing he was certain of was that he had never seen her before in his life.

Melody made a faint sound, like the stutter of a duck.

She averted her eyes by pressing her cheek against the side of his jaw, and spoke to him rapidly. Her words were breathless, but now barely audible.

"Don't go to the corral," she said. "Don't go any place. Keep your backs against the wall, here. They'll never dare come at you from in front."

"Whut?" Over her shoulder Melody saw George Fury's blank misery.

"I'll get your ponies and bring them here. Don't move until I come."

George studied Melody's stupefied face, and conceived that their case was desperate.

"Naow, mam," George Fury said, "yew jest looky here—"

The girl flashed George Fury a smile of dazzling warmth. "Howdy, Roscoe," she said.

George made a noise like a man kicked in the stomach.

She disengaged herself from Melody, gave his arm a little fluttering pat, and hurried on past the Grand Eastern, toward the alley to the corral. Just before she disappeared around the corner of the Grand Eastern she turned back, and tried to convey something to Melody silently, by an exaggerated lip pantomime; but Melody didn't catch it.

George Fury had glued himself to the wall of the saddlery, as he had been told. "Dear God up a pole," he whimpered. "Who's thet?"

"I swear to great Gawd, and you be my judge, I never seen her before in all my born days!"

Taking off his battered old hat with a hand that shook, George Fury mopped his head. But even while he did that he was still rolling his eyes right and left, up the street and down, like a critter cornered.

"I wish I was daid," he said. "At this rate I'm li'ble to git my wishin's, too. *I don't aim to stand fer it!*"

"Relax yourse'f," Melody said mildly. "Like me."

A roaring flub-dub of hoofs sounded in the corral alley. A two-pony buckboard swung out of the alley into the street, nearly turning over as one wheel hooked the high edge of the boardwalk. The girl was driving, and having plenty of trouble, because the horses were half broke, and she was trying to drive them with one hand while leading George's and Melody's ponies with the other. They stepped out into the dust and helped her stop the team.

"Ride close by my wheel," she said as they took their horses from her. "Don't ask any questions. Believe me—please believe me—it's your one best hope!"

There was a singular meekness about George Fury as he swung into his saddle and obeyed. Melody stared obstinately at the whole arrangement for a moment or two, then he shrugged, stepped aboard Harry Henshaw, and followed.

Nothing happened to stop their ride out of Payneville. George Fury, who had decided he had to die there, felt as if he had slipped a stirrup, which is about the same as missing the top step in the dark; but in half an hour Payneville was a peculiar memory, lost behind the lazy roll of the plain.

Riding at the hub of the buckboard, Melody kept sliding sidelong glances at the profile of the girl as she drove the team. Her mouth was drawn down a little at the corners, and her eyes were hidden by her hat brim; she avoided looking around at him. She was watching the badly broken mustangs, which were slashing about in the harness as they loped.

He let his pony drift sideways until he was stirrup to stirrup with George Fury.

"Looky," said George, talking through the frazzled end of his mustache. The noise of the buckboard covered his words. "If you don't outright *know* this girl—you sure she ain't some relation? Some cousin, like, or something, you had once and slipped your mind?"

"I got no relations," Melody said. "I already told you I never see her before. If I lie, the Injuns can take my haid and make a dance-rattle."

"It would make a good one," George said. "What's she want out of us? Where's she drawing us into? No girl is going to come up to *you* out of a clear sky, and kiss you right on the street, without some powerful reason."

"Oh, I don't know."

"Loco weed never drove no critter *thet* crazy. Thet girl knows you, and knows you good—too good to be fooled. Looky here, Melody—you mind last year when you was kicked in the head at Cheyenne? You was missing four days. You sure you didn't marry nobody, or nothing, while you was out of your head?"

"I wasn't any more out of my haid than you," Melody said coolly. "Anyway," he added with less confidence, "I thunk of that. She says she's never *been* in Cheyenne."

"What else does she say, for Gard sake?"

"Nothing. I just said, 'How's all the folks in Cheyenne?' and she says, 'All whut folks? I never been there.' That was the last squeak out of her. She ambition-ized them broom-tails, then."

George Fury looked hard at Melody, He shrugged his gaunt shoulders, and looked grim.

Now the girl beckoned to Melody to ride closer; she pulled the team to a slogging trot.

"Do you want to do one thing for me?" she asked him.

"Mam?"

"Take off your hat."

He looked at her in bewilderment.

"I want to see something," she explained.

Melody slowly took off his floppy sombrero, and she looked at him closely, with such concentration that he reddened.

"I want you to keep your hair clawed down over your left eye," she told him. "Just like it is now."

"Mam?" he said; and she repeated it.

Slowly he put his hat back on. "Why?" he asked at last.

"As a favor to me. A personal favor. Is it a big thing to ask?"

"Hey look," he shouted over the trundle of the wheels. "Hey—"

She shot him an inquiring smile, but as she turned her head, she let the driving lines slack, and the mustangs plunged into a run. The buckboard careened and bounded into the snaky ruts.

"What?"

"Nothing!"

It was hard for Melody to believe that this was what a girl looked like who was fixing to get a stranger feller into trouble. But as he swung off to ride beside George Fury again, he was looking so thoughtful that George wondered if he was sun-tetched.

Absent-mindedly Melody dragged a folded piece of paper out of his hip pocket. He straightened it out and read it slowly. George watched him, burnt to a crisp with curiosity.

"Don't mind me," George said bitterly. "But if I have to drag along and look out for you like a Ga-a-ar' damn uncle—"

"Speaking of uncles," Melody said, "I fetched this here off a post down in the town." He gave George the bit of paper.

It turned out to be a handbill, such as is tacked up in post offices. Apparently it had been printed locally; the type was some that Columbus must have found the Indians using, for it was over a hundred years old, and should have been in a museum.

For murder, robbery, and diforderly conduct—
MONTE JARRAD

5 foot 10, 140 pound, ftraw color hair, fcar over left eye. May be travelling with half-wit uncle name of Rofcoe fomething. Laft feen going over Syke Mt. on a bald-tail horfe.

$1000 REWARD DEAD OR ALIVE
whichever way he packf beft.

"What the heck is a horfe?" Melody said. He swiveled in his saddle to study his pony's tail with melancholy. "I reckon they mean Harry Henshaw. But Harry ain't really baldtail. It's just wore off in that one place, from being shet in a stable, that time."

George was turning purple. "Half-wit uncle," he said between set teeth. It was all coming clear to him now. "Half-wit uncle name of Roscoe. I be damned if *any* man could stand fer this!"

"That's whut done it," Melody said sadly. "There ain't any other resemblance hardly, except I got the same initials burnt on my saddle, two-three places."

"Half-wit uncle," George said again, his voice shaking.

"By God, George," Melody said, "I *tried* to get you over that foolish look!"

"Name of Roscoe," George whimpered.

"I been thinkin'," Melody said.

"I suppose," George consoled himself, "to be your uncle a feller would *have* to be a half-wit."

"Of course, George, you know," Melody said, "it ain't as if I asked to get into this."

"The name even had to be Roscoe," George hung on to it. "By-y Gard, I'm going to fill somebody so full of holes you can button him like a vest!"

"I didn't force my way into this here," Melody said mildly, "but if these people aim to drag me in by the slack of my pants, and git me in trouble, and force their-self on me, so I can't hardly *keep* from catching up with him—"

George suddenly became perfectly still. He fixed his gaze on Melody's profile and his eyes were weird. "Melody," he said at last, his words muffled, "what in all hell is eating you?"

"You know, George," Melody said slowly, "in all my life I ain't ever been so low in my mind as I been in this last half hour, here."

"We'll git out of this all right," George said.

"No, George; no, it ain't that. But, you know, back there in Payneville, when we rode in—it seemed at first like the whole world was changed. Nothin' like it ever happened to me before. I taken and walked down the street, and people stood back to leave me pass. I taken and went up to a bar, and people give me room. All of a sudden, it seemed like, everyone thunk I was somebody. I guess it fooled me, George. For a little while there, I guess I thunk I was somebody myself."

George didn't laugh at him. He looked at Melody sadly,

but not without understanding. "Forget it, Melody," he said. "You ain't Monte Jarrad. Don't let yourself think you be. You're only Melody Jones, a tramp cowboy. And useless, too—you know it perfectly well."

"I know all that," Melody said. He turned in the saddle and looked at George queerly. "But George, something come to me."

George waited.

"I can't never be Monte Jarrad," Melody said. "But by God—*I can be the feller that caught up with him!*"

George looked shocked and scared. "You mean," he said, "you'd throw your damn fool life away at the plain mention of a thousand dullars?"

"It ain't that, George," Melody said sadly, "it's just that for one hour there I found out what it was like to be somebody; and I just can't ever feel the same about things again."

George shrugged. Melody would get over it, he thought then.

⚘ 5 ⚘

Around sundown they climbed a quarter-mile of ragged side-trail, the wheels of the buckboard tilting chancily over the rock ledges; and came out on a mountain crag where clung a weathered ranch house, a sagging barn, and some sketchy corrals. Within the erratic fences an unnecessary number of ten-dollar mustangs climbed about the rocks and steeps. The smallest bear cub Melody had ever seen was chained beside the back door. The place appeared unprosperous, and shiftless; but the fact that the girl seemed to live here gave it imaginary possibilities. In the red sunset light it looked okay to Melody, even attractive, in a go-to-hell sort of way.

George Fury spoke to Melody through a buttonhole in his gaunt cheek, screened by his mustache. "What's the idee stoppin' here?"

"Maybe it's her home."

"Well, it ain't *my* home! Let's hear you name just one thing it could get us to off-saddle here?"

"A meal," Melody said.

"Goodbye," said George savagely, making as if to turn his horse.

Melody ignored the threat. "I been thinkin'," he said. "George, you know something? I'm bait."

"What?"

"I figured out the reason she drug us all the way out here. I see now why she run up to me and made out like I was Monte. I see it just as plain. It's so's the posse would take out after me, and chase me."

"It took you all the way out here to figure out that?"

"Well, it's some forwarder than I was when I started."

"This is wonderful," George said. "This is the best thing happened yet. So now you and her have got it fixed that a posse takes out and runs us to hell and gone!"

"I don't see how they kin," Melody said.

"Why can't they?"

"Because I don't aim to go no place. You can git them to chase you, if you want to, George."

Melody's restless eyes were at work, but differently now. For this one time, as he rode into the little lay-out,

43

he forgot to be Unsmiling Jones. George Fury was looking at Melody with pity, but was still at his stirrup as they pulled up near the house.

Now a rangy, gangling figure came out of the ranch house, letting the broken screen door slam to with a bang that lifted the bear cub a foot. The man who came toward Melody with enormous looping strides was of exceptional height, of the high-pockets design—spidery of limb, narrow-chested, with a small head. The gun that slatted against his bony thigh looked out of place, as if hung upon a tree.

"Howdy, boy, howdy," he bawled nasally. His long slit of a mouth was bracketed by a mustache so narrow and drooping it was almost Chinese. "It's good to see you. It's been a long time!"

As he drew closer and got to windward, Melody noticed the smell of forty-rod. He looked the tall man over coolly from the saddle, but as the stranger came to his stirrup he could not refuse the offered hand. It felt like a fistful of dry mesquite.

"Cherry sent Avery out with word you was here. Come out here, Avery! He's spilin' the grub," he explained to Melody.

So her name's Cherry, Melody thought. He looked at her to see how the name fitted. She had stepped down, and was unharnessing the buckboard team.

George Fury had been watching Melody to catch any sign of recognition in Melody's face. George was looking very grim.

"I crave to ask jist a couple o' things," George said, carefully polite; then hesitated. Since this afternoon he had a sensitivity about certain questions. "What ranch is this," he got it out, "and who are you?"

The girl called Cherry spoke in a quick mumble from behind her horse. "You've heard speak of Roscoe Symes, Paw. I guess you never ran into him—but that's him. Remember?"

George could not see, but Melody saw, as she tapped her forehead. Her lips formed the word, *"Different."*

"Shore, I remember," the tall man said. "Monte's uncle, eh?" He slid off into the patronizing smile that George Fury had seen before, and spoke as if to a child. "I'm Fever Crick de Longpre," he told George. "Reckon you heard Monte speak of me. *You* know—Cherry's paw?"

Cherry de Longpre—Melody thought—that's right pretty; and this long mix of chills and snake-oil is her old man. Well, you never know.

"This here little lay-out," Fever Crick de Longpre was saying, "we call the Busted Nose, on account of our brand. We started to have it the Flying W, but Avery tripped and fell, and bent our branding iron on a rock, while it was hot. It won't burn a 'W' any more. But it looks as much like a busted snoot as a man could ask."

"Oh?" Melody said.

"What's the matter with him?" Fever Crick asked Melody now. He was staring candidly at George Fury with a speculative detachment. "He going into a conniption, likely?" George was turning purple in the face again.

"Pay him no mind," Melody said, shooting George a glance of warning. "Hello, Avery."

The man who came out of the ranch house now was of unplaceable age—he might have been years older than

Melody, or he might have been eighteen. I can't tell, Melody thought, without I taken a look at his teeth. Even before he appeared, Melody had sensed him lurking behind the ill-matched boards of the kitchen, watching Melody Jones and George Fury, estimating them both. And when he left the ramshackle house he left it empty; somehow Melody knew that, too. His strung-up senses were telling him things he could not have decided with his head.

Avery de Longpre was middle-sized and well set; there was power in his shoulder, and hard-packed strength in the slow set of his heels as he walked. But what made Melody's scalp crawl was something else. This was the man Melody had been waiting to see— whom he must inevitably meet if this thing went on: The man who knew that Melody Jones was a stranger, unidentified, and not the man Cherry de Longpre had set him up to be.

He watched Avery de Longpre's face. He didn't much like the flat-muscled cheek bones, nor the hard line of the jaw, bulged faintly by a meager chew of tobacco. But especially he didn't like the small pale eyes, expressionless as gooseberries, and the same color. There was a weight of immovable sullenness behind Avery de Longpre's unfetching pan.

"Hello, Monte," Avery said. He made a vague gesture of salute, but without coming near enough to have to shake hands; and the green eyes dropped away from Melody's flat stare.

"Chuck's up," Avery said. His speech was dull and thick; he hardly opened his jaws for it. "Light and we'll eat."

George Fury's Adam's apple bobbled, but he didn't say anything else. He unsaddled, and rubbed his pony's back with a piece of gunny sack for a long time, while Melody waited. When he finally turned and followed Melody to the house his gloved hand trailed lingeringly along the pony's quarters, as if he were leaving forever his one best hope.

Within the kitchen, with his knees under the plank table, George Fury stoked himself doggedly and methodically with the de Longpre's salt pork and pan bread, but only to keep up his strength. His mouth was dry, and he swallowed with difficulty. Darkness set in; and while moths found their way into the hurricane lamps and the chuck-will's-widows were calling outside, George Fury was straining his ears for the approach of trouble, and watching the two de Longpre men.

Avery, at least, was waiting for something, stalling and listening, like himself. More than once George saw Avery's jaws stop their motion while he listened hard, with unfocussed eyes. The old man, Fever Crick de Longpre, George could not make out, except that he evidently had a jug in the lean-to, and visited it often enough to mellow slowly. As this process continued, it seemed to George that Fever Crick looked more and more like a harvester bug. Either he didn't know what was happening, or he didn't give a damn. Probably both.

Melody Jones paid less attention to the men and more to Cherry de Longpre; she met his eyes seldom, and her face was still. She busied herself waiting on them, and the poor light from the hurricane lamps helped her face to be undisclosing.

She had got a clean red-checkered cloth on to the plank-and-trestle table, and the cooking stuff on the wall—copper, brass, and iron—shone very clean. This streak of good order suggested that these things were Cherry's, though the ranch itself, with its shaky tilt and dilapidation, was the men's responsibility. She was prettier than he had thought, much prettier, and he was sorry to see this. If a girl had to set out to do him wrong, he wished it could have been a homely girl, with one of these here hay-bag figures, and a hostile look.

"Now you take if a hoss has got to throw me," he said to George with his mouth full, "I want to git throwed by the best hoss there is. But now you take a girl—" He saw that Cherry was looking at him oddly, and he dropped the whole thing.

Fever Crick, who was talking continuously, in an obvious effort to make a good impression on Melody, kept apologizing for the wretched lay-out, and trying to explain it. It needed all the apology it could get. It was less a house than a shack, and, except for a broad gallery on two sides, would never have been mistaken by even a wandering cowboy for anything else. Fever Crick said it was "previous to the summer," whatever that meant, and obscurely necessary for horse ranching. But Melody could feel the girl's disdain, whenever her father spoke.

"What's the world's most necessary critter?" Fever Crick asked owlishly. "The horse," he answered himself. "What is man's best friend?"

"His mother," George Fury said sourly.

Melody caught Cherry looking at him; he winked at

her, and tapped his forehead. He saw astonishment cross her face, and knew that he had her for a minute, there. She dropped her eyes, and was expressionless again.

But now he perceived, unexpectedly, that he had the girl in an even more puzzling position than that in which he found himself. She had set him up to be Monte Jarrad, for purposes of her own, without even knowing his name. But probably she hadn't figured on his just casually insisting on being the exact person she had made him out to be.

"It's certainly nice of you people to take me and my uncle in," Melody said with a complacence that chilled George Fury. "I expect we can just as well stay on a while, if it's all right with you."

He let his eyes wander off into the night as he spoke, but he sensed the stillness that instantly came over Cherry de Longpre and her brother.

"Might even be," Melody went on, "me and my Uncle Roscoe could bring ourself to do a little work around here, to kind of pay for our keep. I see you got plenty horse flesh out there; maybe me and Uncle Roscoe will set in to break a few haid, come morning."

He smiled a little, contentedly, and let his eyes slide across the faces of the others to see what effect this announcement had taken. He got his answer at once.

Cherry de Longpre looked Melody squarely and blankly between the eyes. Her tone was cool and perfectly level, but there was a shakiness behind it. "Monte," she said with finality, "it's time to be on your way."

"Oh, I ain't in any hurry," Melody said.

Avery de Longpre's words came in a slow whisper.

"Oh, yes, you are!" Until that moment Melody had not known that Avery's gun was in his hand under the edge of the table.

Melody didn't believe that Avery would actually shoot; at least not while everyone sat quiet. It was George Fury who scared Melody. George's hands gripped the edge of the table, and he had got his heels under him; he could uncoil like a spring from that position. And he was watching Avery like a pointer. Melody knew what George was going to do. He was going to overturn the table on Avery, making the gun miss as it fired, George would hope. That would put out one of the lamps, and probably the old fool would try to kick down the other lantern, which hung from a rafter eight feet from the floor. There was a moment of paralysis.

"Take it easy, Uncle Roscoe," Melody said to George Fury.

"He's got his gun in his hands," George grated.

Cherry said quickly, "You shouldn't clean your gun at the table, Avery." She sounded out of breath.

"He's holdin' it in his two hands," George repeated.

"Where did you figure he would be holding it," Melody said, "if he's cleaning it? In his mouth?"

Cherry's eyes were fixed hard on Melody, ignoring the others. "Saddle your ponies," she ordered him. "Saddle up and get out of here! Right now!"

Melody looked at her without hurry. "You look right pretty when you spark up like that," he said.

"There's a posse after you," Cherry said desperately. "Can't you get that through your head? The Poisonberry country is full of men who would be glad to kill you on sight. You'd be dead now if it wasn't for me! Now you get out of here, while you still can!"

"Shucks, now," Melody began.

"You heard her," Avery spoke.

Fever Crick was sitting goggle-eyed, and his jaw was wobbling; but Avery was steady as a rock.

Slowly Melody stood up, and George got warily to his feet beside him. George never took his eyes from Avery for an instant.

"Ride fast," Cherry said, "and keep going! Don't turn your horses this side of the line, if you want to live."

Melody looked at her a moment, then back to George again. He said sadly, "Well, come on, Uncle Roscoe."

Melody and George rode off into the dark at a sullen walk, resenting the push-around. Five hundred yards below the Busted Nose they splashed into a little thread of mountain stream, and let their ponies stop to drink, since the riding ahead promised to be both long and slow.

"Far be it from me," George said, "to stick a spoke in your Goddam wheel. Well do I realize that you're three hoots and a yelp too smart for a man to tell you nuthin'. But a half-wit Injun that got hisself in your fix would have sense enough to die by his own teeth!"

"Oh?" Melody said.

"One man has got more people trying to kill him than any other man in the world. So naturally, it is pure instink with you to get mistook for that one feller."

"Oh, well," Melody shrugged it off, "they're pretty near bound to find out their mistake, later."

"It must be a great satisfaction to a dead man to have his killers find out their mistake!"

"Oh, well, now, George, maybe they won't actually—"

"Even without you're mistook," George went on bitterly, "you fixed it up to get everybody sore on your own. See what you done. Slapped some jigger alongside the snoozle, and brung him down on the palm of his pants. Bluffed a whole bar, and never paid for your drinks. All on Monte Jarrad's credit. So next you haul off and kiss Monte Jarrad's girl, right on the open street. And foller up by forcing right on into her home, by God! Why, you ain't got no more chance than a one-legged Injun at a ass-kickin'!"

Melody wasn't listening to him. "I been thinkin'," he said now. "You know somethin'? I don't think this Monte Jarrad is up here at the Busted Nose at all."

George Fury's hat seemed to rise slowly on his head. "You rode in there because you thunk he *was* there?"

"Sure. But I see different, now. She wouldn't never of brung me here, except unless the real Monte was the farthest away place he could get. She's trying to use me to lead the posse *off* him, not *at* him."

George stared at him angrily. "Let's get out of this," he said gruffly, pulling up his pony's head.

"It just comes to me," Melody said. "I come up here to find out where Monte Jarrad is. And I come away without finding out."

"Why didn't you ask them people?" George said with all the sarcasm he had. "Them's the ones that know! Are you going to set there all night, or come on?"

"Neither one," Melody said, gathering his reins. "I'm going back."

He turned Harry Henshaw, and started back up the trail.

George sat for a moment or two looking after him. His lower lip drooped pendulously, and trembled. He pulled at it with gloved thumb and finger. Then he followed Melody slowly, limping stiffly in his saddle.

❧ 6 ❧

Cherry and Avery stood listening to the receding hoofbeats of George's and Melody's horses. Avery took off his black California-style hat—the one with the flat top—and scratched his head with the same hand. When they could no longer hear the hoofbeats, Cherry and Avery looked at each other sidelong.

Avery's rugged but dull face was perfectly blank. "God Almighty," he said, without any expression.

"If I were doing it over," Cherry said slowly, "I would leave those people alone, completely."

"Why didn't you tell me," Avery said, "you told that simpleton everything you knew?"

"I didn't tell him *any*thing!"

"Then how did you coach him up to play Monte like he's doin', and how you git him to do it?"

"I tell you," Cherry said, "I didn't coach him up! I've hardly spoken two words to him since I picked him up off the street!"

They stared at each other blankly. They had never understood anything less.

"I swear, Avery," Cherry said at last, "I don't know what got into him. Part of the time it seemed to me as if he thought he *was* Monte. I never saw such a thing. He just stepped in, and played it out, as if it were the most natural thing in the world for him to be Monte. It was enough to scare a person."

Avery scratched his head again and gave up. "What's Monte going to do when you tell him all this?"

"How much have you told him so far?"

"Well," Avery thought a bit. "Well," he began again, "I told Monte how this feller was mistook for him, down in Payneville; and how I spread the word that this feller was him, like you told me—"

"You don't mean to tell me," Cherry cut in, "you did something I said?"

"I swear to Christ," Avery said, "after I was done, the feller don't live in Payneville that don't think Monte was right amongst him this afternoon!"

"All right," Cherry said. "What did you tell Monte?"

"Well—I give him a general idea of how we thunk of this feller as sucker bait, suitable for leadin' posses, and such-like, off of Monte."

"So far, so good," Cherry said.

"But," Avery said, levelling at her, "*but*, when it comes to going back to Monte now, and tellin' him how this feller horned right in and played it all up, I don't want no piece nor price. I think *you* best tell Monte, Cherry."

Cherry looked as if she didn't want to be the one, either. "We don't want to get him upset. You just keep your mouth shut, Avery. I'll do the talking to Monte."

Side by side they walked out to the barn now, moving a little reluctantly.

"It's over with now," Cherry said, with more hope than

conviction. "They're on their way; we'll never see them again, nor hear any more about it—I hope."

Avery shrugged. When something bothered his head, he got around it by not thinking about it at all.

They went into the ramshackle barn. A three-quarter moon was coming up, and the cracks between the warping boards let in thin stripes of the horizontal light; but the interior was very dark. They felt their way around a considerable hoarding of weathered hay stacked in bales, and came to what had once been the wall of a stall. The baled hay was piled against the other side of the old timers now.

Here Avery took down a canvas wind-breaker, and pulled out the nail upon which it had hung. A hidden latch lifted, and some of the boards swung inward—a make-shift trick door.

Beyond, an unexpectedly spacious cave was revealed under the hay tiers, made by blocking up the bales only one deep, like masonry. Avery had built this, and built it fast, while his father was off chasing wild horses. Fever Crick, whose jug-loose tongue was trusted by nobody had taken Avery's story that he had hauled in more hay. This crude hide-out was nothing anybody could have trusted long; the cool, brazen guts of the very idea was its only hope.

The space under the hay was lighted by a kerosene storm-lantern, burning poorly in the bad air. As Cherry and her brother stooped and entered, Monte Jarrad let down the hammer of his cocked forty-four, and laid it beside him.

Monte Jarrad was on a pallet of grain sacks, his head

propped on his saddle. He lay on his back, very still, with the slack relaxation of a man who is saving every pulse-beat of his strength. He smoked a rolled cigarette as slender as a match, and looked at them with humorless eyes.

Cherry wanted to tell him again that he would burn himself up, smoking here under the hay; but there was no use saying things like that to Monte Jarrad.

Monte Jarrad took no notice of Avery at all; but he looked at Cherry with a certain gleam of warmth, if anything.

"What the hell is the matter with you?" were his first words.

Cherry stood quiet, and waited. She was thinking how different two men could be, and yet be mistaken one for the other. Monte Jarrad had the same hard-to-curry shag of sandy hair as Melody Jones, and the same eye-colored eye, the same set of bones in his face. Both had the same spare, horse-transportation build, cut to the same height, and the same weight within a pound.

That was all, though; and Cherry marvelled that it had proved enough. For the man who lay wounded in the hideaway had the unmalleable, gritty quality of gravel in a mouthful of beans. From his light eyes he looked at the world with a narrowed vision, as if squinting through the barrels of a shotgun; and a sort of permanent truculence was his key.

"Haven't you got any sense at all?" Monte asked her. He had the pepper of a man outraged by his own physical weakness—astonished, irreconcilable, at being held down. "You know what you went to Payneville after!

You was supposed to fetch holt of Lee and Virg!"

"Monte," Cherry said, "Lee and Virg positively have not showed patch or pants in Payneville. I don't know why, or where they are, or anything about it."

"And so," Monte said, "so long as you was down there, you had to figure out the worst thing you could of done!"

Cherry stood looking at this man who lay helpless, yet whom nothing could please. "Monte," she said, "you don't need to holler at me in any such tone as that. Maybe it scares the good God out of Avery; but it don't ride any circle on me. I remember you back in Pike county, years ago. I remember when your paw used to tan you with the slack of the thresher-belt, and we could hear you beller clear down to our place, three miles away."

A flicker in Monte's eyes showed that he remembered, too. He could still feel the looping flap of the loose belt which drove the thresher. His strong but lazy father used to hold him up to it pants first, to save the effort of paddling by hand. "Leave my old man out of this," he said.

"All right, Monte," Cherry said, "I'll leave him out. You're not here because I'd give two cents for your old man, any more than for my own."

"Why, Cherry!" said Avery.

"You're here because you're the only man I ever looked at in my life," Cherry said with all flatness, "and because I've always thought you were all hell, from before I was fourteen years old."

Monte said, "Oh."

"It's not my fault that some tramp cowboy wandered into Payneville," Cherry followed up, "and it's not my fault that Payneville mistook him for you. Word ran all over town. Homer Cotton laid for him at the Denver Corral, hoping to kill him. He hadn't been in ten minutes before a rider went walloping out of town to fetch back the posse. The way he rode, I could hear his hat whistle a block . . . Maybe there was holes in it," she explained, as he looked at her queerly.

"No feller looks like me. No feller looks like *any* feller."

"I didn't say he did. He has the same initials, is all." Then as she looked at Monte, her eyes turned strange. "He looks—he looks something like you used to look."

Monte didn't go into that.

"Avery and I did the only thing we could have done," Cherry went on. "The whole thing was a bad cut, that's all. Except for him, the posse would have dusted right on through to California, I suppose. As it is, they'll be back here by tomorrow night. They'll comb this basin until a coon-cat couldn't hide in it. The only thing I could think of doing, so long as they're dead set on thinking he's you, was to *help* them think so—and send him tearing on his way. He's plenty stupid; but even *he* knows he's in trouble, now. He'll pound out of this country as fast as horse flesh can take him. The posse will be *days* catching up with him."

"They'll find out who he is quick enough, once they lay hands on him," Monte said.

"Of course they will. And they'll come flogging back. But you will have had a week to get clear."

Monte looked at her a long time and his eyes were narrow. "You figured good," he said but with cinders under his tone. "You figured fine, except for one thing. That ain't a tramp cowboy!"

"You haven't even seen him!"

"I don't need to see him. I've got enough sense to know that the man couldn't live who's such a damn fool as you make *him* out to be!"

"I tell you," Cherry argued, "he isn't anything but a stupid, ignorant, useless bronc stomper, with fifty per cent less sense than he was born with!"

"I ain't so sure," Avery said.

"Avery," Cherry said wearily, "will you please keep the hell out of this?"

Monte said, "Shut up, Avery!"

"Well, all right," Avery backed up. "I will if you want me to. But I thunk they was something funny about this whole deal, from the time he hit Ira Waggoner."

"He what?" Monte shouted. He rolled up on to his elbow with a jerk that brought the cold sweat.

"Huh?" said Avery, startled.

"He hit Ira Waggoner," Cherry said.

"Why?"

"Didn't come out with no reason," Avery said.

"Damn it, he *must* of said *some*thing!"

"I swear, Monte, he never said 'Hurrah,' or 'Excuse me,' or 'Go to hell,' or nothin'! He Just walked up to him, and—boom—he's endways. I never see such a business."

"It was a picture," Cherry confirmed.

"Naturally," Avery pointed out, his tone aggrieved, "everybody knew that you was the only one would have the nerve to hit Ira. Even Ira thunk it was you. He just picked hisself up and offered you a drink." Avery looked puzzled. "Offered *him* a drink," he decided.

Monte Jarrad laid back against the saddle. His eyes pinched shut for a moment and he locked his fingers over his side; but he gave no other evidence of pain. "This is what I get," he said, "for making a deal with a snapper I don't even know. This is what I get for trying to let people off easy, in place of shooting 'em right in the stummick to start with!"

"Sure, Monte," Avery said.

Cherry shot her brother a contemptuous glance. Sometimes she could nearly forgive Monte's outlawery, because she considered he had been harassed and driven into it, in bitter injustice; but Avery felt just the other way.

"I should have known Waggoner had no sense," Monte blamed himself. "Why was he a stage driver if he had any sense?"

"Sure, Monte," Avery said again.

"It was Lee and Virg picked him," Monte said. "Waggoner was supposed to see that the shotgun messenger got left behind at Stinkwater. He was supposed to drive the stage alone. It's Waggoner's fault that the shotgun rider got his. It's Waggoner's fault that I'm lying here!"

"Sure, Monte."

"And it's his fault now that the posse's on top of me again."

"Sure, Monte."

"Quit saying that!"

"Okay, Monte."

"Don't you see," Cherry said, "that the posse will only

take off after this tramp cowboy?"

Monte fairly yelled at her. "Tramp cowboy, hell! How do you know he isn't one of Luke Packer's men, sent by the express company? How do we know he isn't Luke Packer himself—the God damnedest luckiest blood-money-chaser-upper that ever dry-gulched his granmaw for a quarter?"

"I doubt if this boy even heard of you before."

Monte Jarrad was incredulous. "Never heard of— Where's he been?"

"He's been running cattle, somewhere."

"Cattle run in strange places," Monte said, his voice weird.

Cherry shot a sidelong glance at her brother. "You know that," she answered Monte. "Or you knew it once."

"Why do you think he lets *you* push him around, unless he was sent?"

"Because I can wrap him around my finger," Cherry said contemptuously. "I knew it the first second I looked at him."

Monte looked at her steadily for a long moment. "So that's the tune," he said queerly, as if to himself. He turned his head to Avery. "Get back on your horse. Get down to Payneville. Make one more try to find out if Lee and Virg have come in; wait for 'em until morning. If they don't come in tonight, I'll slope out by myself."

"Sure, Monte," Avery said.

"Move!"

But as they stooped and wormed their way out of the hide-out under the hay, Monte called Cherry back. She turned reluctantly, anxious to be away.

"There's something you might better know," Monte said, "and guide yourself according."

Cherry waited.

"Never mind this wrapping nobody around no finger," he said. "Unless you want to get them shot right in the stummick. Understand?"

Cherry looked at him steadily, for quite a bit. She pinched her lids together, but when she opened her eyes they were dry. "I don't know about you," she said at last. "Some days, I don't think you try."

❦ 7 ❦

Nobody was in the lighted kitchen of the Busted Nose as George and Melody returned to it, leaving their horses hidden in the brush. Fever Crick, who now seemed to have passed out, was snoring in the lean-to; but otherwise their reconnaissance raised no one. Avery and Cherry de Longpre had disappeared.

Mystified, Melody Jones walked into the kitchen and sat down. He tilted back his chair, crossed his ankles on the table, and picked his teeth with the nail of his little finger.

George joined him here, uneasily, after an extra look around. "You ain't got no more worry about you than a hog on ice," he complained, standing himself against the wall in the safest-looking place.

"I'm thinkin'," Melody said. "The girl knows where Monte is. So she's the one I got to find out from."

"So naturally all you got to do is ask her," George said.

"Well, no; that's the part I ain't got figured yet,"

Melody admitted. "I don't rightly judge she'll say. That's where the hitch comes in."

"Oh," said George. His eyes were flicking around the kitchen, tirelessly hunting a ray of hope. "Ain't there some way to git you out of this?"

"Oh, now George—*don't* start all that again. I'm tryin' to find out somethin'."

"Then we might jest as well try to git 'er done," George said grimly.

Melody looked surprised, but he didn't question the change of front. George was moving around the kitchen with a vague caution, as if looking for something. "Lost somethin', George?"

"Shet up!"

Melody slowly untracked himself and began to help George hunt, as well as he could, without knowing what George was looking for. He found a cold biscuit, though, and filled his mouth with it, so that it wouldn't go to waste.

George had come to the foot of the ladder nailed to the wall; it gave access to the loft above the kitchen. "Don't make a sound," he whispered; and suddenly skinned silently up the ladder into the loft.

When George had disappeared, a considerable silence followed, during which Melody had no clue to what George was up to, nor what was happening. Melody began to show nervousness for the first time. He called up the ladder in a reaching whisper. "Hey, George!"

There was no answer from above. Perhaps nothing in the world is so creepy as calling into the dark to some one you know is there, and getting no reply. And now

Melody heard the voices of Cherry and Avery, outside; they seemed to be some distance off, but coming closer rapidly.

"Hey, George!" Melody called again.

"For Gard sake," came George's whisper, "come up here!"

Melody Jones swung up the ladder in a couple of long pulls, and stuck himself half way into the loft.

"Come on! The rest of the way!" George spoke close to his ear. "Quick!"

"Why?"

"Look at how you're fixed! You want to get shot square in the palm of the pants?" He hauled Melody bodily into the loft. "We can listen to 'em here," George explained, "if you're so hell-fire curious!"

Melody considered this. "George," he said, "you should otter of told me. I wouldn't of come up."

"Not without argyin' all night. I knowed that."

"This here," Melody said, "ain't hardly any better than a daid end."

"Hesh!" George snapped at him. "These damn people been short-cardin' you all day. By Gard, they're gettin' me mad!"

"Yes, but—"

"Hesh, and listen! What do you hear?"

"Fever Crick snoring in the lean-to," Melody said.

"What else?" The question was necessary; George never admitted it, but he could only hear on one side.

They were still for a moment. "Avery and the girl are standing back of the house," Melody decided. "Sounds like he's saddling up, and her holding the pony."

"Foller me," George said. He wormed off into the dark.

"Now look where you got us into," Melody whispered. "You old fool, we're treed like a possum up a rope, that's whut! You reelize there's no two ways out of this loft?"

"I can tear out through the shakes of this roof," George whispered back as he crawled, "with my bare hands."

Melody thought that over. "It would make a noise," he concluded.

Even in the dark, Melody could feel George Fury's glare. "Hesh up and come on!"

George Fury was snaking along the shaky floor on his belly. At the back, where the lean-to had been tacked on with afterthought, only a twelve-inch slit opened into the air-space above. A flimsy board ceiling had been tacked up in the lean-to, but on the under side of the joists. George Fury set his jaw and crawled painfully into the air-space, every joint complaining as he negotiated the splintery beams.

Melody followed, bumping his head. Moving more nimbly than George, he pulled alongside under the flat cramp of the lean-to roof.

"One thing," George whispered, "they'll never be figgerin' on us *here*."

"Nobody but a couple o' ratchet-haids *would* wedge theyself in here," Melody said, bumping his head again.

"Hesh!"

At the extreme limit of their compression they were at the eaves. Through the misfit of the overhang they could see the top of Cherry de Longpre's head, amazingly bright in the light of the three-quarter moon; and the black California-style hat of her brother.

"He's changed," they could hear Cherry saying, her voice very deep in her depression. "He started out the only man in the world I ever saw who could really get things done. I'd go to the ends of the earth, for a man like that. But you can't tell me he's driven to *all* this shooting stuff!"

"Why, Cherry," her brother said uncertainly.

"He's got to quit this shooting business," Cherry said in so intense a whisper that it carried better than her spoken words.

"Why, Cherry," Avery said again, shaken by this heresy, "You—you wouldn't go back on Monte, would you, Cherry?"

Cherry's answer came late, but clearly spoken. "No; I wouldn't go back on Monte. I couldn't do that. But he makes me tired, worrying about that grub-testing horse-breaker!"

"That bronc-stomping punk is the bunk," Avery said with conviction.

"You got that, did you?"

"He's too foolish acting to be true," they heard Avery say crossly. "The old one—of course he's another matter. There you got the real thing."

George Fury nudged Melody, to be sure he was getting this.

"Anybody can see the old one is a genuine half-wit, all right," Avery added.

Melody was going to nudge George this time, but he heard George's breath suck through his teeth. "Why them G-a-a-r—"

"Shet up!" Melody hissed. "Or I'll hesh you with this gun bar'l!"

"There's more rats in that roof every year," Avery said, looking up at the eaves. For a moment Melody thought he was being looked between the eyes.

"The old one," Cherry contested, "is virtually a brilliant mind, compared to what the young one is. What's the matter with you and Monte? Don't you know a common simpleton when you see one?"

"Monte ain't seen him."

"I wish he had. He sure wouldn't worry about *him* any more, if he got one look. It beats me how the punk gets himself fed. He came when I called him, and he left when I turned him out—and he's sheriff's bait for the next three hundred miles. Now will you forget it? And get down into town!"

"Mark that well," George Fury whispered to Melody. "I want you should remember every word!"

"Now see what you done," Melody answered. Both Avery and Cherry were looking up at the eaves this time. George and Melody began inching back.

"Fetch out my spurs," they heard Avery order his sister.

"Fetch 'em yourself," Cherry's voice said; and a moment later they heard her walking into the kitchen.

George Fury was whispering to Melody Jones again. "*That's* what I brung you up here to hear! You're messing into this on account of you're sweet on that girl. And you see? That hell-cat would just as leave see you hung. *Now* will you come out of this damn thing?"

"You're just up-ended because she spoke poorly of your haid."

"Why, Ga-a-ard dammit, yew befewzled numpus—"

Avery's heavy voice came to them very plain. "There's rats moving up there big enough to cast a bronc," he said.

"Avery," came Cherry's weary tone, "will you put that gun away and get gone?"

When Avery got hold of an idea he hung onto it. "If there ain't a rat up there I can shoot by ear," he said, "I hope to never shoot another."

Above the thin boards, that were no protection at all, Melody Jones and George Fury froze to the rafters like lichens. Directly beneath them they heard Avery's spurs ring as he stamped his heels to settle the straps. After that the gourd dipper rattled in the bucket as Avery got himself a drink of water. Simple motions seemed to be taking Avery a long time.

A small sage-beetle was crawling on Melody's nose, walking round and round the tip. Every time it came to the lower side of his nose Melody tried to blow it off; the bug would cling more tightly until the gale was past. Then Melody would have to wait for it to finish another walk-around, so he could blow at it again. But he would have felt worse if he had known the difficulty that George was in.

At the moment of Avery's announcement George had been crawling backward upon knees and elbows. One gangling leg, groping for a toe-hold, had found the edge of a stringer, and he had just shifted his weight. So now George found himself in the form of a looping bridge, supported on his elbows and one far-off toe. Not even his leathery years in the saddle could hold up a contraption like that for very long. Yet he knew that he had to sustain it. He had imagination enough to picture a forty-five bullet blowing a hole in the roof, having passed through the spare frame of George Fury on the way.

His natural objection was complicated by the silliness of his position. After all the chances he had had to die bravely, even spectacularly, it was unfair that he should at last come to his end ridiculously, packed head first into a space too small for him, like a man trapped in a folding bed. . . .

Sweat broke out at the roots of George Fury's thin hair, and trickled down behind his ears. The small of his back began to ache first, then the cords behind his knee; then swiftly a strained fatigue swept all through his frame. His stringy old muscles began to quiver with the tension, and red moons began to weave before his eyes. The toe of George Fury's boot balanced on the edge of the feeble stringer as unsafely as an egg on the edge of a cup. He knew this could not go on. He knew what the end must be. In the next few minutes George Fury lived one thousand years.

An outrageous crash shook the whole house as George's boot slipped. The whole weight of his body drove his foot through the flimsy ceiling, protruding into the room below.

Instantly a burst of gunfire exploded in the lean-to beneath. Avery had snatched his forty-five and fired upward as instinctively as a mule lashes out. A splinter stuck in the skin of Melody's thigh. George Fury felt the hard jerk of a bullet that grazed his leather cuff.

Avery fired three times, as fast as his pistol hammer could cock and fall; and instantly afterward a general tumult broke out below. They heard Fever Crick de Longpre bound out of bed with a yell. They heard Cherry running across the kitchen. And close to him in the dark Melody could hear George cussing in hoarse whispers.

Melody said, "Are you hit? Did he git you?"

"No, I ain't hit, but—"

"Then back out of this, you old fool, before he lets go again!"

"I cain't! My boot's wedged by the spur!"

Below, they heard Avery shouting at his sister, "Stop hollering fool questions, will you, and bring a light out here!"

"Then pull your foot out of the boot," Melody urged George.

"What the be-Jesus dew yew *think* I'm tryin' to dew?"

"They's a corpse—" Fever Crick de Longpre shouted hoarsely—"they's a corpse up thar!"

With a supreme effort George freed his foot, and they went floundering and scrambling back into the main loft.

Cherry's voice came choked and strange. "You've killed somebody!"

"Well, what in hell-damn were they *doing* up there?" Avery and Cherry were at the foot of the ladder to the loft. "Stand back and hold the light!" Avery started up the ladder slowly, well shaken now, his six-gun in his hand.

"Pull off your other boot, George," Melody suggested. "You can anyway try to have your feet *match,* cain't you?"

But George Fury had recovered his boot. He pulled it on with a savage wrench, and drew his gun. Crawling on hands and knees, he reached the top of the ladder to meet Avery de Longpre. Avery reluctantly lifted his head above the floor of the loft to find a gun like a cannon staring him squarely between the eyes.

"What in Gardlemighty's the matter with yew?" George demanded furiously. "Ain't yew got no sense at all?"

Avery looked blankly from one to the other of them. "So it's you," he said. Dazedly he withdrew, and backed down the ladder. He and Cherry stood staring inanely upward at the two faces which now looked down at them from the trap. "It's them," he told his sister.

Cherry's voice came faint and small. "What you doing?" she asked Melody, not unreasonably.

George Fury tried a foolish bluster. "A man has to sleep somewheres don't he?"

Melody Jones lay at full length, relaxed, his chin on his arms, as he looked down. He didn't contribute anything.

A slow anger was turning Avery's eyes green. "I guess you better come down here," he decided. "Back down slow, without any false moves. And one at a time," he added unnecessarily.

Melody and George Fury exchanged a slow look of mutual dislike, then holstered their guns and obeyed.

"So now there's three of you," Avery said. "How many more is up there?"

"Didn't see anybody but us," Melody said. "You see anybody, Uncle Roscoe?"

"Then whose foot is that, sticking through that there ceiling, in that there shed?" Avery wanted to know. As they stood silent, looking at him dead-pan, Avery motioned them toward the lean-to with his gun. "Go on out there!" They did as he said.

"Look up at the ceiling," he ordered, bringing the lantern to the door of the lean-to behind them. "What do you see?"

"Cracks," Melody said.

Avery's voice dropped lower, as his anger sharpened. "You see a boot," he said, disdaining to look up. "You see a boot, sticking through them broken boards."

Melody studied the ceiling, then looked at Avery with sadness and pity. "You're all wrought up," he said.

Everyone looked upward now, at the hole where George had broken through.

"Roscoe has them fits, sometimes, too—sees all kind of things," Melody said to Cherry.

Avery spoke faintly, staring upward. "I'd of swore—I'd of swore—"

"Don't let it worry you, Avery," Melody said kindly. "That shadder looks a *leetle* like a boot. For a second I kind of thought I seen one there myself."

Avery sat down weakly on the edge of the rawhide bunk. "This beats me," he said. "I throw in . . ."

Cherry took the gun out of Avery's limp hand, ejected its remaining cartridges, and put them in her pocket. Then she stood looking at Melody, and he could almost see her mind work. One thing he did not see, however, was any trace of a misgiving that she might have misjudged him.

"Sometimes," Melody said, "I feel kind of low in my mind."

She drew him away from Avery now, into the kitchen. "Don't you ever stop to think," she asked him quietly, "about what-all I've done for you?"

"Whut?"

"You were in the soup-kettle, down there in Payneville. Half the town was after your scalp. You couldn't even get your ponies out of the corral without getting hurt. I got them for you. I got you out of there alive. Didn't I?"

"Well, you see," Melody said, "I kind of got mistook for a feller name of—"

"Monte Jarrad," Cherry said. "I saw that. And ever since then, everything I've done has been to help you, and undo that mistake!"

"Was that why," Melody asked her, "you run up to me on the street, and called me by Monte's name?"

Cherry de Longpre wavered a moment. "Won't you do just one thing for me?" she asked finally.

"Whut?"

"Get out of here," she said, her voice rising with the strain. "Won't you please, please get out of here?"

And then Melody astonished her again. "Sure," he said.

She stared at him blankly. "What?"

He looked her over sadly. "Come on, George."

She was still staring as he turned and walked out of the house. George Fury backed out after Melody, his gun on Avery until they were well into the dark.

❦ 8 ❦

fter Melody Jones and George Fury were gone again, Cherry went back to the job of getting her brother started to town. There was a short struggle. Avery had become confused, and didn't want to move until he was straightened out.

First of all Avery had to search the loft; he couldn't get it out of his head that there was a dead man up there. When he found nothing he was just as bewildered as before.

"How did they get up there? What was they doin'? Cherry, I ought to foller them fellers."

"Look, Avery," Cherry said. "Suppose they are peace officers. Suppose they're express company men. Isn't that all the more reason why Monte needs Lee and Virg? You've just *got* to get down there to Payneville and see if they've come in!"

Avery started uncertainly out of the house, but turned back. "What I want to know," he said, "is how they got that dead man out of there?"

"Avery, do I have to tell you a thousand times there wasn't any dead man?"

"Look," Avery said with a great show of patience. "Didn't somebody stick his foot through the ceiling? And didn't I drill him dead center with three shots? So what become of him? Do you figure he blew up, or floated away, or—or something, or what?"

"Either you get started for town," Cherry said through her teeth, "or I'm going out and tell Monte you won't go."

Avery looked hurt, but he was convinced. "All right, Cherry." A few moments later he went hammering down the trail.

Cherry listened long enough to make sure that Avery had really taken the Payneville fork of the trail instead of switching off again on some idea of his own. Then she stood for a few moments in the middle of the kitchen, looking about her vaguely. She was tired, but too much upset to rest. She began to putter around the kitchen, clearing up the things without any notion of what she was doing. She made as long a job of it as she could, because she couldn't imagine ever getting to sleep. She managed to fritter away the better part of an hour before she finally turned to the only other room, which was her own.

Carrying a lamp, and leaving the kitchen dark behind her, she opened the door of her stall-like bedroom. Instantly she almost dropped the lamp. The body of a man was stretched full length upon her bed.

Cherry bit her knuckles in a belated effort to keep herself from screaming. It was not necessary; Cherry didn't go around screaming very much.

The figure on the bed was sprawled loosely, one hand trailing palm up upon the floor, the face covered by a tattered hat. Cherry moved slowly into the room, and set the lamp down on the washstand. Gingerly she lifted the hat away.

Melody Jones lay sound asleep, with his mouth open, a look of placid incompetence upon his unconscious face. Cherry stood looking down at him for several moments before he opened his eyes.

"Hi," Melody said.

Cherry tossed his hat on top of him and turned away; she had never been more discouraged in her life. She sat down on a soap box by the washstand, looking mostly unravelled.

"I don't suppose," she said dully, "it's any use asking you what the hell?"

"I been thinkin'," Melody said.

"I don't believe that, either," Cherry said bitterly.

"You know somethin'?" Melody said. "I believe you're in some kind of a fix, around here."

"If I'm not," Cherry said, "I'm going to be, if I can't stop you from haunting me like the living dead! Once and for all, and for the last time—will you, for God's *sake*—get out of here?"

"Cain't."

"Why not?"

Melody Jones lied to her then. "My hoss run off," he told her.

Cherry stared at him, then dipped her hand in the pitcher and stroked a little water onto her forehead with her fingertips.

In a moment of silence Melody looked around the room. He hadn't seen it before in the light. He had kind of expected this room to tell him something about the girl, since it was her own. The night breeze was lifting the curtains at the wide-open window. He had reckoned there would be curtains here. They were made of blue and white gingham, instead of the red-spotted stuff he had imagined, but it came to the same thing. A place to put clothes had been made by hanging some of the gingham in front of a shelf. On the very plain washstand, beside the bowl and pitcher, a collection of bright-colored pebbles lay in rows, set off by some quartz crystals, and bits of native turquoise—Cherry's substitute for the jewelry nobody had ever bought her. That was about all.

"What have you done with your partner?" Cherry asked him.

He evaded that, partly. "I reckon he's settin' around somewhere, countin' his teeth. That's most generally what George is li'ble to be doin'. You see, George didn't want to come back here, seems like."

"George?"

He told her George Fury's name then, and his own. He was beginning to tell her the history of how they had come to Payneville, starting back two or three years before; but she didn't seem interested very much.

"Look," she cut him off. "I'll give you another horse. I'll give you some kind of a saddle, too. I'll give you anything we've got around here!" Cherry was making a last desperate stand; she looked like a kit-fox at bay. "I'm through trying to explain to you that you're in trouble; I've given up trying to get it into your head. But if you're caught here, and killed, I don't want it to be because you were afoot!"

"I couldn't go to work and abandon Harry Henshaw," he told her, "and him with his bridle on."

She looked at him blankly, and there was another detour—mind-destroying for Cherry de Longpre—as he explained to her about Harry Henshaw being the name of his horse.

"I suppose," Cherry said, her voice shaking a little, "I

ought to be glad you know who you are. *You* have a cheek, pretending to be Monte Jarrad—even trying to fool *me!* Just because I mistook you for some one else, at first—"

"No, you didn't," Melody said.

"What?"

"The whole thing is no better than a hoe-axe," he said. "You knew from the start I wasn't anybody in particular. You cooked the whole thing up in your own haid, and I knew it at the time."

She stared at him a moment more, then turned away, baffled by that mild, effortless lack of pressure.

"You're nuts about this Monte, aren't you?" he asked without prejudice.

"What if I am?"

"Seems like every guy has some gal goes ridic'lous about him," Melody said, "Except—except—"

The corners of Cherry's mouth turned down. She knew he was going to slide off into self-pity, then. But he fooled her.

"Except George," Melody said. "I never knew nothing short of a old bag to go for George. But I reckon we shouldn't expect no miracles, should we?" he asked. "No," he answered himself, "we sure shouldn't."

"What the hell goes on here?" Cherry said, a little wildly.

"Whut?"

"You—you make a person forget what she was talking about," Cherry said crazily. The strain was burning her out. She picked up a hairbrush from the washstand and looked at it as if she had never seen it before. She shook out her hair and began to brush it mechanically, looking at the wall.

"You got pretty hair," he said. "It's the color of—of pretty good timothy hay."

Cherry's voice was gritty, and held low with difficulty. "I'll gladly pull it out," she said, "or set it on fire, if you'll only get out of this country before something happens to you!"

"You're in some kind of a box," Melody told her. "You been mixing with the wrong people, or something. I don't reckon you'd have turned the sheriff on me, and fixed me up to get shot, and maybe hung, without even knowing who I was, unless something was bothering you. I'd feel like a nump, if'n I just high-tailed over the hill, with bullets smoking up the tail of my coat. If I was wearing a coat."

Cherry studied the hairbrush through a long moment of quiet; then she threw it down beside the pitcher and turned on him. "All right."

"Whut?"

"I'll make a deal with you."

"Wait a minute," he said suddenly.

Out by the kitchen door the bear cub had uttered a little explosive snarl, almost like a bark; and it was growling through its nose now, in a high trill, very shrilly. Melody swung his feet to the floor, took a long step to the lamp, and blew it out. As he sat down again on the edge of the bed there was a moment of complete stillness, so that they could hear each other breathing in the dark.

Then he heard her come close to him and drop to one knee, so that they could speak even more softly than before. Her hands found his arm.

"Why did you do that?"

"That bear seen somethin'," Melody told her.

"I suppose he did," she said, at the limit of exasperation. "He's always seeing something; There's coyotes all around here."

"It was something else," Melody said vaguely.

"Couldn't it be," Cherry asked uncertainly, "your partner prowling around out there, looking for you?"

"Who, George? If George was looking for me he'd be giving out with a kind of a hoot-whistle. He thinks it sounds like a owl. You cain't tell him different. And when that fails him, he tries yapping like a coyote, And next thing after that he falls over something. You can count on it. You see, I been through all this before with George."

They were quiet again, and he could almost hear her thinking.

"What was it you wanted me to do for you?" he asked her.

"It's changed," she said. Her breathing had altered, so that he knew some new angle had come up to frighten her. "I'll tell you about it. I'll tell you the whole thing. But I have to show you something first. I can't show you until morning. So you'll have to stay right here until daylight."

"Whut?"

"You can sleep right where you are. That's what you want, isn't it? It is, isn't it?"

"I don't believe this," Melody said.

"I'll make out all right somewhere else," she said

shortly. "Will you do it? Will you do what I ask, and *stay put,* for something new?"

"Don't you even want to set and talk a spell?" Melody asked dolefully.

"God forbid," Cherry said. "I'll wake you before sunrise. Now, for the love of heaven, don't make another move until I come for you!"

She moved softly to the door, and he heard it close behind her.

As soon as she was gone, Melody pulled off his boots, laid them on the bed, and went out through the window.

❧ 9 ❧

The moon was well up now, and very bright. Its gun-metal half-light, color blind to all red or yellow tones, was so clear in that dry desert air that he could have read an obituary notice by it; but the shadows were as black as if they were painted out with soot. Keeping to the band of darkness close to the house wall, Melody Jones moved around the corner of the house to the back, where the bear cub was chained.

The bear cub growled at him once, and then accepted him, perhaps because he had come from within. While it snuffled at the wool socks in which he stood, Melody sifted the night with his eyes.

Where he now stood he faced the barn and the broken up-country. He combed the foreground first, then the distant contours; and he had time to estimate this country into which he had ridden by mistake, sensing its shape. The faint trace of far-off peaks gave him the feeling that he was seeing a thousand miles of this broken land; it lay vast and very still under the cool moon. This was a country for horses and long-riding men, because the cattle would run gaunt, and few to the mile. No wheel would ever touch the most of those broken reaches, not until the world upheavals that tossed these ledges up should come to wreck them down again. No plow, even by dry-farming, would ever stir up anything but alkali dust. A whole empire of this clear-aired, rock-ribbed land would remain a preserve for lean and lonely men on ponies, ten centuries after city men would suppose the riding days were gone. . . .

The bear cub stopped snuffling, and began to worry at Melody's sock. Melody moved out of reach and sat down. The cub followed to the end of its chain, then sat down beside him with its hind feet in its paws, and looked at the country like Melody. It both looked and acted like a very little, potbellied dwarf of a man, so much as Melody could see.

A man could make a living in this country, all his life, and never have a worry in the world. He only needed a friendliness with horse flesh, and a respect for the scarcity of desert water, and a love of the desert land. With these things, this land would take care of him. For this was calf-producing land. The lank and long-boned cattle which knew this range should never be shipped for beef. But the long miles of the desert could produce incredible train-loads of calves, young stock, that could be brought to beef on the banks of the Washita, and the plains of Dodge.

Fever Crick de Longpre only understood the nuisance

herds of mustangs which traveled this country by night, and creamed the feed. If you wanted to give the name of horse to a wild animal as tall as your shoulder, with a head as long as your leg, and five-inch fur, you naturally chased wild horses, here. . . .

Melody first knew something was wrong again because the bear cub was so still. Leaning hard upon pure instinct, Melody centered the whole soul of his attention upon the shadow of a rock, half way up a hill behind a steep corral. The shadow could have held a man. It could even have been the shadow of a man who stood beside a horse.

As Melody watched it seemed to him that the outline of horse and man became more and more clear. It was four hundred yards away; yet, when he had looked at it long enough, he saw clearly the flick of a pony's ear. Just about then an owl flew out, spoiling the whole imagining.

Then, fifty yards away, just within the shelter of the barn, a shadow broke. It was no distant illusion this time, but a plainly visible movement, nearly under Melody's nose. A man, or something the size of a man, was moving through the slim bars of moonlight within the barn, and the shocking thing about this activity was its unexpected nearness. It was as if you were watching for danger two blocks away, when a hand with a knife in it crept quietly under your shirt.

The bear cub said no more. He had been talking about this in the first place, and had known about it all the time.

Melody felt both astonished and humiliated. A superstitious notion offered itself to him that he was looking at a ghost; but he discarded this. When the movement within the barn had passed out of sight, Melody scratched his head and stood up. His eyes ran along the barren, vertical steep behind the barn, and saw no cover there. He similarly prospected the gully far to the right, and concluded that nothing could reach that, without his knowledge. Whatever was out there would have to wait for him, if he went to see what it was.

Not because he was brave, not even because he was curious, but because it seemed to be the next thing to do, Melody Jones relaxed his hands and stepped into the moonlight. He knew he could be killed from almost any place, within reasonable gunshot; but nothing happened. After a moment or two of standing there, Melody walked forward, silent in his sock feet, toward the door of the barn.

Once within the big main door it was better, and at the same time worse. You could be potted from fewer places here, but in the dark it was creepy. What he saw, when his eyes were fully adjusted, was not very much. A lot of the space was taken up by the horse-ranch hay, stacked in bales; and his cattleman's nose told him that the bales were old, and doing no good here. Dim in the foreground, considered late because they could not conceal a gunman, were the saddle racks, carrying a few old hulls; a futile, broken hay rake; some great wheels, from long abandoned Conestoga wagons, and such-like junk.

What worried Melody was not that he couldn't see, but that he thought he could. There didn't seem to be anybody in the barn. He stood well inside the door and scratched his head again.

As he raised his arm, his elbow was perhaps seven inches from the left eye of Monte Jarrad.

Melody Jones' vague bewilderment was a wild and casual thing compared to Monte Jarrad's total astonishment. Monte had not seen Melody moving in the black shadow of the house. He had not even seen him when Melody silently crossed the thirty yards of open moonlight between house and barn. In those moments Monte had been standing braced between the bales, and he was holding his eyes shut while he waited for a certain amount of thunder and lightning to stop playing around in his wounded side. He was mending very fast, much faster than he could have hoped, but the first exercise in three days was something he had to pay for.

Then he thought he heard breathing, where no breathing should have been, and he opened his eyes to see Melody Jones silhouetted in the moonlit door, easily within reach of Monte's hand.

Monte Jarrad had no notion of who Melody was; he had never seen him in his life. He failed to match up this unaccounted visitor with the tramp rider who had been mistaken for Monte himself in Payneville. Beyond the fact that the figure was that of a stranger, and had appeared with amazing stealth, identity made no difference. The country was full of people hunting for Monte Jarrad.

One of them was now standing about three feet away, and Monte was counting his chances. Since the intruder knew his business so well, it was a safe bet that he had not come here alone. It would have been easy enough to kill the stranger, in these moments while Monte remained undiscovered; but there was no way of knowing what kind of a general gun-battle would follow on that. Monte waited. Melody Jones finished scratching his head and wandered off a little way through the tangle of impedimenta in the barn.

As soon as his back was turned Monte drew his gun. Melody seemed to hear the faint whisper of the leather. He turned back, looked about him suspiciously; and then walked straight toward Monte. The man between the bales could not believe that he was unseen, the thin stripes of moonlight made the figure of Melody Jones so plain. Monte's six-gun centered on Melody's belt buckle, and the hammer moved back silently, just short of the click.

Six feet away from Monte Jarrad, Melody Jones wobbled, and turned about uncertainly. He turned his back directly upon Monte, and slowly sat down on a bale. He rested his chin on the knuckles of both hands, his high heels rolled over on their sides, so that he sat bowlegged; and seemed to give himself to thought.

Monte Jarrad's first astonishment had passed off, and he knew now what he had to do. He still did not dare to fire. He believed now that his one best bet was to brain the stranger with his gun barrel, as quietly as was practicable, and hide him under the hay.

Melody Jones, with his back to Monte, was sitting just out of Monte's reach. Monte Jarrad took a long step forward, fitting his boot-heel very slowly into the dust. He managed a second step, undetected; he was close enough to breathe down Melody's neck. His gun came up gradually, until it was higher than his head.

Melody Jones unhurriedly stood up. Casually he hitched up his belt as he strolled to the moonlit door. Monte subsided into the shadows as Melody took one more leisurely look at the hay rake, the wagon wheels, and the dark space where Monte stood. Then Melody left the barn, and moved without haste toward the house.

Changing his position, Monte watched Melody as he walked past the door of the de Longpre house, and proceeded without any particular caution along the house wall. He saw Melody come to the window which Monte knew belonged to Cherry's room. Nonchalantly, as matter-of-factly as if he were vaulting onto a horse, Melody put his hands on the window ledge, and swung a leg over the sill. Still unhurriedly, he disappeared within. Monte's breath sucked in through his teeth.

❧ 10 ❧

The first grey light was hardly beginning to show beyond the gaunt rock of Holiday Ridge when Cherry de Longpre, sleeping on a cot in the lean-to, was wakened by the sound of a ridden horse coming in at a walk. She raised herself on an elbow and looked out through the hole in the board wall which served as the lean-to window.

George Fury was riding in, relaxing caution as he came close. His carbine was in his hands, but he was now in the act of putting it away in his saddle boot. This nonchalance puzzled Cherry until a moment later when she saw, with a keen chagrin, the reason for George Fury's assurance. Melody Jones was up already, and sitting on the kitchen steps in full view. He plainly had been up for some time, for he had had time to find and catch the horse he called Harry Henshaw. The pony was saddled and packed with Melody's bedroll, and was now finishing a heavy bait of oats laid out on a gunny sack at the edge of the rickety gallery.

Cherry lay back soundlessly, more than willing to hear what Melody and George Fury had to say to each other when they thought they were alone.

George Fury looked Melody over ironically, which was mostly wasted in the bad light. Then he stepped down, dropping his split reins to the ground, and loosened his cinches with elaborate deliberation before turning upon his partner.

Melody Jones, who was whittling himself a mestook, acknowledged George's arrival with a silent gesture of his knife. Nobody ever knew what a mestook was except Melody, who had left a trail of them all over the West. In general the mestooks seemed to be little carvings made out of mesquite roots, which come gnarled and twisted in all manner of nearly recognizable shapes. With his knife Melody improved these into peculiar faces and nonexistent animals. The one he was whittling now looked something like a nervous elephant at one end, but the other end bore an odd facial resemblance to Fever Crick de Longpre. Sometimes people asked him what was his theory, working so careful on such a darn thing, and he tried them with any answer but the right one, which was that he didn't know.

"I went and looked for you by the crick where I left you," Melody said, "and I found Harry Henshaw where you tied him. But you was gone."

George eased himself stiffly to the step beside Melody. "Expect me to set there all night?" he grunted.

Melody looked at him gravely. "George," he said, "I've rode with you a fur piece, and I swar a feller don't live that can say you would or you wouldn't."

George's customary snort came out only as a long sigh; he needed his coffee. "I been down to Payneville."

"I figgered that. Liquor's sure a curse."

"I brung you a message." George began digging in his various pockets. "I got it somewheres here."

"Message? I don't know anybody in Payneville."

"You know one feller at least—the feller you hit. This here's from him." He handed Melody a balled-up wad of wrapping paper. "You better read it—if you still can read."

Melody could read very nicely; his father had taught him from some old copies of Godey's Lady's Book. Melody could read words like "bombazine," and "reticule." About the only other literary material that had fallen into his hands, though, had been on the labels of tomato cans. A tomato label packs a lot of information, but it is mainly beside the point.

The note George Fury had brought from Payneville didn't have much in it either. It simply said:

You better come down here and talk.
And quick.

"T'ain't signed."

"Name's Ira Waggoner. He was the stage driver on the

coach Monte Jarrad held up, on the Stinkwater road. 'Give this to Monte Jarrad,' he says. He still thinks you're Monte Jarrad."

"Oh," said Melody. After some thought he decided he ought to have eyebrows on his mestook, and began engraving them with the tip of his knife. A band of scarlet had appeared in the sky to the east, tinging the grey light; and the quiet air held the freshened smell of the faint dew upon dusty brush.

"I finally found a man a feller could talk to down there," George Fury went on. "The town is just as crazy as it was; their minds is et out by drinking water from the Poisonberry River, I figger now. But this feller was a bullwhacker, just passin' through, and he hadn't drunk any water, so he was all right."

"Is he the one that give you the black eye?"

"That come later. . . . This feller told me a pile of stuff about this Monte Jarrad you're supposed to be. Everybody in the Gardam whoop-hurrah country knows more about him than you do. I don't know how it is, but somehow you are the one blink that don't never seem to get the word."

Melody started to explain that to George, but let it pass.

"Monte Jarrad was in a war around here, three-four years back," George told Melody. "Seemingly this war was made up of Monte Jarrad on one side, and a ranch family name of Cotton on the other side. Old Man Cotton had six or seven boys, and a lot of hired help. Monte Jarrad killed him three or four of them cowhands, and a couple of Cottons. But this country is run by the

Cottons now. That's why most of the town was out looking for Monte Jarrad with the posse. And there ain't a Cotton alive who wouldn't give his eyeteeth to git a bullet into you. Naturally," George finished, "if you had to be Monte Jarrad, you would pick the middle of a whole nest of Cottons for it. That follers as a matter of course. It wouldn't be like you if it was done any different."

"Heck, George." Melody seemed depressed. "I don't know why you talk thataway. A feller would think I done something."

"A feller would think so," George agreed. "The sheriff has got near the whole country in his posse, without no aim in life but to git you and hang you. Providin' the Cotton family don't dry-gulch you first. And excusin' that the express company detectives don't grab you out from under their nose, because you taken their strong box, with forty thousand dollars in it. Some say they was forty million dollars in it, but this is likely overthrifty. Failing any of them set-backs, you always got the United States Cavalry to fall back on, because of course they was mail on that stage. They got an up-coming court case they're sweating to try, called People of the United States agin Melody Jones. By Gard, Melody, this here's a record!"

"I don't see somethin'," said Melody. "If I'm such a popular, well-known kind of a jigger, how come I get mistook for somebody else?"

"Because Monte ain't been back here in three-four years. And you ain't run into nobody that knew him good. You ain't fooled anybody that really knew Monte."

Melody studied the note from Ira Waggoner again. "Cherry," he said, without raising his voice, "come out here a minute."

There was a moment's silence, and Cherry sounded chastened, as she answered him. "All right, Melody."

George Fury jerked to his feet. "How long she been listenin'?"

Melody shrugged. "All the time, I reckon. You know how women are." He got to his feet unhurriedly, pocketing the mestook, as Cherry came out of the house, dressed as she had slept.

Cherry looked pale, and showed blue circles under her eyes. Her hands were trying to unrumple her hair, which still looked lighter than her face. There was no exchange of greetings. Melody handed her the note George had brought.

"You know somethin' about this?" he asked.

Cherry studied the message for a long time. "This isn't for you," she said at last. She looked humorless and scared.

"Is that what you wanted me to do," Melody asked, "go down there and straighten this feller out?"

"For God's sake *no!*" Cherry's nervous balance was breaking up. "That's the one thing you must *not* do!"

"Well," Melody said slowly, "if you don't want me to go down there, I suppose we could have him come out here."

"You mustn't talk to Ira Waggoner at all!" Cherry insisted, on the verge of hysteria. "Not now or any other time, no matter where you run into him next!"

"What fur not, Cherry? He know somethin'?"

Cherry looked as if she were going to burst into tears, but she pulled herself together. "I didn't say that."

"All you said was," Melody admitted, "you was going to show me something you wanted me to do."

Cherry snuffled back the threatening tears and made her voice quiet. "I'm going to. Hook up the buckboard for me—you know the team I use. I'll get you some breakfast while you hitch. And I'll take you to where—where we have to go."

"All right, Cherry." He went to get his lariat off of Harry Henshaw.

"Melody," George said when Cherry had gone into the house, "you going off some place with that girl?"

"Ain't you comin', George?"

George seemed weary and old. "Melody, I ain't."

They stood there awkwardly for a few minutes. George's eyes wandered vaguely over the distance, and Melody made marks on the ground with the heel of his boot.

"George," Melody said, "I tell you what I believe I'd do, if I was you. I believe I'd high-tail like all heck. But not in just any old direction, George. I believe I'd haid northeast, and swing past Stinkwater. Seemingly Monte Jarrad come here from that way. So the geenral hunt ain't likely to turn thataway—especially with me somewheres else."

"Keep your silly, befewzled idees to yourself!" George exploded. "I ain't ast nobody to tell me what to dew, yew least of all!"

"And one other thing," Melody said. "For gosh sake try to stay sober, will you, George? Until you've rode a piece. Don't forget for one minute that you're known as Uncle Roscoe."

George Fury's temper died out. "I ain't goin' to kill you, Melody," he said drearily. "I'm goin' to take that there in the sperrit you meant it at." He turned on his run-down heel and went stomping off.

❧ 11 ❧

When they had got the buckboard down the axle-cracking trail to the valley floor, with Harry Henshaw on lead behind it, they drove about four miles along the twisting Poisonberry River. Then Cherry de Longpre turned the team out of the ruts, into the unbroken sage. They presently came out into an open space in which lay the charred, weathered ruins of a ranch. Cherry pulled up, and sat listening.

She asked nervously, "Did you hear a horse whinny?"

"No," Melody said, "because there wasn't any done so. If they had, this team would have knowed it, whether we heard it or not. Whut's the matter? You expecting to meet somebody?"

"No—of course not—"

"Then why did you bring that six-gun?"

Cherry looked startled.

"I see you put it under the seat," Melody explained.

"I brought it," Cherry said slowly, "because you're in bad trouble. If you had to fight, I meant to help you."

"Honest? You did? You mean you know how to fight a gun, same as a man?"

"I know how to fix 'em," Cherry said sheepishly,

94

"because I clean 'em for Fever Crick and Avery all the time. But I don't like guns very well. I've only fired one off about two or three times."

"The main thing about a gun," Melody said reminiscently, "is that it don't hit whut you point it at. Not as a regular thing."

"You found that out, huh?"

Melody shrugged. "I pretty near shot a man, once," he said. "I'd of done it, too, only I didn't have time. So I just whammed him with a chair. They taken and slung me in the trap."

"I don't understand you," Cherry said, looking at him strangely. "Why are you just waiting here to be killed? Any one of the rocks you can see from here, any bunch of greasewood, may have one of the Cotton boys behind it, waiting to kill you. We might have been bushwhacked on the road we just drove. What's the matter with you? Are you *trying* to die?"

"*Huh*-uh," said Melody. He cocked his hat to one side, to block the flat rays of the sun.

"Then what in the name of heaven—"

"Well," Melody said with reluctance, "I'll tell you, if you got to know. It's because there's a couple things I don't understand about this here."

Cherry de Longpre looked at him for a long time with blank eyes.

"I never saw anybody like you before," she said at last. "But I'll tell you why I brought you here."

She drove the mustang team forward a little way, in among the ruins of the ranch. "This is called Burnt Ranch now," she told him. "But it used to be the Rowntree."

"I heard of them old pirates," Melody said.

"Then forget what you heard," she told him shortly. "That used to be the springhouse, there; cowboys used to ride in for miles for a cup of that water. But the spring is ruined, too. You see those dead skeleton trees, killed by the fire? Those used to be the prettiest trees in the whole valley. This was about the nicest ranch there was. But the people who built it, and the people who tried to save it—they're all dead. Except only one."

She moved the buckboard a little farther into the ruins. "Newton Rowntree built this part with his own hands. Look close at those big half-burned timbers, and you can still see the adze marks he made, thirty years ago. That long black slab is what is left of the table. Forty people have sat down at that table, many and many a time. The Rowntree only kept half a dozen cowboys, but everybody who passed by used to stop in."

Melody rolled slow eyes at her with more wonderment than a little. "How you kin *talk*," he said.

"Back there behind that big chimney arch, where the adobe still stands so thick—that used to be the fruit cellar," Cherry went on, with such stubbornness that she seemed unperturbed. "Mrs. Rowntree was a great hand for canning stuff. If you hunted under that rubbish, you'd find the broken cans, with labels on 'em that Mrs. Rowntree wrote."

"Canning stuff is a fine thing," Melody said. "Did you ever put up any cinnamon pears?"

"What?"

"Nothin'. Excuse me, ma'am, and go ahaid."

Cherry went ahead and told him what had happened,

according to her. The Cottons, she said, came into the valley much later than the Rowntrees. Anybody would think that there was enough land around there for everybody, such as it was, but the Cottons didn't feel that way. They set about driving the Rowntrees out, and their methods were an old story all over the West. They started with the handy use of running-irons, and the laming of horses, and sometimes a night stampede; and worked up to a full range-wrecking war, with the killing of an occasional cowboy in what is known as "a fair shoot-out" in some places, as yet.

Then finally a kid cowboy came along, after the Rowntrees had lost about everything they had, and the Rowntrees gave him a job. For a little while things seemed to change; that one cowboy almost reversed the whole course of the war. He had the Cottons so well backed up that it looked as if the Cottons, and not the Rowntrees, were going to be driven out of the valley.

Cherry told all this earnestly, with slow-worded strength of effect.

"The name of this cowboy," Cherry said at the end of it, "was Monte Jarrad."

"I kind of thought," Melody said, "it was going to be him."

In spite of Monte Jarrad's amazing rally, Cherry went on to say, the end of the war had been very bad. The Cottons swarmed down one night with more than forty men. Some of them made pretense that it was an Apache raid, but they turned out to be Cottons when they were dead. They laid siege, intent upon wiping out the Rowntree once and for all, in a single night. Old Newton Rowntree and his wife had only a couple of cowboys there, besides Monte Jarrad, but they fought well, from behind the walls.

One of the cowboys was killed first. Then Newton Rowntree was hit; Cherry showed Melody the angle of the wall where he went down. He was shot in the throat, she said, and bled to death in his wife's arms. Mrs. Rowntree took up his rifle then. Cherry pointed out the window ledge where her head had laid as she died. Monte and an old cowboy called Davy kept on fighting most of the night, until the fires were set.

After the roof was ablaze, and no chance was left, Monte and old Davy broke out of the burning house and made their rush. Old Davy was only trying to get away, now. He made a break for the shadows, and was shot down. It turned out he was shot eleven times. They must have kept shooting him for a long time after he was dead.

"But Monte, he ran straight at the place where he had spotted the Cotton boys," Cherry said. "He had a gun in each hand, and he was firing as he ran. Their gun flashes must have been all that he could see; but he killed two Cottons and hurt another. And somehow he broke through, and got away.

"So that's why Monte Jarrad is an outlaw now," she finished, snuffling a little. "Old Man Cotton had got himself made sheriff the day before the raid. So now every law in the world is against Monte Jarrad, and always will be. And the southwest won't be satisfied until he's dead."

They sat quiet for a little bit. "This Newton Rowntree," Melody said at last, "he wouldn't be the one I heard about—the one that scalped his grandma, that time?"

"*What?*"

"I'm sorry, honey," Melody said. "I just had to see the look on your face." He tilted his hat down on the side toward Cherry, so that she could not see his expression.

"Melody Jones," Cherry said dangerously, "if you're laughing at me—"

"I wouldn't laugh at you, Cherry."

"Then—" her tone was scalding—"how do you dare—"

"You talk good," Melody said with respect. "I've heard lies to trip a bull. I've heard lies that paid off bigger than a hundred dollars. But I never heard no such lies as that lie there."

Cherry turned white; she looked as if she were about to go up in smoke. "You dare use that word to me? You say I—*lie*—"

"Uh-huh," Melody said. "I reckon you was thinking of Billy the Kid—he used to come up with them kind of monkeyshines all the whole time. How was you to know I always stop by and grub-test at the Rowntrees, whenever I winter in California?"

"You—you do?"

"They raise chickens now," he told her. "*They* was some of those folks that come out West to get rich. So, they got rich, and moved to California. Or at least," Melody amended, "they moved. Old Man Cotton bought this whole spread for a hundred dollars and a buckboard team. Newt Rowntree says he's sorry it burned, seeing it was Cottons'; for hisself, he was glad to see the last of it."

They looked at each other strangely.

"Main place you was wrong," Melody said, "was

about Mrs. Rowntree putting up preserves. Newt cooks for the two. Ma Rowntree cain't fry a aig, without she busts the yelk. And when it comes to the part where her pore old hair was shot down onto her rifle butt—she would of told me. She would of said something, when I seen her last year. Monte must of just shot up the Cottons on a whim, or something. And when it comes to—"

"Let it go," Cherry said in a dead voice. "I quit."

They sat silent, a certain awkwardness between them.

"I'm hongry," Melody said.

"I'm sorry," Cherry said, without having heard him. She sounded as if she were going to cry. "I got myself into something, and I tried to talk my way out. That's all."

"So I seen," Melody said.

"My family's known Monte Jarrad since he was so high," Cherry said in the same dead voice. "He rode in hurt, and I tried to help him. That's all there was to the whole thing."

"Did he get away okay?" Melody asked with interest.

"They're about to get him. He *would* have been safe—but you drew the posse back, by being mistaken for him. So now he's dry-gulched and through. It wasn't your fault. You didn't mean to draw the posse in. But you did. I've been trying to make you lead the posse away again. But you bucked me down."

"Oh," Melody said.

Cherry put her chin in her fists and seemed to think out loud, unhurried. "If you had been my friend—but you weren't. If I had one friend in the world, that wasn't known around here, I could get him to lead the posse off.

He could mark himself as Monte, someway—Monte's saddle on his horse would do it. Later he could prove he wasn't Monte, and they'd let him go. And Monte would get his chance to make a new start. Only there isn't any such friend to turn to."

"You'd do just about anything for that belly-gunner, wouldn't you," Melody said, out of his dejection.

Cherry snapped out of it; she lowered her voice. "I want you to know I'm sorry I hauled you into this. You've been pretty nice about it, according to your lights. And this is goodbye."

She put her arms about his neck, pulled his head down, and kissed him. Melody made no move for a moment. Then he awkwardly took off his hat, and took her in his arms. "Well, goodbye," he said; and kissed her again.

"Listen," she said, still in his arms. "I don't want you to think I brought you here to ask you to help Monte."

"Well, goodbye," Melody said again, but this time she ducked.

"I want you to know," she whispered desperately, "that I'm not asking you to help Monte. Nothing was farther from what I meant."

"Oh?"

"Such a thing never entered my head."

Melody released her, slowly. "Then why," he asked her, "have you got Monte's saddle here in the buckboard, under that there blanket?"

Cherry gasped. "I—I didn't know it was there," she faltered.

"I'd of thought," Melody said, "you might of noticed it, while you was tying that sack of flour to it, just before we left."

Cherry's eyes dropped. "I don't know why I lie to you," she said after a pause.

"Neither do I." He swung down off the buckboard. "Hold them broom-tails a minute."

He went to the tail of the buckboard, and unsaddled Harry Henshaw. Then he got Monte Jarrad's great silver-mounted saddle from the buckboard where it was hidden, and swung it aboard Harry. Monte's saddle weighed better than sixty pounds, and Harry Henshaw looked a little bit as though he were looking out of a dog house. Somehow it also made Harry look pigeon-toed on both sides, instead of just the one.

When Melody looked up from tying the latigo, Cherry was staring at him in utter dumbfoundment.

"You're—you're going to do it?"

"Whut? Change saddles? Oh, sure. Ain't that whut you wanted me to do?"

"Yes," she admitted, in a very small voice.

He went back to his own saddle, which he had slung onto the buckboard, and got a purple scarf out of his saddlebags. "I kind of value this," he explained, knotting it around his throat. "I won it for bronc-stomping and roping, in the all-around-best-cowboy contests, back in Cheyenne." He hesitated, and looked embarrassed. "Maybe you're thinking they generally have better prizes than this, at Cheyenne," he said. "Well, they do. But I slipped a stirrup, and come seventeenth." He saluted her with one gloved hand, and reined Harry Henshaw away. "I guess I got to be going, now."

"Wait!" Cherry called sharply; and he turned back.

"That—that's the wrong way! You can't ride down that way! That's toward Payneville!"

"I know," Melody said. "You see—I got to talk to a feller."

Cherry's mouth opened wide with horror. "But I thought—but you were supposed—you've got to—"

Melody grinned feebly. "Huh-uh," he said. He wheeled his pony without hurry and jogged away.

She tried to shout after him; she made a move to whip up the team, and overtake him with the buckboard. But in the end she just sat staring after him, with flabbergasted eyes.

❦ 12 ❦

As soon as Melody was out of sight, Cherry turned and went whaling back to the Busted Nose. She got there with her ratty team blowing and lathering; and Monte Jarrad was at her buckboard wheel, even before she could jump down.

Monte Jarrad was mounted up on the best horse on the place, and his bedroll was strapped behind him. Avery was in the saddle, too, in the background, but before she gave him a second glance she was searching Monte's face, estimating whether he could possibly be fit to ride. Monte's face was a broken grey color, like oysters sprinkled with meal; it was surprising how rapidly he had bleached, in the short time he had been out of the sun. He sat stiffly, and braced a hand on the saddle horn when his pony moved. But in the saddle he was straight and compact.

"I'm glad you're ready to ride," she said before he spoke. "It's time to be out of here, Monte. Avery, how in time did you get past me on the road?"

The deceptive thing about Avery was that he made his long, sullen silences and his secretive eyes suggest a singular wisdom; people always listened when he spoke, because it was seldom. Then they were let down by the triviality of the long-awaited remark.

"Oh, I got ways," he answered her.

"Where's my saddle?" Monte Jarrad demanded. His voice was flat, and slightly nasal, with a hostile edge.

She told him what she had done. "As many people are chasing that flashy saddle as are chasing you. There isn't another like it in the world. I got the stranger cowboy to put it on his horse, and ride it. The posse will be pulled half across the country, following that saddle."

She did not tell Monte that Melody had inexplicably ridden down to Payneville, instead of going over the hill as he was supposed to do. She did not dare tell Monte, because she did not understand it herself. Cherry was beginning to be badly shaken by the whole thing.

"Avery," Monte said without looking around at him, "start moving south."

Avery started to say something, but shut his mouth and obeyed. He turned his pony and went slantwise downhill at a long walk, avoiding the trail. In a few moments he had disappeared.

"You lied to me," Monte said to Cherry. "You told me he was on his way last night."

"I swear I did everything I could to get rid of him!" Strain was coming into Cherry's voice, because of the way Monte was looking at her. "I had to let him stay—in the house, even—simply because the fool wouldn't travel until daylight."

He looked at her steadily for some moments. "You'd better be telling the truth," he said. "Do you know what I'd do to you, if I caught you in a double-cross?"

Color came into Cherry's face, across the cheekbones. "Now you look here, Monte! If you think I like the sound of that—"

"I didn't ask you what you like," he said in that same flat tone. "I haven't time to deal with this so-called stranger. Not right now. But I'll take care of his case later. I know how to bust him of this fooling around. And you too!"

Cherry stared at him in bewilderment. "Why, Monte," she said unsteadily, "why, Monte—"

He looked at her for a long time, and his face changed. Uncertainty came into it; then a faint admiring surprise; then the rocky sullenness came back, just a half-point sharper than before. But it was Cherry who spoke, at last.

"Yeah," Cherry said, and her voice was very empty. "Yeah, I know. So you'll 'shoot him right in the stummick.' And me too. And yourself, too, I hope."

"How's that again?"

"There's a couple of things you need to know," she said, looking him directly in the eyes. "Neighbors used to mean a lot, back in Pike County. Because people were few and far between. And they hung onto each other, for better or worse. So we were there; so we broke a colt together, when we were eleven years old."

"Named him Dusty," Monte said.

That made Cherry falter a little. "I didn't reckon you'd remember."

"I remember, Cherry."

"All right. All right, Monte. But you've got to know something. I wouldn't risk one thread of that stranger boy's shirt to pull you out of this!"

He stared at her blankly through most of that, but on the last of it a kind of humor came into his eyes. "You done that already," he said.

"I didn't," she said breathily, as much to herself as to him. "I didn't—I didn't, and I won't."

His stiff-cheeked smile pushed up the lower lids of his eyes. "It'll be a long day, the day you ever quit me," he said.

She stared at him defiantly; but presently her eyes dropped. "I guess so, Monte."

"There's only one thing you got to be sure to do," he said clearly. "After they get him you got to go and identify him."

She shrugged that off, almost with contempt. "He can easy enough prove who he is!"

Monte's eyes snapped back to her face. "I reckon he isn't going to prove much, after he's dead."

"They—they aren't going to—"

"I should judge they'll bring the body in. But if they don't, you've still got to make sure they bury him as me."

Cherry was staring at him as if she couldn't believe her ears. She managed a shaky flare-up. "Nothing like this is going to happen! Even if they should catch him—"

"Of course they'll catch the damn fool. Why, he can't

even get horse relays!"

"They won't kill him," Cherry insisted desperately, "because he won't fight. He doesn't even know how to fight! And they certainly won't hang him—without even any trial—just because he's riding the wrong saddle!"

"What did you think they was goin' to do?"

"He might have got the saddle in a trade, or found it, or—or anything!"

Monte's eyes crinkled with his stiff grin. "Listen, honey," he said, almost with indulgence, "them Cottons is nervous people. For about five minutes they'll think they've got me, and they'll be the happiest jiggers alive. Then it'll come over them they haven't got me—they only got the feller that led 'em off, when I was right in their hands. I wish I could hear the yell that'll go up when they realize that. And on top of that, they can't even convict him of nothin', like you say. That's goin' to be the most sudden-hung cowboy ever was seen!"

"I don't believe you."

Monte chuckled, but it hurt his side, and he finished straight-faced. "All he better hope is that there's a tree handy, so they don't have to hang him by draggin' him."

"I don't believe you," Cherry said again. He could hardly hear her this time.

"This is the break in the luck," Monte said; "and it's you that done it, honey. I got plans for burnin' this country to the ground, once I get in the clear!"

Cherry sat perfectly still, as if she were hypnotized; she seemed to have lost any ability to move or speak.

Monte started to bend in the saddle; he meant to kiss her. But his wound stopped him as if he were caught with a fishhook. "I'm headin' south for the border," he told her; "I'll send for you as soon as your job here is done."

He forced one more grin, then lifted his reins and followed Avery, his pony at a running walk.

❦ 13 ❦

As he swung down in Payneville's Court Street, Melody Jones took one more look at the low sky beyond the town. A haze to the southwest might or might not be the dust of the posse coming in. He could not tell how far away it was, but he judged that what time he had would be none too much.

He could feel a hundred pairs of eyes upon his back, but the many who must have been watching him were making themselves as inconspicuous as they could, so that Payneville seemed nine-tenths deserted. He hitched up his chaps and pulled down the old cowhide vest with the brands burnt on it. Monte Jarrad's tremendous black and silver saddle, with its deep-carved pattern of twining roses, made him feel shabby, as he turned away from his horse.

Melody crossed the boardwalk and went into the Last Chance bar, walking with such slow, light steps that the spur-irons hardly whispered at his heels. He had pulled the buckskin glove from his right hand and stuck it in his belt as he supposed Monte Jarrad might do in walking into uncertainties. His knees were stiff as boards, but his face was as blank as could have been wished by Unsmiling Jones. His intent watchfulness had left it empty, except for the restless switch of his eyes.

Desert-country shadows seemed blackest in full day-light, by contrast to the white blast of the sun, so that a man needs a moment to accustom his eyes. But even without knowing what was waiting for him here, Melody felt a certain broad relief to be within the walls, out from under the eyes he had felt in the glare of the street.

His entrance was immediately spoiled by a trivial impasse. A round card table was planted in the narrow space just within the door, to take advantage of what breeze there might be; and here three slouch-dressed cowmen sat, tied up in a game of draw. The tilted chair of the fattest one blocked the way by which Melody might have passed.

Melody stood looking at them in a baffled sort of way, hoping they would let him pass. Either these were men who knew he was not Monte Jarrad, or they did not even know that he was supposed to be. Melody cleared his throat. The fat one in the titled chair looked up at him with a leisured insolence, and went back to his hand.

"Can I git by, please?" Melody said.

"Raise you five," said the man in the tilted chair, tossing a chip onto the table.

Melody's mind stopped turning, then, something like it had in the moment in which he had hit Ira Waggoner; except that this time the reason was that he was scared. He took a half-step backward, to give himself room.

"I call," Melody said. He took a long step forward, boot swinging, and kicked the table straight up, out from among them.

The table banged against the ceiling, splitting down the middle, and its wreckage went spinning into the shadows, with further sounds splintering. Cards, glasses, chips, and spilled liquor flew all over the place. The crash brought Melody to his senses. He stood dumbfounded by what he had done, and looked at the shock-silly faces of the card players. They sat with their cards still in their hands, staring at him, but they made no move. He walked between them into the bar, his scalp tingling. He knew that when he had passed them it would be no good to look back. But no gun spoke.

The bartender, the same one who had served Melody before, looked as scared as a man could look. His hands were held a little above the surface of the bar, not exactly raised, but ostentatiously in view. He made a motion toward the back room with his head.

Nobody else was in sight as Melody slowly walked the length of the room toward the indicated door. When he faced the door he thought for a moment that he was going to be unable to bring himself to thumb the latch and walk in. Obviously the man who had sent for him had spotted him from a long way off, and fitted his arrangements to his plans, whatever these might be. A blast of gun-fire might immediately follow his opening of that door for all Melody knew.

Melody wanted to turn back to the bar for a drink, but the card players behind him might be pulling themselves together now; lingering might be bad medicine, too. He put his right hand lightly upon the latch; then drew it back and opened the door with his left hand, so that his right hand would be free; and went in.

The back room of the Last Chance was used for poker by men who wanted privacy because of their high stakes.

Professional gamblers sometimes made this room their hang-out while passing through Payneville, each making a nice thing of it, before he decided it was time to move on. Cattlemen played here when their pokes were heavy with money from newly sold herds, and travelers were welcome while their money lasted. Sometimes a man had got himself killed in this room.

The place itself had nothing but a round table covered with a worn blanket, nailed down, and a lot of straight-backed chairs. Some pictures of actresses were nailed to the board walls, mostly hippy women in enormous hats. The place didn't look like much; but so much money had changed hands across the threadbare blanket that the walls could have been sheeted in gold.

Ira Waggoner sat alone beside the table, now, in the dim, stuffy quiet of midday.

His long, flat-boned frame was arranged on the small of his back, on a chair turned sideways, so that one ankle could rest upon his knee. His thumbs were hooked into his belt, not lying along the edge of it as a gun fighter is supposed to fix his hands, but hooked there solidly.

He looked Melody Jones steadily in the eye, without any expression, as Melody came in. He gave no other sign of recognition. He was one day behind his shave, and his cheek lines showed more hard-weather riding than feeding; but his eyes were the kind used for seeing the actual, as a profession.

All Melody knew about him, except for the note that George had brought, was that this was the man he had hit so hard, and so unexpectedly, without hardly noticing what he looked like, before he hit.

"You want to see me?" Melody said. He had wanted to make that sound hard, and kind of relentless, but the best he accomplished was to make a mumble.

"Sit down," Ira Waggoner said.

Because he had not foreseen this correctly, Melody was caught unawares, and obeyed.

"You know what I want with you," Ira Waggoner said.

"Do I?"

Waggoner leaned across the table to pull Melody's tobacco sack out of his shirt pocket. He rolled himself a cigarette unhurriedly, and tossed the sack back with so contemptuous a flick that it hit Melody in the chest and dropped. Melody automatically caught it as it fell.

"You don't need to keep watching my gun," Waggoner said. His voice was low and flat, but inexpressibly bitter. "When I figure you need it, you'll get it all right. And you know that, too. There's only about three men in the southwest I can't swap lead with. One of them is Monte Jarrad. But you ain't him."

"No?" Melody said.

"No," Waggoner repeated. "I don't know who you are, and I don't give a damn. And I don't know why you're sucker enough to front for Monte, either. But it don't go with me. There's one thing I want to know from you, and you know what it is; and I'm going to have it, now."

"Oh?" said Melody. He kept wondering whether he could shoot this man, if he had to. It was a sickly sort of a wonder, because the answer was so plain.

"There's one thing in this country that will get a man salted down quicker than stealing a horse," Waggoner said. "That thing is a double-cross. I could have shot

Monte in two, easy, the morning he come aboard the stage; and it come to my mind to do it, too. Monte should have drew out when he saw I hadn't been able to get rid of the shotgun guard. But I went on and played my half of the game; and now you fellers have got to play yours!"

"I kind of thought you might be off-center," Melody said, "when she didn't want me to talk to you."

"What?"

"Wasn't any reason I shouldn't talk to you," Melody said, "*unless* you had holt of something."

Waggoner looked puzzled. "What the *hell* are you talking about?"

"I don't know how it is," Melody said. "Cain't anybody understand English any more? Seems like everybody I talk to gits to looking kind of bitched and bewildered."

"By God," said Waggoner, "I can understand it!"

"Have a drink," Melody suggested.

"The hell with it. I want to know where that strongbox is. You're going to take me to it. If you think you ain't, try to walk out that door, without I say you can!"

"This here is disappointin'," Melody said. "I was kind of hoping you would have some kind of idee of what I seemed to have did with it."

Waggoner was looking baffled again. "What *you* did with it?"

They stared at each other. "I see what's the matter," Melody said at last. "I keep forgetting that you don't think I'm Monte Jarrad any more."

Waggoner reddened. "You never fooled me, except for

that couple of minutes," he said.

"That throws me sideways," Melody admitted. "I hadn't figured on this. I don't hardly know what to say next." He took his hat off, and looked inside it, and wiped perspiration from his forehead with his gloved left hand.

"That phony scar," Ira Waggoner said with irony, "is beginning to rub loose."

Melody put his hat back on without comment. He had figured out why Cherry had wanted him to keep his fore-lock down; but he had forgotten for a little while that he had made a crooked blue mark on his forehead with the indelible pencil he carried for calf tallies. He thought of rolling a cigarette, but was afraid the tobacco would chatter in the paper.

Ira Waggoner brought his heels to the floor and faced Melody squarely across the table. "I'm waiting for you to talk," he said, as if he didn't mean to wait much longer.

Melody Jones had never felt so alone in his life. His mind was running all over that sun-hating room, check-ering over everything in it which his eyes had reported to him when they were restlessly all over the place. He was hunting for some kind of an idea—something to do, something to say—anything. The silence dragged out while Ira Waggoner watched him.

His observation had been thorough enough. He knew everything that was in here, and could see it as well as if he were looking at it. The placement of the chairs, the brass cuspidor in one corner, and the sawdust box in the opposite. And as his mind went all over these meaningless things, he could feel Ira Waggoner's patience running out.

"You figure I know where it is?" Melody asked pointlessly.

"I figure that you better."

"Mister," said Melody Jones, "you are easily the worst damn fool I ever see in years of riding. And I've rode from hell to Sunday."

Ira Waggoner stared at him blankly. "What?" he said.

"Think where you be," Melody Jones suggested. "You're a free man, and you can go where you want to. You could be in Tucson, or Seattle. But allowing that you got to be in the Last Chance bar—don't you ever look where you set? You could just as well have set over there with your back to plain wall. Or you could be standing up, where you could look all around you. I swear I don't know how you've lived as long as you have."

Ira Waggoner showed exasperation. "I don't aim to give you all day."

"There used to be a great fighter named Morgan Earp," Melody said. "He had his spine cut in two by a gun."

"Everybody knows that," Waggoner snorted.

"Then," said Melody, "maybe you remember how come that happened to him. He turned his back on a door that had glass in the upper half."

"Well?" Waggoner smiled a little, knowing what was coming now.

"Look behind you," said Melody, "and you'll see just such a door."

Waggoner grinned a little on one side of his face, but

did not take his eyes from Melody Jones. "Look at it again yourself," he said with a weary contempt. "The glass is painted over."

Melody did look at the door again. What he had said was true; there was a door behind Ira Waggoner with glass in its upper half. But the glass had been fogged solid with a streaky white paint.

"That's the oldest trick in the book, sonny," Waggoner said. "Monte will spank your little behind if he hears about you trying that."

But as Melody looked at the painted glass in the door he saw something else now. A clear place the size of a quarter showed where the paint had been scraped away. And as Melody looked at that peep-hole, the peep-hole blinked. After a moment Melody was able to make out the eye that was looking at him through the peep-hole in the door.

There was an ugly patronizing complacence in Ira Waggoner's tone now. "There ain't anything behind that door," he said.

"I'm right sorry," Melody heard himself saying with flat candor, "to hear you take that view. Because I have an idee that somebody's number is coming up, in about two seconds, now."

"Yours, maybe," Waggoner said, tossing aside his patience.

"It might be mine," Melody said. "But there's just one off-chance that it might be yours. I sure wish you'd give a little thought to that. We can always talk later on—if only some bad accident don't happen to—"

Ira Waggoner said savagely, "I've heard enough of—"

And then he broke off suddenly and sat utterly still, as if he were holding his breath.

The door behind him was opening gently; and a soft voice said, "So have I."

Ira Waggoner moved his hands slowly and placed them in plain sight upon the table. Then even more slowly he swung his head back to look over his shoulder.

"Hello, Lee," Waggoner said queerly; but he left his hands where they were, only stiffening them a little so that they pressed more tightly upon the wood.

The man who stood in the doorway behind Waggoner was one whom Melody Jones had never seen before. The stranger dropped a quick glance to Waggoner's motionless hands and then stood looking at Melody for what seemed a long time. Melody Jones thought he had never seen such desolately empty eyes; they gave the impression of being slit-pupiled, like the eyes of a lynx. Nothing else distinguished the stranger's appearance much. He had the slat-like build of a Texan, and wore the common clothes of a cowhand, without chaps.

"Who's this?" asked the stranger of Waggoner, without taking his eyes off Melody.

"God knows, Lee," Waggoner said. By the placating note that came into Waggoner's voice, Melody knew that whoever the stranger was, he was one of those few others beside Monte Jarrad whom Waggoner was afraid of. "All I know is he tried to pass himself off for Monte."

"I know that already," the stranger said. "He's got Monte's saddle on his horse." He drew a hard breath through one nostril, and it drew up one side of his mouth in what looked like a sneer. Later Melody found out that this was caused by the fact that this man could breathe through only one side of his nose. He shifted his eyes to Waggoner now and they had less warmth than the eyes of a Gila lizard. "What kind of a deal are you making with this punk?"

"No deal, Lee," Waggoner said doggedly. "I want to know what kind of a score is being run up, that's all. There's things I got a right to know."

The stranger's words came a little more softly. "What kind of things?"

"If anything's gone wrong—" Waggoner started to say.

"Pray Gawd there ain't anything gone wrong!" His face contorted again in that unexpected combination of a sniff and a sneer. "If I find out it did, and you was mixed up in it, I'll come after you, and I'll get you; and I reckon you know I keep my word."

"I know that, Lee."

"Set here where you are until you hear me ride off. After that, stay in this town. Be where it won't be any trouble to find you, if you're wanted."

Ira Waggoner hesitated for perhaps three seconds more. "Okay, Lee," he said.

Lee turned to Melody. "Let's go," He indicated the door with a sway of his head. "Walk ahead of me until we're in the street."

Melody Jones thought this over only briefly. There are men who do not get their results from being either tall, or powerful, or any particular thing. Lee was tall, and perhaps strong, but his authority did not live on that. Lee was one of those men who just quietly get done what they start to do; you can see it. If you've seen it, you know. Melody saw it.

The card players were missing from the bar as they passed through. The bartender, sweeping up the wreckage of the card game, worked busily, and pretended not to see them go.

In the street the man called Lee picked up his reins where they lay loose across the hitch-rail, turned his horse so that his animal was between himself and Melody, and swung up. "Mount your pony," he said.

Melody mounted.

"Ride by my nigh stirrup—close."

"Mister," said Melody Jones, "I sure appreciate you fetching me out. I was gitting mighty restless, setting there."

"You don't know yet why I done it, huh?"

"No; because I haven't got the faintest kind of idee who you be."

The stranger studied him for a moment. "I reckon that might be so," he decided. "God knows I never set eyes on you before. I'm Lee Gledhill. That mean anything?"

"No," Melody said.

Sniff-sneer, went the stranger's face. "This ain't easy to believe."

"Believe what you want," Melody answered.

"I've side-rode Monte Jarrad a long time," Lee said. He seemed to have decided that he did not care whether Melody spoke the truth or not. "Just lately we got divided. I been trying to find him. I reckon I just found out, for sure, why it couldn't be done."

"You did?"

"I'm through looking for him," Lee Gledhill said, "because I know now that he's dead. But I guess I found the man I wanted worse." The empty eyes held on Melody; they held an unconsciously long time without having to wink. Sniff-sneer.

"Who, me?" Melody said.

"How come," Lee Gledhill asked curiously, "that a punk like you found a way to kill Monte Jarrad?"

❧ 14 ❧

So I killed Monte Jarrad," Melody said, with a certain amount of stupor. "That's what you figure, huh?"

They were out of the town, by this time. Lee Gledhill took a look back the way they had come; then his eyes ran around the perimeter of the hills.

"Well, I never done no such a thing," Melody declared.

The other gave no sign that he had heard.

"What makes you think I done a thing like that?"

Lee was looking at him steadily, now; but he still said nothing.

"What makes you think he's even daid?" Melody demanded, flustered by the silence.

"His saddle is on your horse," Lee answered him at last. "You wouldn't ever have got Monte's saddle off him without you dry-gulched him first, and he was dead."

"Well, I know good and well he's alive," Melody contended.

"You do?" Lee said with ugly disinterest. "You do?

Where is he then?"

Melody hunted for a plausible reason not to answer. "How long you been a peace officer?" he asked.

No reaction from Lee came out of that. "I told you who I am," Lee Gledhill said.

Some day, Melody thought with self-pity, people are going to realize this country isn't run right. But it isn't going to do me any good, because I won't know about it, then.

"What makes you so daid sure," he offered with faint hope, "that I *ain't* Monte Jarrad?"

"You don't look nothin' like him to me. I don't know how anybody mistook you for him, even with his stuff."

"Okay," said Melody. "I want to ask you just one thing more. Who do you think was quickest with a gun, you or Monte?"

"The man never lived that could match him," Lee Gledhill said. "Not even me."

"And according to you, I am the man who shot him down," Melody said. "By your own way of figuring, you ain't got any more chancet with me than a yaller gal at a squaw sale. What's the matter? Don't you want to live no more?"

Melody Jones felt his scalp creep as he heard how silly that frail bluff sounded, even to himself.

No smile crossed Lee Gledhill's face. He evidently took the threat more seriously than Melody could. He continued to study Melody unhurriedly, and his heatless eyes looked thirty years older than his face. "I thought of that," Lee said. "If you outshot a man like Monte in a fair fight, and can do it again, you'll kill me like a duck. But

I don't think you did. I'm gambling that you shot him from in back."

Melody knew by this time that he was up against something that was less a fight than an execution. In a country so vast, where the law was spread so thin, this loyalty to a friend who was dead was a necessary thing, without which nobody would be safe.

Lee Gledhill's way of looking at it was widespread, even common. Melody was pretty sure that George Fury would do the same for him, complaining bitterly to the last, but going ahead with it just the same.

It's no way possible, Melody thought, that this here thing is about to happen. But nothing else *can* happen, if this man means business; and business is what he means. . . . Yet even then he could see that nothing could be more outlandish than the plain fact that he was sitting there in Monte Jarrad's saddle. Once he admitted that, everything else here was inevitable, he supposed.

"What you aim to do?" Melody asked, seeking information.

"I'm waiting for that squaw to get by," Lee Gledhill said. A little squaw four feet tall was trudging past with about three dozen bushel baskets, apparently empty, on her back and head. She was a pretty little squaw, with slanted eyes the color of frosted plums. She looked at Melody shyly, sideways from under heavy lashes, as she passed. If ever I get out of this, Melody thought, I betcha I don't neglect 'em like I done here before. She got on over the rise.

"Give me Monte's lariat," said Lee.

Melody obeyed. "What's that for?"

"To catch your horse with, Mister. I aim to get that saddle off him. It's too good a hull to have him wear it back to the wild bunch, and lose it in the hills. Go ahead and draw, if you're ready."

"And supposing I don't?" Melody asked.

"You might just as well," Lee Gledhill said, his words sounding weary now. "I don't see I got any choice anyway; I know plain enough what Monte would do for me in the same place. And I haven't got all day. If you ain't got the guts to make a play, all I can do is get it over with."

"Only you won't," Melody said.

"No? Why?"

"Because you don't know where the strong-box is."

"So you know that, too," Lee Gledhill said, wonderingly.

Melody said nothing.

"I can't make a deal with you," Lee Gledhill decided. "Not across Monte Jarrad's corpse. I wouldn't trust you if I could." He drew in one long, lip-pulling breath and then his face became still. "I'm going to throw this cigarette down now. It's up to you to take care of yourself in any way Gawd tells you to, as soon as it leaves my hand."

Melody Jones watched him motionlessly as Lee drew one last drag of smoke, and blew it out in a single stream from one side of his nose.

"Just a minute, wait," Melody said. "Just a minute, wait, wait a minute, wait now, just a—"

"What's the matter?"

"They's a digger-Injun coming yonder with a load of

wood," Melody said. "Do you aim to git dropped right in his lap?"

Lee Gledhill considered a moment or two, listening to the creaking wheels of an approaching cart, and he went sniff-sneer twice. Gledhill was getting nervous with the prolonging of delays. Melody had a farfetched hope that the nervousness might catch up with him—even with this man as cold as yesterday's buckwheats—if it went on long enough.

"Ride on past," Lee decided. "Ride past like nothing was happening. Then turn off into that drift of brush."

Melody lifted his reins, minding again. The passing of the wood cart gave him a little time to think, but he couldn't seem to find much use for it. He noticed the beadwork on the bridle of the tiny donkey which pulled the wood cart, and identified it as Arapahoe. The cart had two wheels, home-made solid, and was loaded to the sky. A slim young Indian, beak-nosed, with a rag around his head, sat behind the donkey's quarters on the lowest tier of wood.

"Look," Melody began.

"Turn off the road," Lee Gledhill told him.

"Look," Melody said again. He pulled up his pony, but failed to obey. "You want to know where Monte is?"

"What good's the corpse of any man?" Lee Gledhill asked. "No, I don't want him. Leave him stay where he lays."

"Where *you* got off the trail, you bull-headed bazoop," Melody said, "is on this here idee I killed him. I never done so. Because he ain't daid. He's a hell of a sight more alive than one of us is going to be, if you keep on like you been. Blame it," he finished, "I'm getting tired of this!"

"Then how come you got his saddle?"

"I got it off'n his girl, damn it."

Lee Gledhill was beginning to glare with that look of outrage which comes to a man who is becoming bewildered, and bitterly resents it.

"I'm supposed to think *she* was wearin' it?"

"I put it on Harry—on my pony—as a favor. The idee was maybe it would fool some jackass like you, long enough for Monte to get away. But I'm blamed if I'll go through with it no more. If I'd of knowed the botheration this here was going to be, I wouldn't of tetched the whole thing with a prod-pole."

Lee was looking at Melody weirdly, now. "How *well* do you know Monte Jarrad?"

"Don't know him any. I never seen him, yet."

"So you aim to have me think—" Lee Gledhill's voice was strange—"you want me to think—you was damn fool enough to let some *girl* talk you into a thing like this here? You figure I'll believe that such a damn fool could ever have got his full growth?"

Melody thought he had him there. "Here I be," he said, "ain't I?"

"Good God," Lee Gledhill said, looking almost frightened. "I never listened to nothing like this." He turned cadgy again. "What's the name of this girl?"

"Monte's girl? Cherry de Longpre."

"That's her name, all right," Gledhill admitted, worse bothered than before. "Monte spoke it frequent." He stared hard at Melody as if looking at an incredible, perhaps dangerous monstrosity. "I don't believe you, natcherly," he said. "It ain't in human reach to swaller no such a lie as that lie is. But you never killed him. That I know, now. Nobody with the brain it would take to kill Monte Jarrad could even think up such a God damn thing. That I grant you!"

"It's a wonder you don't sprain somethin'," Melody said.

Lee Gledhill threw away his cigarette now, but he made no move for his gun. He spoke with a taut, slow wariness. "I guess I better talk to this girl. Lead out, some. Not too much. And remember there's a gun looking down your neck, every foot of the way from here in."

"Well," Melody conceded, "all right. But don't try any funny business." He would have said more, but he caught Lee Gledhill's eye, which was cold as the nose of a winter wolf.

He shut up and led out.

❦ 15 ❦

They did not have to ride far, as it worked out. Cherry de Longpre was already nearing Payneville, powdering the road.

As Melody and his captor topped a long rise, a tower of dust was boiling toward them. Lee Gledhill drew Melody off the road into the brush; but Melody almost immediately recognized the de Longpre buckboard, with Cherry driving, and George Fury beside her on the seat. George's horse was tied on behind.

Melody was able to apprise Lee Gledhill in time for Lee to flag the buckboard. Cherry had a hard time pulling down the hard-run team, but got them stopped a hundred yards beyond. Her hands kept tensing and slackening the lines, to hold the rebellious horses, and she looked at Melody and Lee with poker-faced questioning as they came up. "Well?"

Lee Gledhill took a good look at George Fury, then reached over and took Melody's gun out of his chaps pocket. He stuck it into the loose top of his own boot. George stayed quiet, but his eyes were bright and awake, like a watching owl.

"You again, huh?" Melody said to George.

George looked sheepish. "I come back," he grunted.

Lee Gledhill went to the buckboard wheel, backing his horse around in such a way that he could watch both Melody Jones and George Fury at the same time. "Your name Cherry de Longpre?"

"Might be," Cherry said sharply, like the snap of fingers. "Take off your hat, if you want to talk to me!"

Lee Gledhill hesitated, annoyed that she should catch him up, and make a thing of it, when he was thinking about something else. Sniff-sneer. Sulkily he obeyed, and started over.

"You maybe heard of Lee Gledhill," he said. "Uh huh—I see you have."

"Anybody's heard of him," said Cherry noncommittally. "There's handbills out, even, offering a reward."

A faint insolence came into Gledhill's tone. "Been readin', huh? All right. Good. Because I'm him. And seein's you study up every handbill you see, I reckon you know I side-ride Monte Jarrad."

"I'll have to take your word for it," Cherry said without the least expression.

"Thanks," said Gledhill drily.

"I'll also have to take your word," Cherry said, "if you tell me you're Rutherford B. Hayes. Because I don't know you from a flea in Adam's whiskers."

"You mean," Gledhill said edgily, "you *don't* take my word for it?"

"You're quick," Cherry affirmed. "Personally," she added, "I like the old custom of everybody just calling himself 'Smith.' Easy to keep hold of."

Gledhill looked at her queerly for some time. He was irritated, but reasonable. "I see how you look at it," he conceded at last. "All right. I'm some doodle name of Smith."

"You might even be named Luke Packer, and work for the express company," Cherry said, with a lump of ice in every word.

"All right," Lee said again. "Never mind who I be. It don't change what I'm here for, any. I want to ask you one thing. *What become of Monte Jarrad?*"

Her hands were motionless now, and the whole girl was motionless; she watched the riders sidelong, and for moments did not seem to breathe. "I suppose I must have seen him about twice in three years," she said at last. She looked at Melody with a hard, blank stare. "Who's that you've got there?"

Lee Gledhill studied her steadily for a long space. He was looking at her squarely now, holding George Fury in discount. "You mean to tell me," he said slowly, queerly, "you set there and tell me—you don't know—you don't know who this man is?"

Cherry de Longpre looked Melody Jones straight in the eyes, but her own eyes were blank. There was no message in them, either, any more than he could have found in a couple of puddles of grey rain.

"I never saw him before in all my life."

Then for a few moments a quiet clamped down like the quiet of the rocky hills beyond. Everybody held steady, however, locked motionless in the harsh sunlight.

Lee Gledwin said thickly, "Maybe you know the saddle he rides."

"Yes," Cherry admitted.

"It's Monte Jarrad's saddle."

"But," said Cherry evenly, "he isn't Monte Jarrad."

"There ain't but one other jigger he could be," Lee Gledhill said, watching her face as intensely as a ferret. "He's the man who killed Monte."

Once more a long moment of quiet held, until the team tried to start again, and Cherry had to work on them. "Whoa!" she shouted, "Goose! Bucky!" Then she turned on Gledhill coolly. "Well, what do you want me to do? Have him arrested?"

"There isn't nothing more you need to do," Lee said. He began backing his horse away.

Melody Jones stared at Cherry de Longpre unbelievingly. Cherry looked sad and dreamy, showing no sign of tension.

Now George Fury came straight up on his heels, shouting as he stood up. If the team had jumped then, he would have been pitched out crop over kettle. Instantly

Gledhill's gun came out, clicking to the cock in the same motion; but George Fury ignored the gun, and Gledhill did not fire.

"Yew befewzled numpus!" George Fury shouted at Gledhill. "Has everybody gone crazy here but me?"

"Who the hell is this?" Gledhill demanded of Cherry. He kept his gun on George Fury, and the corner of his eye upon Melody.

Cherry looked at Gledhill with ostentatious significance, and tapped her forehead. "Different," she told him. "Confused like, but helpless."

"Never you mind her," George shouted at Gledhill. "She's in it with the rest. Monte Jarrad is alive and kicking, what's left of him! He's layin' low in a hide-out, nursin' a wownd—and I can show you where he be!"

It stirred up Lee Gledhill. "How far away?"

" 'Tain't so fur but what we can make it in time to eat!"

"What's this?" Lee snapped at Cherry. "What's this now?"

Melody had had time to think it over by this time, and he esteemed that George Fury was getting himself into trouble. "Shorely," he dabbed in his rope, "shorely you remember Uncle Roscoe? You must of heard of him many a time. You know, the famous half-wit feller?"

"It seems to me," Lee said grimly, "a couple of you people are mighty anxious that I won't listen to this feller!"

"You bet they be," George insisted loudly. "But I can lay my hands on Monte Jarrad within a couple of feet! Gimme them lines, and I'll drive straight to him!"

Melody started to say, "Don't pay any attention to

the old—"

"Shut up!" Lee stopped him. To George he said, "Take the lines, Mister. You're on your way. . . ."

Lee Gledhill kept them herded together when they dismounted at the Busted Nose.

"Once and for all," George said to Melody, "I want you to take note who does the thinking here. I figured out where Monte is by using my head. I know where he's hid, and even how to git in it. He's been here the hull time, while you was messing around blind. And I've knowed that sence we first rode in!"

"Shut up," Lee told him. "You're *all* going to be in trouble in about two jerks!"

George looked him over with slow dispraise; then led the way to the barn.

The shadows within the barn were cool and black. But the cracks in the weathered walls let in brilliant stripes of sunlight in which dust motes danced. Here, in this altered light, a change came over George Fury. He was moving now with a tense but leisured certainty. Unhurriedly he gave a slight hitch to each of his sleeves, and looked at the others with a brazen condescension, like a man who is about to pull something out of a hat.

George Fury now took down the canvas wind-breaker which hung upon what had once been the wall of a stall; the bales of ragged hay which were piled against the other side overhung the old wall now. There was nonchalance, even a touch of grandeur in George's gesture as he lightly tossed the wind-breaker away. Dramatically, with motions of exaggerated finesse, he took hold of the nail on which the wind-breaker had hung, and pulled upon it. Nothing happened.

Cherry de Longpre's face was quiet, her eyes upon the hills. Melody watched with polite interest, Lee Gledhill with angering impatience as George Fury pulled harder. George stepped back, glared at the nail, spit on his hands and tried it again, wrenching at the nail with violent jerks of his whole frame. He was beginning now to curse a little under his breath. "I'll fix it! I'll fix it!" He put his shoulder against the aged timbers and heaved with his whole strength. He stepped back and charged the wall four or five times like a battering ram. The sweat was standing out at the roots of his sparse hair, and he was whimpering enraged epithets.

Lee Gledhill and Melody Jones found themselves looking at each other sidelong with that blank, silent inquiry of men who can't make out what it is they are looking at.

"George," said Melody sadly, "you been drinkin' somethin'?"

George whimpered, and began to smash at the wall with his high heels. A board split. Scrabbling at it with his fingers, he ripped off a strip of it, and then with frantic effort tore loose the whole board. Then for a moment he stood back, dumbfounded. Nothing faced him beyond the opening but a solid barrier of baled hay, pressed tight against the wall.

He flung himself at it again, trying to push one of the bales out of place, but it did not yield. Instead, one of the overhanging bales toppled from above, jostled George roughly aside as it fell, and burst at his feet. A big rat ran out of it and loped off into the shadows.

Frantic now, George ran around the partition to look at the other side. Nothing but a disorderly pile of hay, a couple of bales deep against the wall, was waiting there. Some small animal might have been concealed there, or a tribe of rats, but not the hide-out of a man.

Cherry de Longpre stood in the broad doorway, silhouetted against the sunlight. She spoke directly to Lee Gledhill, ignoring the others. "There's coffee on the back of the stove," she told him. Her words sounded tired and subdued. "I'll show you the last word I got from Monte, if that will be any help."

Lee Gledhill considered for a long time, looking poker-faced from one to another of them. "All right," he said at last.

"Come on in the house," Cherry said, and led the way.

On the gallery she held the broken screen door open for them while Gledhill made Melody Jones and George Fury precede him into the kitchen, and the chained bear cub scrabbled at her boots, unnoticed.

Cherry stepped through the doorway after Lee Gledhill; and for a moment, because he was watching the others, his back was turned.

Cherry's right hand reached into the corner by the door where her carbine stood. The carbine whipped up, not smoothly, as a rifleman might have taken it, but with a direct, purposeful practicality, as she might have caught up a broom. She planted the muzzle hard in the middle of Lee Gledhill's back.

"Get your hands up!" she blazed at him. "Melody, take his gun!"

Lee Gledhill's whole body went rigid with a jerk, as if

he had been struck by lightning. Then very slowly his hands came up. Melody took Lee's gun, and recovered his own.

She snapped orders at Melody and George, and her cool, indifferent weariness was gone. "Saddle my pony," she flung at them. "I ride that old punkin-seed mare. Then throw down the corral bars, and turn everything out. Put those broom-tails into a stampede that will carry them halfway to Texas!"

"What about this feller's horse?"

"We'll lead him with us."

"Horse thieves hang," Lee Gledhill said, "where I come from!"

"You'll find him tied about five miles down the trail."

George Fury kept Lee Gledhill's hands up while Cherry changed into riding clothes. By that time Melody had saddled her round-bellied old roan, and he held it for her to mount. Cherry came close to the animal, then stood hesitating.

"What's the matter?"

She glanced at him with a shamefaced shyness he had never seen, and started to mount, but faltered. "I guess," she said in a small voice, "I just don't trust horses very well." Then she set her lips and swung neatly aboard. "At least," she said, "if it comes to a pinch, I'll be able to identify you."

"What you aim to do?"

"This time I *know* you're leaving the country! I know because I'm going with you and see that you do."

❧ 16 ❧

High up in the timberless hills, where the manzanita grew shoulder high to a man on a horse,
they had to walk their ponies, mostly. Melody
kept looking back; George had gone off on another trail
to misplant Gledhill's horse, but he ought to overtake
them presently, with the mountain pony he had.

Sunset was coming on. From this high, increasing
angle, as their ponies climbed, the sundown looked
unnatural; the sun itself appeared to stand still, giving the
western ranges the weird appearance of swinging
upward with a slow, irresistible wheel toward the sun
disc.

"I never did anything like that in my life before,"
Cherry said; she spoke shakily. "I scared the hell out of
myself. But if he was really Lee Gledhill, he would have
killed you, for nosing in."

"Who, me?"

"He doesn't know you like I do," Cherry said
obscurely. "If he wasn't Lee, he was a peace officer, and
anything I said would have given Monte away."

"You think a heap of that Monte jigger, don't you?"

She didn't answer him.

Melody looked depressed. "Okay," he decided. "You
love him, then."

"I always thought I did. Since I was fourteen years
old."

"And nothing he done ever changed it," Melody kept
on.

"I don't change easy," Cherry said. "Who ever loved a man for what he did, anyway? That's got nothing to do with it. If it did, the population of this country would die out quick!"

Melody was embarrassed; he shrugged, and changed the subject. "Maybe I should of told George," he said, turning in his saddle to look back again. "If he *really* gets it in his haid he's gone crazy, how do I know he won't shoot hisself, or wander off? I otter of told him he was right about that hide-away under the hay."

"What makes you think that?" Cherry asked sharply.

"The bales was moved recent," Melody said. "And there was a blood stain on the floor, under the chaff."

Cherry was looking at him queerly again. "How long have you known that?"

"Last night, I kind of figured sech might be the case. I didn't say nothing to George. I don't rightly know *when* he could of fell in it."

"You knew Monte Jarrad was there all the time?"

"I didn't want to say nothing, hardly," Melody apologized. "But it kind of looked that way to me."

Cherry's face was turned away from him, so that her low voice sounded far away. "Well—he's long gone now, anyway."

"And so," Melody said when he had thought it over, "there ain't hardly anything left for you to do but get me haided some opposite way, so's he won't be bothered by posses, and such like, any more."

Cherry stole a quick glance at him; but there was no more bitterness in his face than there had been in his tone. She spoke in a monotone, not looking at him.

"There's one other thing I want you to do. Not now—sometime, after all this has blown over. I want you to come back here then, and turn up the express company's strong-box. I want you to give it back to the people it belongs to."

"Cain't."

"I can't make you do it, if you won't."

" 'Tain't that. I jest don't know where it's at."

"I'm going to show you."

He turned and looked at her, but she did not meet his eyes. "Monte told me where it is," she said. "He told me when he thought he was going to die. There's an old, old cabin that near everybody has forgot. Monte's used it before; but he'll never use it again. It has dobe walls, four feet through. There's a slab sill to the only window. Once when Monte was hiding out, he dug a cache in the wall, under that slab. It's near big enough to hide a man, if a man could breathe in there. And that's where the strong-box is, with more money in it than you ever saw in your life. So I guess you know I trust you, now."

"Where did you say this cabin—"

"I'm taking you there."

"Well, heck, then," Melody said, "we'll just give 'em back their strong-box now, and wind the whole thing up!"

Her frayed nerves flared up in a flash of temper. "You most certainly will not!"

"Whut?"

"Monte has to have his chance. They suspect he came to the Poisonberry, but they don't know he did; they're still hunting for him in five states. If they find the strong-box they'll close the country so tight that a jackrabbit couldn't get out. I won't have that! Monte has to have his chance."

Melody thought that over a long time. "Well, I think I better go right ahaid and turn it in now," he decided.

"You can't. You wouldn't dare! I wouldn't have told you if—" She bit her lips for a moment. "You promised me you wouldn't," she finished desperately.

"When was this?"

"Well—you have to promise me now!"

"Oh—well—heck. All right, Cherry."

They rode a mile in silence. The slow dusk of the mountain country was closing in. "I suppose," Melody said at last, "you'll be going back to the Busted Nose, then, after you show me where it's at."

"I don't know. And I don't care much. I'm sick of the whole forsaken thing. But I'm going to see you fetched out of this, before I do anything else."

"Whut? Why?"

"Because you don't know how to take care of yourself, or what's good for you—that's why!"

"I don't know why," Melody said, "you set yourself to all this trouble, now."

He said that in all honesty, without rancor. Up until now he had found her willing enough to get him outlawed, or shot, or hung, without turning a hair. She had coolly drawn him into more trouble than he had ever seen in his life, for the sake of another man he had never seen. So now his curiosity about her change of action was almost scientific. He wondered about her behavior as impartially as he might have wondered why an elk whistles, instead of going "moo."

There was bitterness in Cherry's voice, not his.

"I don't blame you for saying that," Cherry said. "If ever a man had a right to get sarcastic, you're it."

"I didn't mean it that way."

Cherry angered unaccountably. "You never mean any thing," she lashed at him. "You never complain about anything, or demand anything, or let out a holler—butter wouldn't melt in your teeth! But I know what you're thinking, just the same!"

"Whut?"

"What the devil did you expect?" Cherry demanded furiously. "Do you expect a girl to fall in love with every damn fool that lifts his head? Think every girl in the world is going to fall all over herself on account of *you?*"

"No," Melody said.

"What right have you got to expect any different breaks than anybody else gets—and mostly better men than you!" Cherry ranted at him. "Are you better than anybody else? Why shouldn't the same things happen to you as happen to me, and Monte, and everybody else?"

Melody was amazed. "I didn't say nothing, Cherry."

"No, but you're thinking! You're thinking so plain it howls like a wolf! You think what I've done to you is cheap, and low, and snaky!"

"You done something?"

"You know what I did," she said bitterly. "I dragged you into this. If you're killed at the end of it, it was me that killed you!"

"I guess maybe," Melody said gently, "you didn't rightly realize—"

"I realized perfectly!" Cherry's self-accusation was almost savage. "The minute I kissed you, there on that boardwalk, and saw the way you looked at me, I knew I could do what I wanted with you. You were a gone duck—you never had a chance, from that minute on!"

"Shucks, now," Melody said.

"There's one in the Bible where a man did a thing like that," Cherry said. "But I don't reckon any *woman* ever did anything so common mean—" she blew her nose— "since these dirt hills first coughed up the Poisonberry!"

"I guess you don't understand women very well," Melody said.

"I suppose *you* do!"

"Well—I ain't never improved on what paw told me. Paw says, 'Son, if ever you fool with a woman, hide a dollar in the toe of your boot. Then you'll come out a dollar to the good,' he says, 'so long as you keep your boots on.' That bunk of advice," Melody finished mildly, "I ain't never found to fail me."

She wasn't listening to him. "I carved his name on a tombstone," she whimpered, "and dropped it square on top of you! How was I to know you wouldn't run? You spoiled everything, just because you wouldn't run. But I should have told you. I should have told you what I was trying to do, so you could have had open eyes."

Her voice sounded so queer that he leaned forward over his saddle horn to peer into her face; and he saw that she was crying.

"You'd of been wrong," Melody said gravely, "to of so done. Because I'd of told you to go chase a sting-bee, and I'd of rode on."

"I wish I was dead!" Cherry burst out hysterically. "I wish to God you'd shout at me, or take a club to me, or knock me endways—anything—anything but this sorrowing Jesus attitude! I'd feel better if you brained me with a whiffle tree, so help me God!"

"Don't feel that way," Melody consoled her. "I wouldn't of missed it."

She turned to stare at him blankly, the tears drying on her cheeks. "Monte would kill a girl who did to him what I've done to you," she said at last.

There was criticism in that, even a faint contempt. But Melody only shrugged, his eyes searching the hills by the last light.

"Well, I wouldn't," he said.

They reached the forgotten adobe an hour after dark. It was set on a bit of barren ledge, among plunging, tortuous ridges suitable for use by wild burros and goats. Scrub oak, juniper and ground pine tangled with the manzanita along a racy little stream. In the brief darkness before moonrise the adobe squatted like a squared-out piece of the solid hills.

Melody, striding into the black interior with confidence, immediately fell over a slab table with a terrific crash.

Cherry's voice said, with nervous irritation, "Will you wait until I make a light?"

She struck a match, and touched it to the candle she had brought. Melody watched her as she melted the base of the candle first, and stuck it on a shelf, before lighting the wick.

Then they turned and looked at the room.

A tall, gaunt-faced man sat watching them steadily from a bunk in the corner of the room. He lounged back with his knees crossed, to all appearances at home and at his ease. But in his hand was the biggest hog-leg of a six-gun that Melody had ever seen, and it was pointed steadily at the region of Melody's belt.

The three stood and looked at each other through a moment of quiet. The man with the gun spoke first. "Do you happen to know who I am, bud?"

Melody looked the gun in the eye, and his answer was respectful. "No, sir."

"Luke Packer is the name."

"Are you—are you looking for somebody, Mr. Packer?"

Packer stared at him; but the gun did not waver from Melody's belt buckle. "You be the judge," he said.

❧ 17 ❧

First thing of all," Luke Packer said, "you might put your hands up a little bit. . . . That's high enough. . . . No, you stay away from him, gal. I'd be in a hell of a fix, if *you* pulled his iron and flang a shot at me." His voice was conversational and easy, with none of the disused rustiness common to the voices of far-riding men. This would be a story-telling man, given to talking late by drowsing fires, as long as any one would listen. "Now turn around, Monte, face to the wall."

He uncoiled himself with leisure, stretching his joints as he stood up—a lank and angular man, big-boned, and lean everywhere, except for the beginning of a thickening at the waist. Luke Packer was getting old for this sort of work, though it might be a long time before he would admit it.

"That's one thing I never figured out," he said as he took Melody's gun, "what a feller would do if a *woman* hung the drop on him. Okay, you can put your hands down, Monte. It's my idee of one hell of a fix." He stuck Melody's gun in his waistband.

"I know a feller got hoisted by a lady with a shotgun, oncet," Melody offered.

"What did he do?"

"He give in and married her."

"Tch, tch," said Luke Packer. "Don't that just go to show. You people make yourselves as comfortable as you kin. There's liable to be a couple of hours wait."

He moved about the room in lazy, lurching strides, very awkward looking. There can be great deceptiveness in a man with a gait like that. He was lighting stubs of candles he had found some place, and sticking them around. Dim double and triple shadows formed beyond him, cast by the several points of light, until he appeared to be dogged by a ghostly troop.

"I like for a dump to look jolly," Packer said. "These here don't give no light to speak of, but maybe they'll kind of warm 'er up."

About all the added light showed was a heavy carpeting of dust over everything, sifted from the deep adobe walls. It lay half an inch thick on the window ledge that Cherry had spoken of. A lot of the glass was gone from the many-paned frame, but what remained was heavy with cobwebs, as if nothing around that window had ever been disturbed. The ledge itself was a weighty rough-hewn slab, split from a single log. With the dust sifted over it, it made a good cache, much better than it had sounded to Melody when Cherry first had told him of it.

"What are you holding us for?" Cherry demanded now. She held her voice low, but there was a nervous edge to it. Her eyes were too bright, and her lips looked sick and pale. "I don't reckon we're just going to live here, are we?"

"Not for too long," Packer answered her genially. He had holstered his huge gun, and now eased himself down on the bunk again, patient and relaxed. "A few of the boys—part of Sheriff Thingan's posse—are casting up the other arm of the gulch. They ought to be back, directly—in an hour or two. What they want to do then is up to them. I just work for the express company."

Cherry asked sharply, "Are there Cottons with them?"

Packer, loading up a pipe now, looked her over calmly. "Monte was bound to run into Cottons, soon or late," he said. "What's the difference if it comes now, or later in the town?"

"Because," Cherry said, "if there are Cottons on the way he'll never *see* the town, or a trial by law! If you don't know that, you don't know what you're making happen here!"

"I can't see how I'm liable for any possible hastiness on the part of deputies that don't answer to me, and that I don't even name," Luke Packer said.

"The Sheriff didn't appoint the Cottons deputies," Cherry said bitterly, "the Cottons appointed the Sheriff!

You know the Cottons run the Poisonberry!"

"They're legal; legal to the teeth. That lets me out. And out is where I aim to be, Sister."

"But this is murder!" Cherry cried out.

"Monte should know," Packer said, looking at Melody dispassionately. "He's a well-known expert, on all different kinds of sudden death. Shooting 'right in the stummick' is his favorite kind, if I recollect."

"Now, wait a minute, here," Melody said. His words were even and unhurried, and his gaze was as steady as Luke Packer's. The times were trying to change Melody, these last few days, but they weren't getting any place. "This thing's gone fur enough, and ten feet further. It's time people knowed a couple of things, before there's one hell of a mistake made here!"

"Anything - you - say - is - liable - to - be - used - against - you, go ahead, son, I'm listening." Packer lit his pipe from a candle, and idly watched a smoke cloud float away. "And come a leetle farther from that door!"

"I'm not Monte Jarrad," Melody told him now. "My name is Melody Jones, out o' high Montana. I don't know Monte Jarrad; I never set eyes on him in my whole life; I ain't responsible for none of the things he ever done; and I'll be pertically damned if I aim to get hung in his place!"

Luke Packer set his hat far back on his balding head, and looked at Melody with a pity that touched contempt. "Listen, Monte," he said at last. "I can't scarcely read my name. But I can read *you,* son, as easy as a bear trail knee-deep in molasses candy. And I'll go on record that that is the wobbliest darn fool lie I ever had a try at, man or boy, in sixty years of misdoings!"

"He isn't lying," Cherry said; but her words were low with lack of hope.

"I can prove how I come here," Melody plugged doggedly, "step by step. I can prove how come I got hold of Monte's saddle. I can prove anything you want to know, and I'll do anything you want me to do—but I won't be any use to you or nobody if all of a sudden I'm daid!"

"Listen, son," Packer said with grave patience. "I don't care a hoot in hell whether your name is Monte Jarrad, or Melody Jones, or Harmony Smith. You can be old Mrs. Hymie MacStoople, if you want to be. All I'm interested in is forty-two thousand and four dollars and eighty-five cents, belonging to the people I work for; and not another cussed thing on earth!"

"You'll never see it again if this boy's killed," Cherry promised him. "I swear to *God* you never will!"

"I got to lay my hands," Luke Packer repeated, "on forty-two thousand and four dollars, and eighty-five cents. I'll do better than that. I'll settle for the forty-two thousand, just to wind the whole thing up, and pay the four eighty-five myself, out of my own pants. All right, Monte—how's for coughing it up?"

"And supposing I cain't?" Melody demanded.

Luke Packer sadly tamped his pipe with the lead of a fifty-one calibre slug. "It was only a suggestion," he said.

"And what if he *could?*" Cherry asked, almost crying. She sounded as if she were breaking up.

"It's all *I* want from him," Packer said. "Once I get hold of it, he can go on, for all of me. It'll be up to

Thingan to make his own fresh ketch, any way he can. It's the express people pay *me,* and what I want is forty-two thousand and four dollars—"

"—and eighty-five cents," Melody finished for him. "You said that already."

He turned his eyes to Cherry; and was instantly mystified to find her looking at him with an unspoken, almost desperate appeal.

"Packer," Melody said, "is there any way I could talk to this girl alone?"

A gleam of interest showed in Luke Packer's eye. He had an idea that he was about to get some place. "You and her can step in there," he decided. With his eyes he indicated a heavy slab door in the rear wall. "Last year a possum was living there. But I judge she's gone, by now."

Melody rolled his eyes at the door, and his jaw slacked a little. "You mean," he asked, "you trust me I won't slope out the back way, and high-tail over the hill?"

"Son, in this here case, I trust you one hundred per cent to the ton."

"Whut?"

"I kin pretty near bet my life that you ain't going to flapdoodle a pore old trusting detective by busting out no back way."

Cherry de Longpre looked a little queer, and her gaze upon Luke Packer sharpened. But Melody just said simply, "Mr. Packer, I appreciate this. You ain't going to never regret it."

"Better take a candle with you."

When Melody had forced the stuck door, Cherry preceded Melody into a black little room like a moldy cave.

Melody's first act was to crack his head upon a low beam; but when he had wedged the door shut behind them, and they looked about them by their candle's still flame, the reason for Packer's trust became clear. There was no back door, nor window, nor opening of any kind.

"Why, that old rip," Melody complained, "this ain't nothing but a old root cellar!"

"What did you expect? The bridal suite of a hotel?"

"I *thought* there might be a catch to it," Melody said darkly. "But I supposed there might anyway be a weak place in the top!"

He angrily tested the low roof. Its mass suggested three or four feet of packed dirt.

"If a feller would tunnel up, I suppose he'd find Packer waiting on top." Melody seemed unwilling to forgive this. "I never see such a deceitful old jigger. Why, this here is no better than a dang fraud!"

Cherry said in a smothered voice, "What did you want to talk to me about?"

"Oh," Melody said, brought back to the subject in hand. "Cherry, you look here. I would like to hear one reason—just some one reason—why that money shouldn't go back to the people it belongs to."

Cherry wouldn't look at him, nor let him watch her face. "And save you the risk of your skin," she said without expression.

"That ain't got nothing to do with it!" But after Melody had heard himself say that he hesitated. "Yes it does, too," he admitted. "It has all there is to do with it. What I want to know is why in all hell I shouldn't turn that money back?"

"No reason, I guess," Cherry said, "if you don't know any."

"I know what's in your mind," Melody accused her. "You're thinking it will hurt Monte's chances if I give the money up. You figure I should sooner take my chances with the Cottons, than let Monte in for a risk on the trail."

"I didn't say all that."

"No, but you thought it. You think if Monte gets clear, fine, and the heck with my neck! The *hell* with my neck," he improved this.

"I've already told you where the cache is," Cherry said. Her words were very quiet, as if pressed down by the walls.

"I want to hear some reason why Monte shouldn't face this out for himself," Melody persisted. "He got that money by a bloody murder, didn't he? He sure did. He's left me to hang in his place, hasn't he? He sure has! What in all heck, I mean hell, is supposed to be my theory, helping myself get hung?"

"No theory. I didn't say you should." Her tone was flat and dead, without any trace of contention.

"You're thinking about that dang promise you trapped me into!"

Cherry hoisted him with the most infuriating words known to the feminine mind. "Keep your voice down," she told him.

He lowered his voice. "Look," he said with unexpected calm. "You're in love with Monte Jarrad, aren't you?"

Cherry was silent.

"Well, I'm not in love with him! I never even seen him! Can't you get that through your haid?"

"Yes; I understand that, Melody."

"Well, there's absolutely no sense to the idee that I otter lend a hand and virtually saw off my own head, without even one dang reason in its favor!"

"No," Cherry agreed tonelessly, "there wouldn't be any reason."

He looked at her sadly for several moments; then turned with unusual decision upon the door.

❦ 18 ❦

T he inner handle came away in his hands on his first try at opening it, but after some effort he got hold of the edge with his fingers, and wrenched the door open with a violence that broke its leather hinges.

"Shucks," he said.

"Made up your mind, Monte?" Packer asked him.

"I reckon," Melody grunted, "it's as near made up as I'll ever git it."

"I'm glad to hear it, Monte. I thought for a minute, there, we was going to see a pack of trouble, here, when the Cottons come. I do hate trouble," Luke Packer said. "I've ducked it all of my life. . . . Well?"

"Well, whut?"

"Well, where's the money?"

"Whut money?"

"*What* money?" Packer yelled.

"Most money I ever seen in one place was ninety dullers, the time I got snowed in at Lake Lizzie, and my pay piled up. But I ain't got that no more."

Luke Packer turned hard and angry for the first time. "You realize what you're doin'? You realize that posse ain't thirty minutes away on that trail? You realize—"

"To hell with 'em," said Melody.

"So be it," said Luke Packer, sitting back. "I ain't got any way to force you. Though I'm sorry to see a man took apart without any chance. Even such a reptile as you be, Monte."

"Don't call me Monte," Melody said futilely.

"You're dead set you won't tip your hand?"

"I don't know *nothin'*," Melody shouted at him. "Don't people think I *ever* git mad? Jesus!"

Cherry said, "I'll tell you where it is."

Packer was caught off balance, "Where what is?" he asked idiotically; and sat staring at her.

"Forty-two thousand and four dollars, and eighty-five cents," Cherry said distinctly. "What's the matter with you? Can't you keep your mind on what we're talking about?"

Both men were looking hard at her now. Melody's face had gone slack again. "But," he said, in a silly-sounding squeak. He cleared his throat. "But," he said again, this time in bass, but just as vaguely as before.

Red spots had appeared in Cherry's cheeks, and unexpected tears were in her eyes, but her words were crisp and clear. "I know where it is, and I'll show it to you, if only you'll let us get out of here and go on!"

"That's my proposition!" Packer confirmed instantly. He surged up onto his long legs.

Melody turned toward Cherry. "Are you sure," he

asked her, his voice peculiar, "are you sure jest *which* man you aim to be the death of around here?"

"*What?*"

"Jest a little bit ago you was all in favor of hangin'—"

"Will you be quiet!" Cherry blew up. "I can't *stand* this any more! *The express box is under that slab!*"

Luke Packer did not turn to the window ledge at once. His eyes were jumping quickly back and forth from one to the other of them, studying them acutely. He drew his huge gun, very cautious, now that he had come to the end of a weary trail, that no last-minute trick should unseat him. When he moved at last he backed toward the window ledge, still facing them. He bent his knees; with his free hand, but without looking at the ledge, he heaved upward upon the edge of the slab.

The broad timber of the window ledge moved to his lift, not easily, but enough to confirm that it was free.

A faint surprise crossed Luke's Packer's face. He may not have believed Cherry, until then.

Packer half whirled toward the window embrasure, his gun pointed straight upward in his right hand. With his left hand he caught a new grip upon the ledge slab, and sent it spinning to the floor.

A black hole, big enough to close over a couple of stock saddles, was revealed, cut into the four-foot adobe of the wall. As Luke Packer looked into it a blaze of jubilant, incredulous triumph lighted the impassive leather of his face. He said, "Well, *by God!*"

He hardly noticed as Melody, moving at his walking lope, crossed the cabin to his side. Together they stood peering into the black cache. Luke Packer bent to reach in after the steel-bound box that rested deep within the wall.

Then, as he bent, there came an ugly short sound, as when a melon falls and splits; and over this sounded the tinkle of glass fragments. Luke Packer's whole body shocked rigid, as if struck in the middle by a crowbar; and for a moment he balanced there, upon galvanized muscles.

In that moment while he still stood, bent and rigid, they heard the far-off sound of the gun-shot which had sent the lead. Then Luke Packer collapsed and fell, first in a loose sprawl across the black mouth of the cache, then, rolling and sliding, into an angular heap upon the floor.

"God Almighty," Melody whispered. For an instant he stared out through a broken pane into the night, as if anything were to be seen out there in the moonless dark. Then he stooped above Luke Packer.

Instantly a second shot buzzed through the room, and bedded in the floor; followed in a moment by the sound of the rifle.

"Melody! Melody!" Cherry cried out. "For God's sake get down!" She came running to him.

"Get down yourself," Melody said. He deftly tripped her with his toe as he pushed her out of line, so that she sat down in the dust, against the bunk. A drop of blood fell on the back of his buckskin glove as he turned Luke Packer over; but he didn't stop to find out where it came from, then.

By easy stages they worked Luke Packer up onto the bunk. He freed the heavy gun from Packer's hand, working carefully not to discharge it; Packer had cocked the gun by muscle reflex, in the instant he was struck.

"Put out the candles, you—you ninny," Packer wheezed. His words were no more than a soft rasp in his throat. "Put out all but one."

They did as they were told; and then, when they had made Luke Packer as comfortable as they could, they straightened up and looked at each other. Their eyes were grave.

"George Fury," Melody said, very softly, his lips scarcely moving. "He must of come up careful, and saw that we was caught. So this—this is what he done."

"What?" Luke Packer asked, in a ghostly whisper. "What did you say?"

"Nothin'."

Luke Packer's eyes were open, fixed on the beams above, but they did not appear to see anything. There was a strange look of preoccupation in his face, as if the old man had turned inward with an intense attention. "You folks had better be getting on," he said without moving his eyes. "The posse can't be far away."

Cherry and Melody exchanged a quick glance. It was so obvious that they could not leave him now that no words were necessary. Melody began to rake big veils of cobweb down from the beams with a stick.

"What's that for?" Luke Packer asked, more weakly than before.

"If you poke them in a bullet wound," Melody said, "they stop the bleeding inside."

"Keep that trash away from me, you—stalking horse. . . ."

A stalking horse is one a hunter walks behind, to get

near to game.

"Whut?"

Luke Packer did not tell Melody what he meant, right then. He did not take a long time to die, but it seemed a long time. When they had put all the candles out but one the cabin was very dim. There had not been much light in there before, with all the candles going, but it seemed like the merry blaze of a new saloon, compared to the yellow gloom in which they waited now. Melody kept expecting George Fury to come in, now that Luke Packer was down, but he did not come.

They waited. There was nothing to do, and nothing to look at, and nothing to listen to except the slowly changing rhythm of Luke Packer's breathing, which was turning shaky in his throat. But when Packer finally spoke his voice was surprisingly clear.

"So you were telling the truth," he said.

"Yes," Melody answered.

"It's a funny thing," Luke Packer said. "It's easy to tell when a man is lying; but it plumb fails you to say when he's telling the truth. But that ain't any excuse. A thousand things otter told me you was only a stalking horse. No such damn fool *could* be the real Monte Jarrad. But I never caught on. Until the real Monte fired from the slope."

Cherry and Melody exchanged another slow glance, but without conveying much. All Luke Packer's ramblings meant to them was that Packer knew nothing of George Fury.

"I suppose I've done more mean things in my life than one man can remember," Luke Packer said. He was speaking with great difficulty now. "But the mean things you do are brushed over and forgot. The one thing nobody ever forgets . . . and nobody ever forgives . . . is a bald-headed jackass of a blunder. . . . Not even God'll forgive that. Him least of all."

Those were the last words Luke Packer ever said. He died with a strange aboriginal stoicism, without bitterness and without faith. Seemingly he literally believed, as he had said, that the death penalty was a suitable one for a man of his occupation to pay, for the crime of mistaking one man for another.

After Luke Packer was dead, Melody very gently took back his gun. As Melody recovered it he noticed the belt it was stuck in.

Nobody had ever seen a belt just like it before. It was nearly three inches wide, of very thick, hard leather, like the sole of a boot; and all of its outer surface was covered with intricate carvings, worked out with infinite patience and precision with the point of Luke Packer's knife. The figures of mounted men, and men with long rifles in their hands, and Comanche warriors, crowded each other in the minute panorama. There were ox-teams and covered wagons, buffalo, antelope, and wolves—all the animals of the plains. That strip of leather was virtually a history of the things that had made up Luke Packer's life. Part of the carving was old and worn, some of it was smoke-smudged, and some of it was new. The patient knife point must have worked beside a thousand far-separated camp fires, out on many a lonely trail.

And the carving was unfinished; the last of the innumerable figures were sketchily scribed, uncut. Melody wondered if Luke Packer would ever have begun the decoration of that belt, if he had known it would never be done. Probably Packer could have saved himself the trouble of starting a hundred other things, too, that would be unfinished now. A man could get tangled up thinking about things like that. If you thought like that long enough you could prove beyond a doubt that there was no point in looking ahead, or ever starting anything at all. None of your plans are apt to matter very much, ten minutes after you are dead.

Melody Jones shook out a saddle-blanket, and laid it over Packer's body; then immediately forgot the whole thing, for now the outer door was pushed open from outside, and flung wide. Melody thought he glimpsed the hand that swung the door; but nobody stood in the opening that gaped blackly into the night. Melody snatched his gun out in what was intended to be a lightning draw.

❦ 19 ❦

He would have done better to take his gloves off and draw the gun with both hands. As it was, it flew out of his fumbling fingers in the same instant that it cocked. The gun spun in the air, and went off with a thunderous detonation as it bounded end over end along the floor. Probably nobody on earth but Melody Jones could ever have made a draw like that. He often thought about it afterwards, wondering just what was the cause of it, and just how it could have been done. He never did find out where the bullet went.

Melody stood frozen for a minute, and when he decided he should make another snatch for the weapon he couldn't find out where it had gone. He finally noticed a curl of powder smoke coming out from under the table, and went scrambling under the table after it on his hands and knees.

He had got hold of the gun, but was wholly under the table, as George Fury's voice sounded outside.

"Melody, are you there?"

"Oh, it's you," Melody said, with all the disgust a man's voice can convey.

George Fury stepped through the door, and flattened himself against the wall inside, allowing the least possible silhouette of himself in the door-frame until the door was shut. He was in time to see Melody bump his head as he crawled out from under the table.

"It don't do you no good to get under there," George Fury said judicially. "A bullet can run under a table just as easy as it can climb a tree."

Melody looked as if he might either blow up or fall apart. He opened his mouth to explain, but decided in time that the truth was even sillier than the mistake.

George Fury's eyebrows jumped now as he saw the form of Luke Packer under its blanket. He looked at it for a long time, and his face was very grim. "So now they got a corpus delicti," he said at last, hollowly.

"A whut?"

"A dead man," George Fury amplified. "It ain't legal to hang you on account of a dead man unless they can come up with one. Corpus delicti is some foreign way of saying that soon's they got the corpus you're de-licked."

"Oh."

"This here is rock-bottom," George Fury said, completely without hope. "Up until now we was in bad shape, but all right. Even if they hung you for Monte Jarrad, we could of proved the mistake. But what good will it do to prove who you ain't, now that you come fitted up with a corpus delicti of your own?"

Melody put away his gun. "Sometimes," he said, "it don't seem to me like we get the breaks."

"I suppose you realize," George Fury said saltily, "there's a posse pretty near on top of us right now?"

"George," said Cherry de Longpre with deep gravity, "you shouldn't have done this."

"Who, me? What? Done which?"

"You shouldn't have shot him."

"I shouldn't of what? Shot who?"

"The man under that blanket is—was an express company detective. His name was Luke Packer. He was one of the most feared peace officers in the West; everybody knows his name. There isn't a single man in the whole territory who wouldn't have been a better choice for you to kill than this man."

"Yes, but—but—"

"There's going to be such a man-hunting hullabaloo as the West has never seen before. I wouldn't give two cents for the chances of either one of you!"

George Fury looked from the girl to his partner, and back again, slowly, with the dreary disillusion of a man who witnesses an all time low.

"So now," he drawled, "you can't neither of you think of no better out than to blame the whole damn calamity on me, by Gard!"

"It ain't any question of blaming nobody, George," Melody said sadly.

"This sinks the duck, by Gard," George said. He slanted a bitter gaze at Cherry. "I long thought better of *you*. I naturally knew you didn't mean well. But I shore never looked for you to team up in a outrage with no such silly ninny as my partner!"

"What in God's name are you talking about?" Cherry demanded, unstrung.

"And as for you," George said, turning on Melody Jones with deep repugnance, "this is a new bottom. You've hauled off and outdid yourself at last. I would of bet the seat of my pants it couldn't be done, but this beats! Ga-a-rd damn it, you're a walkin' insult to the mind!"

Melody and Cherry looked at each other in bewilderment.

"What's got into him?" Cherry asked. "Does he always holler in a steady yell, for his own benefit, or something?"

"George," Melody said with reproach, "I don't know where you got it, but if you been drinking, I think you ought to come out and say so, so's we can face it."

George reddened. "Why yew befewzled numpus—"

"I guess," Melody told Cherry, "we got him on our hands. That's how come he shot Packer."

Cherry just stood there looking bleak, and stunned—a little glassy-eyed. The full complication of their disaster was still soaking its way into her mind.

"It wasn't the real George done this," Melody said. "It was a bottle of liquor shot Packer, just the same as if it capered in here and popped him with its cork. When George drinks, he ain't nothing but a bottle with laigs."

"I heard you fire the shot that dropped him." George was pitying them now, in a weary, embittered way. "I was right outside. And when I come in, you was under the table, your six-gun smoking in your damn hand."

"You mean, *I* shot him?"

"You finally got it, son."

"Why is a hole in the window, and glass on the floor, if I shot him?" Melody demanded. "You think I run outside, and shot, and sudden run back?"

"I don't know nothing about that."

"Why is they blood on the floor by the window, where he fell?" Melody insisted. "And how does the corpus get from there up on the bunk, if I'm under the table when I shoot him daid? You think the corpus hauls off and *leaps* up under that blanket, when he hears you coming in?"

This gave George pause. He grew suddenly very still as something else that was going on, beyond the range of their argument, beyond the cabin clearing, became plain to him. Cherry watched him.

"Can you hear the posse?" she whispered.

George shook his head. "Something else is tooken place," he said with a new bleak awe. "So *that* was it! I'm sorry, Melody. It wasn't you shot Packer. I should of knowed you wasn't up to nothing so practical as that."

"I don't foller this," Melody said.

"For Gard sake," George pleaded with him, "don't *try* to git it through your head. We ain't got time for no such complicated projick as that! *If* you want out of this, will you please, please do like I say, jest for the next few minutes?"

"What you want?"

"Distance," George gritted. "Quick distance! It's the only hope!"

"That appeals to me!" Cherry breathed.

"Go catch your ponies," George Fury ordered Melody. All the dead-level urgency he could put into his low tones was there. "Saddle 'em both, yours and Cherry's. Then git mine. He's about forty rods down the crick, in a little meadow. You can't miss catching him because he's close hobbled, and he's also short picketed."

"You always was a pessimist, George."

"Shut *up!* Go on, now, as careful as you kin—because there's eyes looking down gunsights at this dump right now. And for Gard sakes try to remember to unhobble my pony! I don't want to go somersaulting down no mountain in the dark."

"It looks to me," Melody said uncertainly, "like we *all* ought to go, and keep kind o' clotted together."

"We got a little housekeeping to do here," George said grimly. "*Will* you git gone?"

He blanketed the lone candle by cupping his hat over it as Melody eased the door open a few inches and slid into the night.

❧ 20 ❧

Out in the fresh dark Melody realized that the cabin he had left had become an unwholesome place. There within the adobe walls was everything needful to put an end to him. His doings were wandering and purposeless, but he valued them; and the living air in his lungs became increasingly precious as his time supply ran short. It was a considerable relief to find their ponies about where he had left them; he was already aware that they might easily have been gone.

His own gelding, Harry Henshaw, took his saddling without any question, but Cherry's pony delayed him by treating him as a spook. After some minutes of thrashing about in the brush, unable to swing Cherry's saddle aboard, he discovered the trouble. His right ear was stinging as if blasted by a wasp, and he found now that it was bleeding. There was a small piece missing from that ear, like the bite of a flying mouse. Whoever had killed Luke Packer had, with his second bullet, put an earmark on Melody that would have been satisfactory on a maverick calf.

Melody now understood the flightiness of the horse. He scraped up a handful of needles from the ground pine, and pressed them to his ear. Their powdery, resinous odor moderated the smell of blood, confusing the issue for the pony enough so that Melody could cinch the saddle down.

After that he found George Fury's pony, after walking past in the dark without seeing it only once; and settled himself to wait for George and Cherry. What he noticed as he strained his ears for warning of an approach was that this was an unquiet night. The tumbling of the name-less creek, rampaging down from level to level through its boulders, filled the dark with a watery monotone, unnoticed until you tried to hear something else.

Melody stood and waited, so sure that Cherry and

George were on his heels that at first he was glad to have got the saddling down before they caught up and found him unready. By and by he sat down, his back against a boulder and one ankle on a cocked-up knee. His bullet-nick was hurting very interestingly now; he idly picked pine needles out of his bloody ear, and wondered if he would lose the whole shebang.

After a long time the three ponies whoofed and hauled on their leads, and Melody spotted a pair of luminous green eyes, amazingly far apart, watching him from across the creek. He pulled his gun for a shot at them, but remembered himself in time. The eyes haunted him, and kept him interested for a quarter of an hour, switching on and off and reappearing in different places, until at last they went away, and the ponies quieted.

Melody was thinking about Cherry de Longpre, and feeling sorry for himself. He couldn't see why his life should not be romantic and fascinating, like a farmer's life. Melody's idea of romance was a farm kitchen with plenty to eat and a hot stove. Failing that, he would have settled for any other situation in which no one was out after him with firearms. The bleakest, most tiresome thing he could think of was to flog all over the country in a darn saddle, on a darn horse with a hay-belly and narrow withers, so you had to re-cinch all the time. Or any horse. And the one thing worse was to get mixed up with people who were fools with guns. So naturally he had worked it out to swap the most dismal kind of thing for the one thing that was dismaller.

"The most miserable feller in the world," Melody told Harry Henshaw, "is a cowboy with a partner that has rheumatiz. And three o' you ratched-haided broom-tails on lead, and his ear shot. And a blond-haided gal circlin' round him like a wolf. If they's anything I hate and despise, it's a gal that gets stuck on Monte Jarrad. You take miseries like I got, and a few posses cain't add nothin' to it, hardly. The average feller should ought to be *glad* to get hung. Damn!"

Melody Jones now got stiffly up onto his heels, and mounted Harry Henshaw. Riding Harry and leading the other ponies, he turned back toward the adobe, on no better theory than that he had waited long enough. He approached the cabin with some caution, riding with his led ponies in places where the animals' unshod hoofs were least likely to clop upon stone. The three ponies moved like ghosts as he rode into the little meadow.

And now a burst of outrage lifted him in his stirrup bows. The adobe was well illuminated now, as if every candle in the place had been lighted.

"Lit up like a new saloon, by God," he breathed aloud. "Couldn't wait until I was out of sight hardly, before they relax completely!"

He made one concession to caution. With the elaborate patience of exasperation, he picketed his ponies and made a careful scout-circuit of the cabin. With some difficulty he made his way to a place from which he had a line upon the interior through the shattered pane.

One figure was included in the segment of his vision. It was that of George Fury.

George stood at ease against the wall; and he was engaged, exactly as Melody might have expected, in making what appeared to be a lengthy speech.

Patience left Melody Jones. Throwing aside all pretense of caution, he went slashing up to the door of the cabin and kicked it in.

"Now you lookey here," he shouted, stepping into the full light.

He stopped then and looked around him. Cherry de Longpre and George Fury were not alone. Three interlopers made the cabin seem packed. Their guns were in their hands; and they had so placed themselves that they could keep an eye on George Fury while their guns converged upon Melody at the door. The body of Luke Packer, however, was no longer in the bunk.

"All right, m'boy," the oldest of the three men said, "I'm Sheriff Thingan—the big end of the law in Payneville. Stick your fingers in your mouth," he ordered surprisingly.

"Whut?"

"Stick your fingers in your mouth. Both hands."

"Whut for?"

"Because I tell you to," Sheriff Thingan said, angering. "And be pert, before I let fly!"

Melody looked with bewilderment at George Fury, who was staring at him ironically. "I never seed so many crazy people," Melody said; but he obeyed Sheriff Thingan and put his fingers in his mouth, all the fingers of both hands. He rolled an eye at Cherry to see if she was laughing. She was not.

Sheriff Thingan now stepped forward, approaching Melody from one side. He pulled Melody into the room by a shoulder, and spun him around, then disarmed Melody from behind. After that he shut the door.

"You can collapse now," Thingan told Melody. "Turn around, and take your feet out of your mouth, and start to talk."

Melody Jones took a slow look at his captors. Sheriff Thingan was somewhat apple-cheeked, but with deep grin lines, amounting to dimples. He affected a neat white mustache, more cleanly trimmed than the old conventional buffalo-horn model, and curled only slightly, after the manner of the better class of Mexican border desperadoes. His hat—not ten gallon, but perhaps two— he wore raked at a sporty angle. Sheriff Thingan had the name of being a profoundly wise, infallibly cagey old man. What Melody saw now was that this was a profoundly silly, infallibly eccentric old man.

Sheriff Roddy Thingan had probably been excessively bright-eyed, at about the age of twenty, with a livelier mind and shrewder intelligence than other cowboys. But there he had stopped. Now white-haired and partly bald, he was still excessively bright-eyed and mentally twenty, with a net gain from experience of nil. Definitely a man whose election by the citizens of Payneville was a cinch.

"Lucky you be," Sheriff Thingan said to Melody, "that it was me caught up with you."

"Why?"

Sheriff Thingan directed a genial question to his deputies. "Ain't this the little punk that's been making out to be Monte Jarrad?"

"So fer as I got any resemblance," Melody Jones said, "to somebody that done somethin', it's a pure coincidence."

"As Gard be my judge," George Fury said fervently,

"that is a true thing. Man or boy, he's never accomplished a Ga-ar' damn thing, either one way or the other. Nothing!"

"Shut up," said Thingan.

Thingan's number one deputy now spoke. He was big and coarse featured, his face crudely and strongly made. He had big aggressive ears, a big craggy nose and jaw; his sparse hair had once been red, but now was greyed to a sandy roan. His rough-cut grin had the expression of a pumpkin face, and it showed yellow teeth as big as an elk's, with gaps between. And his eyes, which were a muddy blue, had about the same expression as holes blown in a roof.

This man's name was Royal Boone.

"I shore don't know what you fellows want," he grinned. "If he ain't Monte, he'll sure do in Monte's place."

"You're just rope-handy," Thingan said, his words bumped by a chuckle.

"Well he's virtually volunteered to get hung, ain't he? Why quarrel with the guy?"

Thingan turned amiably to his other deputy. "Does he look much like Monte Jarrad to you?"

The second deputy, Mormon Stocker, was a swarthy, beery little man with a broken nose. He had a habit of carrying his chin on his chest, which set his mouth in a line of disgust, and gave a peculiar look to his eyes, which were buttony, and had circular lines about them above and below, like the eyes of an owl.

He switched these owl eyes upon Melody through a moment of dark depression. "Nump," he said.

"I suppose," Royal Boone said with sarcasm that killed himself, "you aim to fight it out with the Cotton boys to see that they don't hang him."

"I do like hell," said Sheriff Thingan.

"Them Cottons has waited four years for this," Royal Boone said. "They'll never run a risk that he might be Monte Jarrad and get loose. How you aim to get him back to town, if you don't fight the Cottons? That trail is plumb full of Cottons."

"I aim to let the Cottons take him back to town."

"Oh, of course they'll be glad to do that," said Royal Boone elaborately.

Sheriff Thingan's mild eyes were almost merry. "I admit it is barely possible," he said, "that the Cottons might feel they had to rope him by the neck to a tree, to stop him from trying to escape. But I am only one man around here. Can one man take care of everything? I will gladly try to stop them, if I'm there."

"You won't be there," said Mormon Stocker.

"One man can't be everywhere," Thingan admitted.

Cherry de Longpre began to speak rapidly, in a low monotone. "Why don't you let him go? What kind of murderers are you? Give him a chance to run for his life!" She looked grey faced and desperately tired, but to Melody she had never looked prettier in her life. "This fool kid has nothing to do with anything. Let the Cottons catch him for themselves!"

Mormon Stocker said with deep dejection, "Let the kid slope."

Royal Boone looked at him blankly. "Have you gone out of your head?"

Sheriff Roddy Thingan looked at Cherry de Longpre with all kinds of benevolence. "Crime doesn't pay," he told her. "How come you got your foot stuck through the fence like this? I swear, I'm goin' to stop this corrupting American womanhood around here if I have to hang fellers right and left!"

"Listen you old fool," said George Fury, "don't it never occur to you that you won't never find out where the loot went to, if you let this punk git hung?"

"How's that again?"

"Who do you think is going to tell you where that strong-box is," George Fury asked him, "once this punk is dead? Monte Jarrad? You don't even know Monte Jarrad is alive!"

"Do you," Sheriff Thingan asked Melody cynically, "know what Monte done with that express box?"

"Yes," Melody said.

"What?"

"I can lay my hands on it in less than a minute."

Roddy Thingan's whole outlook turned brittle. He looked much more commonplace when he proposed to go into action than he did when he was posing as genial and profound. "Then come on with it, and come on with it quick!" he said, in the tone of a nervous and worried old man. He shot a quick glance at his deputies. "It's a good thing I flang this posse out in a spread," he told them. "Come on with it, you!"

"I want you to get it through your haid," Melody said, "that I ain't Monte Jarrad. If I show you where the money is, I want you should turn me free. And my gal with me, too!"

It was only later that Melody found that George Fury's knees had sagged under him, just here.

Sheriff Roddy Thingan was ready to deal, and deal quickly. "I know you ain't Monte Jarrad," he said. "It's only the Cottons that get excited, as a general thing. The first minute I get my hands on that express box, you're free to high-tail in all the directions you want."

"Do you swear to that?"

"I swear it on my sacred honor," said Sheriff Thingan piously.

"The express box is right over—" Melody began.

Melody stopped there, with all the wind suddenly gone out of him, as if he had been kicked in the stomach. By a horse. He had caught George Fury's eye, and had seen there such unholy terror as George Fury had never shown before. For only a fraction of an instant he failed to understand what this meant.

Then he knew what was the matter. He knew why Luke Packer's body was no longer on the bunk. And he knew where it must be now.

He let his eyes rest for a moment on the bunk where Luke Packer had laid and then flicked a questioning glance to George. George nodded imperceptibly.

George Fury had put the body of Luke Packer on top of the express box in the cache.

❦ 21 ❦

There was a brief silence while Sheriff Roddy Thingan and his deputies waited. George Fury sagged where he stood, and felt of his head with a wavering hand. He was by long odds the unhappiest man in the world, completely without further hope. Cherry de Longpre appeared to be holding her breath, her eyes slowly glazing, as she waited for the blow to fall.

Melody Jones wasn't waiting for anything. He was standing there paralyzed. There had always been a good chance that he would lose his life in the boots of Monte Jarrad. If nobody else got impetuous and rubbed him out, the Cotton feudists could be counted on for this mistake. But as soon as the body of Luke Packer was discovered, no mistake would be necessary. He could be lynched as himself, or as Unidentified Traveller, as well as for Monte. He had a corpus delicti of his own. And he saw all this, now.

"If ever I git out of this darn country," Melody said, "I ain't never coming back!"

"What?" Sheriff Thingan demanded. "What? What's that got to do with it?"

"Well—nothing, I suppose," Melody admitted.

Royal Boone was staring hard at Melody with those blank, windy blue eyes, and his big gap-toothed grin was gone. Boone's stare was something like that of a mountain lion, hard-fixed and glassy, but full of an explosive vitality. This man liked things to happen, and could make them happen, without any delicate shadings. Even by himself, he would have been sure to force the issue very soon.

But Mormon Stocker was watching Melody, too. He was the only one of the three who had favored letting Melody make a break for his life, and now he was watching Melody in a different way. His chin was lower than ever, and the circular lines above his eyes were higher than ever, so that the shoe-button pupils seemed to float in the stained whites. All the beery cynicism in the broken-nosed face was gone, and the whole sullen weight of the man was concentrated on Melody in a single question.

And the most ineffectual man in the room had now turned into the most dangerous. Deep in the back of his mind the Sheriff must have realized that his long life had accomplished nothing; and he was suddenly seeing a swell chance to bring his percentage up. If he actually laid his hands on the express box he would score on the law officers of four states, many of whom had always held Roddy Thingan in contempt, and had been plain about it. Like most frauds, Thingan could turn mean, and he turned mean now.

"Don't you try balking on me!" he snapped. His eyes seemed to have drawn closer together, and his whole face had darkened as the man changed. The dandyish white mustache remained foolish looking, like something stuck there with paste. "Come on, come on, come on—have I got all night?"

"Come on?" Melody repeated in blank desperation. "Come on how?"

Thingan instantly looked as if he would blow up. "Don't you fool with me!" he shouted. The close, taunting opportunity had him crazy. "I'll tear up a man that'll fool with me! *Where* is that express box?"

Melody's words came weakly. "Well—I'll tell you—"

Thingan came close to him, and thrust nastily burning eyes within a few inches of Melody's own. His voice dropped low, and seemed to loaf, as it conveyed all the threat that he knew how to conceive.

"You said you knew where it was," Thingan said. "Deny that, and I swear, I'll kill you where you stand. You *don't* deny it, do you?"

"No," Melody admitted. "I couldn't hardly go to deny something whut I just now spoke."

"And you didn't lie," Thingan told him.

"No; I wouldn't lie to you, mister."

"Then," said Roddy Thingan, "then, the only thing left is—"

"The only thing is jest one thing," Melody stumbled.

"*What?*"

"The only thing is, I ain't goin' to tell you."

Thingan's eyes showed bloodshot as they widened and popped.

The big gap-toothed grin came back to Royal Boone's crude-built face. Because he was a big iron-boned man, sure of his guns, and with no imagination, he was able to take time to taunt Mormon Stocker. "Still want to turn the pore jigger loose?"

"Nump," said Mormon Stocker.

"This punk knows somethin'."

"Yump."

"Okay, then, we got to bang it out of him, that's all!"

"We otter kill the little pismire," Stocker said. The dregs of used-up alcohol were in his vindictiveness.

"Where you aim to git back your express box," George Fury put in, "if you kill him?" He was rallying a little, not in the light of any hope, but because he was recovering from the first impact of the disaster that had sent him reeling.

"I was thinking more of heating up a brander," Boone answered.

"If you want to burn somebody with a brander," Cherry de Longpre flared at him like a spit-cat, "you can try it on me, and see what it gets you! You three are the nearest thing to no men at all that I ever saw, and I've seen some sorry ones!"

"Shut up!" Thingan bellowed, turning on them all. "You jackasses mean to stand and blab until the Cottons ride up and take over?" He spun on Melody. "Once and for all—do you aim to cough up, or do we have to *git* it out o' you?"

"I—I—I ain't got no sujestions."

"Git holt of him!" Thingan ordered his deputies. He had holstered his Colt, but now he ripped it out again. It came into his hand fast and suddenly, not in a smooth draw, but in a violent one. "Git holt of him! Pin him! Pin him and hog-tie 'm!"

Mormon Stocker moved sidelong, in a sliding lurch, to get between Melody and the door. His gun also was in his hand now, thumb joint clamped hard down across the hammer.

"Who's got a piggin' string?" Thingan's voice crackled.

Royal Boone said, "Don't need it." He came fast around the table. His hands were empty, but they were in front of him a little, big competent hooks, too heavy to tie a knot without fumbling, but good for throwing a steer. His face was dead ugly now, but his eyes had a happy blaze.

In that instant the light went out.

The yellow glow of the candles blinked out in a double jerk, first those on the shelf as Cherry swept them to the floor, then the rest as George Fury kicked over the table.

The last flicker of flame as the candles fell left an arrested picture on the eyeballs, drawn fantastically in yellow ink on blackness. It showed the table high in the air, half turned over; Royal Boone already whirled like a cat toward Cherry; Mormon Stocker with his gun drawn on George Fury. Sheriff Roddy Thingan, slower than the others, remained exactly as he was, as if nothing had happened around him. He looked strangely silly in that last glimpse, before he had moved yet.

Mormon Stocker's gun spoke with a terrific concussion just as the table crashed. Instantly other guns followed, exploding with red stabs of flame as long as a man's arms. A sudden hell of yells, collisions, and smashing blows mixed in with the gunfire; nobody there could have vouched for who was near him or what was happening.

Somebody got the door open. The faint light of the rising moon blinked in the doorway as headlong figures jammed in the frame and fought their way out.

Then sudden stillness, heavy with the gun-smoke, closed down inside as suddenly as the riot had begun.

Outside, for a space of some minutes, sounded hammering boots, random expletives, shots, a few shouted commands; and at last, through a stream of high-tongued cussing, the six-eight drum of a pony's hoofs, busted out in a hard run. A second and a third pony tore away crashing through the brush, splashing through the creek;

and hoofs rang on stone. One more gun spoke, three times, as fast as its hammer could cramp and fall.

Then, an uneasy, winded quiet.

Cherry de Longpre moved slowly, tentatively, out of the corner into which she had packed herself. Her motions were creaky, as if she had been in one position for a long time, so tensely had she stood. Some of the strings seemed to have been cut in her knees; they threatened to bend both ways. She drew a deep, quivering breath of let-down.

She went to the doorway and leaned against its side, sucking in the sweet outside air, and listening to the sound of the galloping horses. It was already dying away, far off, submerging under the sound of running water. She wondered where her own pony was now to be found, if at all. She was more conscious than ever of the dead man in the cache. Now that she was alone, the black room, with a dead man in it, was more than she could stand.

The blackness behind her vanished with a snap and a flare as a match was struck. Immediately the yellow candle-light welled up softly.

Cherry's chin jerked around, her eyes astonished.

The first thing she saw was Royal Boone, sitting against the wall. He wasn't looking happy. A trickle of blood was running into his left eye from a broken eyebrow, and he was fuzzily trying to rub it clear with one straw-haired wrist. His gun hand rested on one propped-up knee, the forty-five trailing idly.

Cherry turned furious, for no logical reason. "So, you brush ape," she prodded him, "they walked over you, did they? Did you think a sorry passel of fakes like you could stop any healthy man and boy from—"

She saw surprise, and a pleasant unbelief, come across Royal Boone's rough-cut face. His dangling six-gun straightened up and levelled rock-steady at the point. Cherry turned and looked at the room.

Melody Jones was there. He had found some of the overturned candles, and was methodically lighting them, one by one.

Cherry looked at him, while slow disillusionment choked her. "What are you doing here?" she asked him without expression, almost without voice.

"Lighting this here candle," Melody said.

"Why—why didn't you slope?"

Melody blew out his match and looked at her sorrowfully, "I tried to git holt of you," he told her. "I felt all around in the dark. But I couldn't find you. What could I do? I couldn't hardly leave you here, in this here mess."

Cherry's voice broke, full of hysterical tears. "You fool—you fool—you flea-brain! What could they do to *me?*"

Melody looked her up and down blankly. "Plenty," he decided.

"If ever you get another chance—get *out* of here!" she screamed at him. "If you hold back for me again I'll—I'll—I'll *kill* you, you *hear* me?"

Melody studied her. "Well—all right," he reluctantly agreed. "Though I don't trust 'em much, when it comes to—" Melody's voice checked momentarily in mid-word as his eye caught something on the floor. One of George Fury's boots lay there on its side. It gave the curious effect of being all that was left of George Fury. This being unlikely, the second impression it gave was that George must have jumped clean out of his boots. Melody shook his head once as he gave up hope of explanation. "Not to no marked extent," he finished.

Royal Boone snickered.

A wild, frantic desperation turned Cherry crazy for a moment. She thought of kicking the gun out of Roy Boone's hand, spinning the table on top of him, making another try with the lights. . . .

Boots sounded outside; Sheriff Roddy Thingan appeared in the door behind her, unexpected. Beyond, she could hear Mormon Stocker in the shadows.

"They stomp-peded our hosses," he said bitterly. He was almost whimpering. "They stomp-peded every last hoss, and got plumb clear of—"

He stopped short as he saw Melody. "Oh," he said faintly.

"I got the one we *need* worst," Boone said.

ᕹ 22 ᕹ

George Fury was doing somewhat better. Once outside the cabin and into the timber, he was delayed by no false notion that Melody Jones would be able to join him. Two men escaping separately, without any prearranged plan, could hardly hope to join forces in the storm of flight and running battle in the dark. Not even if one of them were not Melody Jones.

When Cherry and he had struck the candles out, George had promptly sat down on the floor. This was to let random gunshots pass over in the dark. In this position he unhurriedly peeled off one of his boots, while the location of his antagonists clarified itself in his mind.

Next he made a clean spring from all fours, using the boot as a weapon. His lucky wild swing in the dark brought down Royal Boone. George quickly recovered his gun from Roy Boone's waistband, where Boone had stuck it when George was disarmed. Doing this he lost his loose boot, and wasted several seconds groping about for it. As Boone recovered himself somewhat, George gave up the boot and broke for the outside.

Sprinting into the timber, his sock foot finding every stone and sharp root in the brush, George hunted for whatever foolish place Melody might have put their ponies. He never did find them, but in trying the obvious wrong places he crashed headlong into the horses of the posse. These he promptly turned loose—they set off in brush-popping stampede—except the quietest one, which he vault-mounted at a run, and rode off in yet another direction.

He tore breakneck through the horse-high brush, hanging low to the pony's side. He lost his hat when an unexpected tree-trunk nearly brained him; but after half a mile he was able to pull up, blowing more than the horse, with the situation well in hand, such as it was.

He now set about the plan which was already full-formed in his mind. It was a conception of the utmost bold desperation, only fit for rock-bottom necessity; but he probably didn't look at it in this way. He probably thought of it as the only thing left to do. He set about it methodically, wasting no moment by useless hurry.

He first found an open promontory, from which he could study the throw of the moonlit land. He could not see the cabin from here, but he could closely judge its position. Carefully he calculated the probable trajectory of the bullet which had killed Luke Packer.

When he had placed the likely position of the rifle within a furlong or so, he studied the country a long time. He was thinking in terms of poker now, judging percentages of chance with the same careful accuracy he had used a thousand times when he had staked his wages on the sequence of the cards. He was comparing probabilities of place with the little time he had left, trying to give himself the best stud-poker chances to come out, if it were possible to come out.

After a long time he jogged off through the shrub, riding with one stirrup lest his bootless foot slip through the bow, and get him dragged. But the route he chose, yielding and twisting to conform to the land, was as certain as if he rode a traveled trail.

But down below in the cabin George now left behind, Melody Jones was making no new friends.

"I don't know why I'm not through with men," Cherry said bitterly. "I have a mighty poor opinion of women, what few of 'em I've known. But if they don't have more sense than the smartest man that ever walked, this race is in a hell of a fix!"

"Well, shucks, now," Melody said.

"Shut up!" Sheriff Thingan snapped at him. "How the devil," he turned blankly to Roy Boone, "does it come *he's* still here, anyway?"

Royal Boone was getting to his feet, concealing a certain grogginess by movements of great deliberation. He made it, and stood on spread heels, his back against the wall.

"He's here," he said heavily, "because I kept him here." The disgruntled bad temper of an impact-headache put a saw edge on his voice. "While you fellers was flying out of here, and leaving that old wild cat raise hell like he felt like, and shooting in the dark, and letting off your guns, and losing our horses—it was me hung onto the guy you *really* need."

"Tell 'em how you held onto him," Cherry said to Royal Boone.

He shot her a glance of sheepish hostility. "Well, I—I held onto him," he said truculently. "He's here ain't he? He shore is!"

"He shore is," Cherry admitted, looking at Melody with a disgust that was near to hatred.

"The reason he didn't get out," Sheriff Roddy Thingan suggested with a forced blandness, "is prob'bly that he couldn't get out. Because I'd of shot him if he run out. Why, I'd of shot him like a duck, if he run out on me!"

"Hump," Mormon Stocker said.

"Don't hump *me!*" Thingan jumped him. "Seems like it was you jammed in my way in the door, and pre-vented—"

"Me? Not me! I was standing right over here."

"The hell he was," Roy Boone argued. "That's where I was standing. You was over—"

A brisk heated argument now went briefly round and round, like a bear with a grip on its own tail, as the peace officers sought to determine who was standing where when the lights went out.

Cherry de Longpre took this opportunity to enlarge her opinion of Melody.

"I never saw anyone like you," she told him, "not in all my life." She was cooler now, but her discredit was outspoken. "Another lifetime bronc rider, huh?"

"Sometimes I bust a colt," Melody admitted feebly.

"Uh huh. I knew it! Broncs jolt the brains out of every punk that touches 'em. You might as well let 'em dump you on your head, as get your brains numb from being hit a million times in the seat of the pants!"

"I been dumped on my haid by 'em too," Melody said conversationally.

"Oh Lord in heaven!" Cherry whimpered. "Listen." She dropped her words to a quick whisper. "Try to get this. You've got to get loose—you've got to get gone! Over the south border, or over the north border, or into the Pacific Ocean—but *out* of here!"

"Cherry," said Melody slowly, "I ain't going no place."

"*What?*"

A new peculiar stubbornness came into Melody's words; it changed his face somehow, drawing the skin around his mouth so that he looked older. It had the strange effect of making him look a little like Monte Jarrad, for the first time Cherry had even been able to see it.

"I'm good and sick of this Monte Jarrad," Melody said. "I been trying to figure out what he's got that makes him different from me. So I figured out what it is. And by God, I'm going to take it away from him!"

She looked at him strangely. "Just what," she asked him oddly, "do you think he's got, that you're ever going to get?"

"You," Melody said.

Cherry stared at him with her mouth open, so utterly dumbfounded that his next words were meaningless to her, without any effect.

"I don't trust that guy no more," he told her gravely.

The voice of Royal Boone had lifted to a measured roar. He had shifted so that he had the door braced shut with his back. "—and it ain't me that put us afoot!" he bellowed.

"Then why," Mormon Stocker gritted at him, "did you give the old moss-horn his gun back? *You* had it. Because *you* took it off him. Where is it?"

Roy Boone's left hand made a sneak check-up of his waistband. His lips drew back from his horse-teeth, but not in a grin; and he said nothing.

"Shut up, you both!" Sheriff Thingan snapped, coming back to the world of immediate necessity. He had noticed Cherry and Melody talking with the quick intensity that Cherry had put into it; and now he shouldered toward them.

"What's going on here?" he blustered, glaring from one to the other of them with suspicion. He turned back to his deputies. "For*git* who tripped, will you, you jackasses? You realize them Cottons will be here *any* time now? You think the gunfire won't draw 'em like fleas? Then where are we?"

Mormon Stocker and Royal Boone still scowled at each other, full of black gripe.

"We got a chance of the biggest law-and-order scoop they's ever been in this country," Roddy Thingan pleaded. "We all but got my hands on the express box—that's what we gotta get! What the *hell* does it matter about who stood where? Are you guys crazy?"

The two deputies relaxed the attention they were giving each other, and focused on Melody. Mormon Stocker's pupils looked like two holes burned in a sheet; and Royal Boone's stare slowly took on once more the crystalline glaze seen in the eyes of a watching mountain lion.

Sheriff Roddy Thingan came close to Melody. He lowered his voice to a soft simulation of double menace. What was really menacing in it was not what he thought. It was that they now knew this man to be as irresponsible of a prisoner's life as a seven-year-old child in possession of a bug.

"You was speaking of the express box," he said, his held-down words coming breathily, as if he were panting. "You was saying you knew where it was."

"Oh?"

"You spoke of you could lay hands on it within the space of a minute. All right, boy. A minute is what you got."

"I cain't use it," said Melody.

"You right sure," Thingan said, with an even more ostentatious softness, "you want to tangle with me?"

"Ain't sayin' that," Melody answered, mournfully. "But I ain't going to help you git it; and that's a fact."

"Work on him, Roy."

Royal Boone stepped toward Melody, businesslike

and unhurried. He blew once upon the knuckles of his half-closed hand; then smashed Melody on the mouth with his fist.

Melody spilled back against the wall, hard. A last-instant turn of his head had saved his teeth. He did not entirely go down. He came off the wall with his hands in front of him, charging instinctively. Instantly Mormon Stocker was on Melody's back, pinning his arms with a hay-hook grip upon each of Melody's elbows. Melody was not entirely pinned, but he was impeded enough to make a sucker of him. He relaxed and stood up in Stocker's grip, his eyes on Roddy Thingan.

Cherry de Longpre turned white, but she didn't say anything. A quick trickle of blood ran from the corner of Melody's mouth. By ducking his head he wiped this off on his shoulder, but it instantly reappeared.

"Where is it?" Thingan asked Melody.

Jones said nothing.

Royal Boone stepped in again. He made a quick feint with his left hand, and as Melody ducked, brought up a crushing right uppercut. It looked as if it nearly tore off Melody's head; but Mormon Stocker's hold upon him kept him from falling. A purpling split appeared on Melody's cheek bone, and began to bleed.

Cherry's words seemed to choke her, but her voice was low. She said, "You'll never get anywhere like that."

"I'll bust him down, all right," Royal Boone said. He was just warming up to his work.

"Sure you'll bust him," Stocker said with an ironic slur to it. "But when?"

"Right quick," Boone promised. He blew on his

knuckles.

Stocker straightened Melody up to take the blow. But he said, "I ain't so sure. You ain't got all night, if them Cottons is close as *I* think they be."

"Wait, Roy," Thingan said. "We got to try something different."

"What's the reason we do?"

"Because you're going to knock him out, thataway. Then what good is he?"

"What good is he anyhow?"

"I thought of something," Thingan said, talking quickly now. A desperate hurry was in his eyes. "What was the last thing he said, just before he balked on us?"

"He said he knew where—"

"No, no—*that* ain't what I mean," Thingan cut Stocker off with almost frantic impatience. "He said he could lay hands on the express box in less'n a minute, didn't he? And right after that he makes a kind of a false start—but not toward the door—and he says, 'the box is right over—' "

"And there's where he drew back," Stocker said.

"Yes," Thingan said with bitter sarcasm. "We recall he drew back, but he was right on the ragged edge—he even started to *move* toward it—and not toward the outside! Fellers—that express box is *here in this dump!*"

"You're wonderful," Stocker said sourly. "Pick it up, then, and let's go." He slacked his grip on Melody's arms experimentally, then, as Melody stood there, let go the prisoner's elbows. But he kept a purchase on Melody's belt.

Thingan paid no attention to him. "He was standing

right over here," he began, taking position in imitation of Melody.

"And I was right back here," Royal Boone put in readily.

"For God's *sake*," Thingan shouted, his voice almost breaking, "don't start that again! . . . He stood right here, and he says 'The box is right over—' "

"Over what? He never said."

"Over *here*, you fool! That's what he meant!"

"All right then," Boone blared at him, "he says 'Over here, you fool,' meaning you, I guess, and moves toward the blank wall. Hell! Let's get on with the way we was doing. Hold him, Mormon."

Both Stocker and Thingan ignored this. "Boot in that door!" Thingan ordered, indicating the root cellar.

Boone obeyed. The door, being unfastened, banged wide. Thingan caught up a candle, and both he and Royal Boone jammed into the root cellar, virtually at once.

Stocker started to drop Melody and follow, but caught himself in time. When Melody moved tentatively, Stocker prodded him in the ribs with his gun muzzle, and said, "Huh uh."

Melody looked at Cherry. He knew now that it was only a question of very little time, whether the Cottons came or not. Tears were running down Cherry's cheeks, and this astonished him.

"Don't," he said. "Don't bawl. There ain't much more of this left."

She leveled him a glance of last-ditch encouragement as her lips formed the words, "George Fury . . ." Melody shrugged. George had probably assumed, Melody thought, that they had all got free.

Thingan and Royal Boone came piling out of the root cellar again. Thingan stood pulling at his lower lip, his eyes so avid as they searched the room that he looked drunken.

"Pull this up," he ordered, kicking the bunk.

Roy Boone tore the bunk out by the roots in a couple of splintering heaves. Nothing was under it but a considerable rat's nest, and a litter of such trash as had found its way there.

Melody saw that Cherry had sidled nearer the door; she could almost reach it, from where she now stood, if reaching it would have done any good. You could always get to that door, but you could never get through it. "Still figuring," Melody thought, "still trying. She never gives nothing up . . ."

Royal Boone was methodically testing the packed clay floor, under the place where the bunk had been, chipping at it with his high heel.

But now Sheriff Roddy Thingan whirled upon that deep window embrasure in the adobe wall. Light had come to him, sudden and complete. He laid hold of the great slab that covered the cache, and heaved . . .

Nothing happened.

Incredibly, without any reason, the slab stuck where it was. Thingan tried a few more wrenches, this way and that, but nothing gave.

Melody looked at Cherry. "It's wedged," he whispered.

Cherry bared her teeth at him like a wild cat. "Shut up!"

He feared the sheriff had heard that, but apparently he had not. Thingan stood away from the window ledge. His hands were at his sides, but the fingers were spread stiffly, tense with the frustrated pressure that was about him.

"Ain't no use heaving at that," Roy Boone said. "It's all sewed down with cobwebs."

"You figure," Mormon Stocker said with insult, "the old man can't even tear a cobweb up?"

"Them cobwebs been there for years," Boone explained, in vacuous good faith.

"You don't tell me," Stocker said.

Thingan's voice was low, quick-breathed and shaky. "Work on him, Roy," he said fervently. "Work on him to kill the son of a bitch! By God, I'll have him talk or—"

Roy Boone stepped gladly toward Melody, but Mormon Stocker swung Melody out of the way. "Stop it!" Stocker said.

"By God, Stocker, if you've gone soft—"

"Soft hell! *You* ain't getting no where! Cut out this bashing his brains out. Git some wood in here. Build a fahr—a good hot fahr. Stretch his pants over it. Heat his spurs red hot, and we'll write his name on him! He'll talk—he'll talk like—like—he'll talk plenty," he finished.

"Too slow," Boone objected.

"Try it," Thingan decided. "Try it anyway." Fear of defeat was riding him. "We got to take a chance on it. Git some wood in, Roy. A little otter do it."

Twice Roy Boone made as if to argue, but words did not come easily to the big gap-toothed puncher. He gave up, and turned toward the door.

Thingan had backed up, pulling hard at his lower lip again. Stiffly he eased himself down, sitting on the window ledge. He teetered there while Boone took two steps.

Up tilted the window slab, at the touch of his weight.

The great slab, which had refused to move when Thingan tried to dislodge it with all his strength, now rose perversely, displacing itself with uncanny ease as the Sheriff sat on its edge.

For a moment more Roddy Thingan sat on the edge of the shifting slab, a strange blank expression making his face sillier. Then the slab let go altogether, and thundered to the floor. The sheriff slid with it, sitting down hard and suddenly at the base of the wall. He sat there idiotically for a moment, his legs spread wide in front of him, one pants leg hitched up to his knee.

He turned quite slowly, as his brain almost visibly began to move again. He sighted the black cavity the falling slab had revealed. In a curious, unhurried way, he craned his neck to look into it.

Then suddenly he was scrambling frantically to get to his feet, his hands clawing at the wall to help himself up. His voice exploded in a bawl.

"They's a dead man in there!"

A strangled grunt sounded in Mormon Stocker's throat as he dropped Melody and plunged toward the cache.

The voice of Royal Boone rang out strong and crazy; he was already beside Sheriff Thingan, crouched over the black hole in the adobe ledge.

"It's Luke Packer!"

Cherry de Longpre snatched Melody by the wrist so hard that she almost threw him, as he stood there gaping. She already had the door open. Somehow, with a surprising use of her slight weight, she managed to sling him through the door ahead of her. As he slowed up and caught his balance he could hear her furious whisper.

"Run, run, you damn fool! Run or I *will* kill you!"

He started to say something, but she pushed him violently down slope, and he found himself obeying her. He stampeded a little way into the tall brush, then circled more warily. Watching the cabin, he saw the sheriff and his deputies come trotting out. They made a confused pass at starting in two or three directions, then got together and conferred about it. They ended by going back into the adobe.

Melody Jones looked about him for Cherry, then, but she wasn't with him now. He hunted around for her, a little aimlessly, not daring to sing out; and he couldn't find her. At first he couldn't find the horses, either. He found a place he thought he had left them, but they weren't there; and when he recognized that he was in the wrong place he could no longer be sure what he had done with them.

He whistled softly the call he used for Harry Henshaw. The gelding had never paid any attention to it before, but Melody hoped that this time he would at least paw or something, in this emergency.

Instead, a soft answering whistle sounded in a different part of the scrub; and when he shook off the first fantastic impression that his horse had whistled back at him, he knew that Cherry had answered him. He ran toward her, trotting stiffly to keep his high heels from turning his ankles; but she didn't whistle again, and he couldn't find her.

He did find the ponies, though. Monte's carbine was still on his saddle, so that he was armed again now, and mounted. He left two of the ponies tied there, and scouted aimlessly through the manzanita, wondering what was sensible. Far-off up the mountain, perhaps a mile and three furlongs away, a double pistol-shot sounded, as two guns fired almost together.

⚘ 23 ⚘

Monte Jarrad sat well back in the shadows as George Fury walked into the ring of the fire-light. Monte's gun was in his right hand, where it rested across his knee. The gun was cocked, but it swung nose down, idly, not raised.

Monte looked at George Fury in a puzzled way tinged with admiration. This was mainly because he didn't understand how George got here, let alone how he dared come here to begin with.

"Who sent you?" he asked without expression.

"I come on my own," George said.

"How'd you find this?"

"It's a reasonable question," George admitted.

Monte Jarrad's fire was no bigger than a pair of clasped hands. It was built close against the cut bank of a dry rivulet, well back in an angle; the overhang should have blanked it, even from above. Jarrad sat to one side, not too close, in order not to be blinded. His position was peculiar, propped angularly half across his saddle, stiffly favoring his injury.

"I figured you was up here," George said, "because I figured it was your shot killed Luke Packer. So—"

"Dead, is he?"

"Plenty."

Monte Jarrad grunted noncommittally.

"I already figured out you was wownded. So I knowed you wouldn't travel fur. And I knowed you'd be cold, like any wownded man. So I look in the near places where a fire could be hid, and here you be."

"Smart—maybe." Jarrad said.

"Uh-huh. My name is George Fury."

"I know who you are. You're the old buck that's been palming himself off as my uncle."

"And you're the cheap gun-fighter that has framed up a sap of a boy to take your medicine for you," George said.

Monte Jarrad looked him over with some puzzlement. George Fury did not look dangerous enough to face Monte Jarrad with a comment like that. He wore one boot and one sock frazzled to the shape of a spat. He was hatless, and his thin hair was full of leaf-twigs, and other trash. His knees were muddy, and his shirt torn.

"I don't look nothing like your half-wit uncle," George said.

"No," Monte admitted. "More like a scarecrow, seems to me."

George Fury didn't argue it. He was trying to see what there was in Jarrad's lean, haggard face that made people confuse him with Melody Jones. It stopped him at first;

he couldn't see any resemblance at all. Only the scar on Monte's forehead told him he was talking to the right man. Then after a little while he began to see what it was. The natures of Jones and Jarrad—everything they thought and felt—were nearly opposite; but if both men were dead they would look nearly the same. He could even see how people could be fooled, by allowing too much for the remodeling of the years, while Monte Jarrad had been gone from the Poisonberry.

"What do you want here?" Monte asked him now. The question carried a strangely detached curiosity, as if Monte Jarrad had already decided what disposition he was going to make of George.

"I come here alone," George began.

"I know that. I been listening to you blundering around here for an hour. I could of picked you off any time, just as easy as now."

George reddened a little this time, but he let it pass. "The sheriff and some of his posse are already down there at your cache. That's what that shooting was you heard."

Monte Jarrad's eyes showed a sharpened flicker as George used the word "cache." But he only said, "I figured that."

"They ain't found your express box yet," George went on. "When they do find it, they'll find Luke Packer's body. Because I loaded the corpus in there, on top of your dang box."

"How did *you* find it?"

"The gal showed us."

Monte Jarrad showed a faint subtle change of color

around the mouth, as if the skin were turning green. It may have been only a drawing of the muscles, that made it look like that.

"If the little slut has turned on me—" he said, as if to himself; and let the words trail off.

"She's trying to help you, according to her lights," George said, "only she lacks lights. The woman never lived," he added with casual contempt, "that *any* man dast bank a chip on—you otter know that, at your age."

His eye now fell on some strips of jerky, where Monte Jarrad had them laid out beside the little fire, and he unhurriedly stepped over without being asked, and helped himself. There was insolence in that, the more so in that he had used his gun hand. He stood chewing on the jerky, with his mouth open, and looking down at Jarrad with overt dislike.

Monte Jarrad watched him with amusement, and a faint admiration. "So they *caught* that there imitation of me," he said.

"Seems like so," George Fury admitted. "I thrashed around and tore some of 'em up, and come away. But Melody's no way quick, in a thing like that. Not quick, and not lucky. He *seems* lucky, many a time, but he ain't. So they still got him by the neck, I judge. In a little while more they'll find your dang cache, and when they do, they'll find the corpus of Luke Packer. About then, them Cotton friends of yours are due to show. So now they got Melody Jones four ways from the ace; he ain't got no more show than a one-laiged buck at a pants-kicking."

"You don't mean to tell me," Jarrad said, greatly entertained.

"Either the Cottons rub him out in hopes he's you; or else they cancel him anyway, for getting mixed up with you; or else the whole posse gets hasty because he won't show 'em the cache, which he cain't hardly do, owing to the corpus is in it; or else they find the cache, and hang him for killing Luke Packer. Seemingly they's seventeen reasons why he's up against a sudden finish; and the only thing lacking in the whole befewzled situation is one single, solitary way for the boy to ever get out of this here thing alive."

"That is too bad," Jarrad drawled.

"Yes," said George Fury.

"And you took all this trouble, just to come up here and tell me this!"

"I come here to make a reasonable demand," George said, biting off more jerky. "This here boy is only a boy, and he ain't got the sense he was born with—that's a living fact. He don't know which is up, or what the score is, or what's good for him. I'm the first to admit all that, and freely tell him to his face, for his own good. But leave me tell you one other thing."

"Make it short," Jarrad said. He readjusted his position, moving carefully, as if his wound might be stiffening again.

"There ain't a mean hair in that boy's head. He never done no harm to nobody in his life, nor thunk of any. He's in this because of you, and because your gal hauled him into it, and made out she needed him to help her. You and her rigged up all this between you. So there ain't but one right thing you can do, now. You got to whistle up your bullies, and go and get him out of this."

"I swear to God," Monte Jarrad said, "I don't believe my ears!"

"Or anyways make an honest try," George finished.

"You come up here to pull a sob like that?"

"That's what I come for, partly," George said.

"You mean to tell me you didn't know the answer you'd get?"

George Fury tore off one more bite of jerky, looking down at Monte Jarrad sardonically. "No," he said; "no. I wouldn't lie to you like that." His words sounded odd, coming muffled from a full mouth. "I knew the answer I'd git."

"Then why in the name of all—"

"I had to give you a chance to do a right thing once," George said, "if it was in you. It's a superstition with me. I'd give a chance to the worst skunk alive; even you, Jarrad."

"This beats me," Monte Jarrad said. His breathing was quickened and broken by a silent laughter.

"Git to your feet," George said, chewing.

Monte Jarrad stared up at him, unbelieving; but the twisty laughter left his face as if he had been struck.

"You heard right," George Fury said. "I'm taking you down there, Monte."

Jarrad still stared at him, thunderstruck, unable to conceive of this.

"They're going to hang you," George said; "and it ain't going to be in effigy, with the effigy consisting of Melody Jones. You cheap gun-throwers don't make no impression on me. I've seen you come and go. So git up out o' that—before I smoke your carcase!"

All expression had left Monte Jarrad's face, except for a clear brightness in his eyes, as in the eyes of a lynx. "Crazy," he murmured, as if talking to himself. "You crazy son of a bitch!"

He fired, then. He hardly seemed to go through the motions of a draw at all, the weapon came so smoothly from the tied-down holster at his thigh. All George Fury ever saw was a general galvanizing jerk of Monte Jarrad's whole frame, and instantly the gun blasted in Monte's hand, as if it had been there all the time.

George Fury doubled and pitched forward as if he had been struck in the middle by a swinging log. His gun, which he had somehow grabbed out of its leather, fired only a bare instant after Jarrad's weapon; but it exploded downward, blowing half of the little campfire away; and the recoil almost tore it out of George Fury's slackened hand.

Monte Jarrad reclined motionless, his face impassive, but his eyes awake, watching the man who was down. His gun was cocked and steady. After a moment or two he noticed that George Fury's right hand half covered a living coal from the little fire, but did not draw away. When he saw this, Jarrad let the hammer down, easing it gently.

He turned the cylinder of the six-gun until it rested on an empty chamber; then got out a stiff wire and a bit of rag, and cleaned the gun bore, before he reloaded. His hands did these tasks automatically, long practiced; his eyes stayed upon George Fury, but the old man did not move.

When his gun was returned to its holster, Jarrad put the

last of the fire out. He left the place stiffly, half carrying and half dragging his saddle by one stirrup.

❧ 24 ❧

Morning was leaking out of the far-off Drag-onette ranges as Melody Jones drew near the ramshackle ranch house of the Busted Nose. First a dull green illumination appeared in the eastern sky, without in any way lighting the soot-black trail; and as this appeared the red-poppers began to go "zeep" in the brush. After a time this first effort withdrew, so that the night seemed blacker than before; but a muddy grey-ness was beginning to pervade the ranges, as if seeping up out of the ground. By the time this had increased to full dawn, Melody was sitting his pony behind a stand of locust, watching the ranch house from a respectful dis-tance of more than four hundred yards.

When the Busted Nose showed no sign of life at this range, Melody moved closer by easy stages, watching his back trail as much as he watched the house, and lis-tening to the morning warily.

So far as he could find out he was alone in the world entirely. Even the bear cub had been turned loose, or had worked its way free, from its chain beside the broken screen door. As Melody prospected closer, a late-ranging armadillo trundled around the corner of the house, and disappeared without hurry. Melody was satisfied with that. The animal would have known, better than he could, if anyone were around. He rode to the back stoop of the house without further caution.

He unsaddled Harry Henshaw, watered him, and rubbed the pony's back with handfuls of dry straw. He brought hay and a bait of grain from the barn, and fed Harry on the back gallery close by the door. While the horse dug into it, Melody loose-saddled him again. He left the bridle dangling by its head-stall from Harry's head, the bit clanking free as the pony shook the hay, to dust it.

Jones went inside after that, and moved disconsolately through the house. He stood for a while in the door of Cherry's room. In the grey depression of early morning the whole house felt like some kind of shell which had quartered people never to be heard from again. He propped the broken screen door open with a rock, so as not to be impeded by it in a beeline for his animal, and he took Monte's carbine—the only weapon he had left—from its saddle boot, and stood it inside the kitchen, in the angle by the door.

After that he walked a little way out from the house, to get away from the sound of the pony's munching, and listened a while longer, very lonely in the dawn; and then made a fire in the stove, with more than necessary thuds and bangs, to be rid of the insufferable quiet.

A hot smell of coffee, smelling ten times better than it would ever taste, began floating down-wind from the Busted Nose. Melody rummaged for something to eat which would take no work to fix.

His back was to the door, and his hands were pawing over a shelf of canned goods, when the kitchen darkened faintly.

His hands faltered, but only for an instant. He went on

with what he was doing without looking around, stalling over the labels. Somebody was standing in the doorway. He knew that much, though he had heard no approach. Melody's right hand weighed a can of tomatoes, testing it as a weapon. But he set it down.

Melody turned slowly, empty handed; and, for the first time in his life, faced Monte Jarrad.

"Hi," Melody said. The man in the doorway grunted.

Even if the light had been better, instead of directly behind Jarrad, Melody might not have recognized him yet.

"Looking for somebody?" Melody asked this stranger.

Monte Jarrad took in the whole lay-out coolly, the room first, then Melody Jones. Melody saw him notice where the carbine was.

"Just passing by," Jarrad said, watching Jones oddly. His voice had a soft lack of tone to it, very unsettling.

"You don't need to be so edgy," Melody said. "We don't ask no questions here. Want some coffee?"

"I'll get it myself . . . Don't go over there. Don't go any place. Stay against that wall. Back up against it a little closer." He gave these orders casually, not even bothering to look closely at Melody. His eyes kept wandering around the room, checking, and checking, and re-checking.

"Now you looky here!" Melody began.

"Want to play like you don't know me, huh?" Jarrad commented, his eyes still wandering.

"I never seen you before in my born days."

Jarrad's gaze stopped wandering. "Nor heard of me, neither, I suppose."

"I can't keep knowledge of every grub-testing punk that—" He stopped short.

"What's the matter?" Jarrad asked sardonically.

Melody looked puzzled. "It come to me for a minute that you might be Monte Jarrad. But you ain't."

"No?"

"No. This Jarrad weasel looks somethin' like I do—it fools people even."

"It's a hard thing to say about a man."

"Whut?"

"When I think of being mistooken for the kind of chuckle-head that you look like to me—it's enough to turn a feller sick, by God."

Melody looked at him with pity. "Don't let it worry you," he said. "Nobody ever mistook *me* for no such limping wreck as you be. It's small wonder you got strucken by lightning, or something, the manners you got. And here's another thing—"

"Well, I'll be damned," said Jarrad.

"And here's another thing. Keep on like you're haiding, and you'll think lightning hit you again!"

The two looked at each other strangely across the kitchen table.

"A feller never knows," Monte Jarrad said obscurely, as if to himself. "Don't make much difference, in the long run, I reckon . . . Stand closer to the wall. I don't figure I got much better than an hour, here."

Jarrad took off his hat and laid it on the table. He ran a finger around his neck cloth, to loosen it, and wearily put one hand through his hair, like a man trying to rouse himself after sleep.

Melody saw the scar on his forehead, then.

The carbine was a long way off, beyond Monte Jarrad. Jarrad picked it up now, and pitched it into the yard.

"I been watching you think," he said, flattering Melody a little. "You don't need to figure no more how to lay me out with one of them cans. You can't reach the stove poker, neither; I seen you measuring for it." He drew his gun now, unhurriedly, spun it on one finger by the trigger-guard, and clamped the hammer to full cock. His tone was dry and crusty as a horntoad. "Even if you knocked me out, this here iron would get you."

"So you're him," Melody said, as if he couldn't believe it. He stood staring idiotically, as people look at some great mysterious phenomenon they have heard about all their lives. "It's a hell of a disappointment," he said at last.

"Take off your boots," Jarrad ordered.

Slowly Melody unbuckled his spur straps. "It beats me," he said, "what she sees in you, Jarrad."

"I'll take your belt; and your hat; and whatever trash is in them pockets. Good God! I suppose that bone pile out there with my saddle on it—you call that your horse . . ."

"And that carbine you slung out in the dirt was your carbine!"

"You can have it now. We'll get your own saddle on that old hide. You can have mine."

"This won't do you no good," Melody told him. "Even if we swap every stitch we own, there still won't be any scar on my bean."

"No," Monte admitted. "No; there never will be. But I suppose there can still be the place where one was . . ."

When the meaning of this soaked in on Melody he studied Monte Jarrad for a long time. "You got clammy idees," he said at last, without much assurance. "I'd ruther be daid than in your place."

"You can have both," Jarrad said.

Jones obeyed as Monte Jarrad swapped boots, hat and equipment with him; and finally switched his own old worn hull to Harry Henshaw. After that was done Melody was kept standing against the wall of the kitchen while Jarrad, one-handed, drank his coffee.

There was still something Monte wanted to know; but he didn't know how to get at it.

Some very peculiar things were running in Melody's mind just then. He knew he was going to make some kind of a play; and he knew it wasn't going to be any good. He entirely believed what Monte had said—that he might knock Monte out, but not fast enough so that Monte's gun wouldn't get him.

"Where did she say you was from?" Monte asked him.

"Montana. A place called Two Lance. But that ain't what you want to know."

Melody had been thinking about Montana, in a kind of a way, while at the same time he was trying to think of what he'd better try, any second now. That was the way most of Melody's thinking had always been done—by wandering off from the thing in hand. When Montana lay under a February thaw, and the frosty edge was melted off the air, and you could smell the grass opening out to get itself blighted, there was more lift to Montana air than any air on earth. He should ought to have breathed deeper while he could. With six feet of dirt close-packed above you, no air even gets to your bones, unless the coyotes have you out of there, which most fellers would sooner they didn't . . .

"You ain't fretting over where I come from," Melody said. "What's eating you is something else you want to know, while you still can find out."

"Oh?" Monte Jarrad said.

"I aim to make you ask for it," Melody said. "I ain't going to help you out."

Monte came out with it then. "What was going on," he asked, "the night you was in Cherry's room?"

"Which night you mean?"

"*Which?*"

"Oh, you mean *that* one? Nothing. Nothing then."

Jarrad's eyes looked as if they could eat through a horse blanket. "Just what the hell do you mean by 'then?' "

"Listen, you wrong-haided bastard," Melody said. He spoke in a nerveless drawl, and it stung worse than contempt. When a man has no chance at all the fear goes out of him, sometimes, for lack of anything left to be afraid of. "Maybe you got me over a bar'l. But you ain't going to forget me, what short time you live. Because that girl ain't yours no more, and never will be again."

Monte Jarrad stood and stared at him, glassy-eyed.

"It don't matter how daid I be, or nothing," Melody said, pouring it into him slowly. "Daid or alive, I'm your finish. You ain't never going to get nothing you want again. I can stand in your light ten times better when I'm daid than I ever done yet. And when you finally puke blood and die, you'll know it was me that done it, some way."

Monte Jarrad stared at him dumbfounded, too profoundly shocked to explode. Nobody had ever talked to
him like that in his life before.

"You'll be an earmarked ghost," Monte said, looking
at Melody's ear. "I already got my notch on you, I see."
But his mind was not on it.

"Reckon it won't show with a coffin on," Melody
answered. "Different with the mark I got on you.
Because I taken her away from you, you hear? Whether
she knows it or not."

He had not meant to add that last. It slipped out of him.
He tried to think of a way to swallow it back. Then he
saw that he didn't need to. Monte Jarrad was no longer
hearing him, because he was listening to something else.
His eyes, fixed hard on Melody's face, were faintly
glassy, still watchful, but only mechanically so. The
intense core of his attention was turned elsewhere, to
something that was happening outside.

When Melody had got that through his head, he realized that he had begun to listen also, before he was
aware.

Two riders were coming in, walking their horses. The
stride of the ponies, conveyed to the listeners by the
hoof-rhythm, was unhurried; yet they moved in boldly,
with no pauses to spy out the situation into which they
headed.

Melody shifted to crane his neck.

"Stand where you are!" Monte snarled at him. Monte
backed across the angle of the room until he could flick
a glance through the door in the direction of the corral
without giving Melody a chance to make a break.

"You don't see 'em," Melody drawled, without sighting anything himself. "Because they gone in the barn. I can tell that by ear. And I can tell you something else. You don't need to look so sceart. Because one of them is Cherry's horse—I can tell because I know he threw a shoe."

Monte Jarrad didn't look scared; he only looked intent, more keenly concentrated than a knife point. He knew how to focus completely what faculties he had, in his own physical defense. He knew how to go into a cold sweat of fear, too—there was never any resignation in Monte Jarrad; but the fear usually came when he looked back on action that was past. And when he looked ahead it was without imagination.

He didn't bother to answer Melody.

"So now you can ask her for yourself," Melody said. "She'll walk in here in a minute. Ask her if what I told you is so. Ask her what that gun will get you from here on in. If you had sense you'd turn it on yourself, and duck a peck o' misery."

"Shut up!"

Monte's eyes, carefully watching Melody, kept flicking toward the barn; and presently Melody knew by Monte's face that he had been right, and that Cherry had come into Monte's view.

Very slowly Monte Jarrad put his gun away; but as it settled into its holster he tested it to be sure that it rested there lightly. He could draw it again much faster than another man could spit.

They were standing there like that, silent and watchful in suspended motion, as Cherry de Longpre came across the gallery to the door, and stopped there.

Cherry's face had no color, bloodless because she was tired. Her hair was tumbled and her clothes hard worked; but her head was up.

"Hello, Cherry," Monte Jarrad said.

"So you lied to me," she said tonelessly. "You lied about where you went."

He did not answer, and she stood there looking from one to the other of them. Blue circles underlay her eyes, and their mistiness showed her need for sleep. But some kind of a live smolder was behind her gaze. Very plainly, she had stood all she intended to stand.

"I can't remember," she said, "why I ever thought you looked like each other."

"God forbid," Monte said with a hard irony.

"Me too," Melody said, more conversationally. "If I had realized what kind of tizzick-looking jigger I was mistook for, I sure would of high-tailed out of here to begin on. By God, there's some things a man *shouldn't* put up with, and that's a fact!"

"Be still," Cherry said, disdaining to raise her voice to him. "You'd better go out to the barn. George Fury is out there. He's hurt."

Melody stared at her while this soaked in. "Bad?" he asked finally.

"He's dying, I think."

Melody shifted his eyes to Monte Jarrad, and held them there while he moved sidelong to the door. She made room for him to pass. Once outside Melody took a chance on turning his back, and moved toward the barn at a run.

Cherry looked after him for a moment, without any change of expression.

"Cherry," Monte Jarrad said, "are you crazy?"

"No," Cherry said.

"Sometimes—a couple of times lately—it's sure seemed like there was something pretty funny in the slant you take about him."

"Is there?"

"He's useless," Monte said, low voiced, without heat. "He's got less natural sense than a fresh-dropped calf— and ain't worth half as much. You could study him a life-time, and never find something he was good for."

"Yes," Cherry said. "Monte, why did you shoot George Fury?"

"The old one? He come looking for it," he answered shortly. "Cherry, if ever I catch you fooling with a squirt like this Melody, I won't stop with killing him. I'll kill you, too. You know that much, don't you?"

"Yes," she said again. "I know that, Monte, I guess." She turned toward him unhurriedly, and looked at him steadily and hard. "But I'd give anything in the world if you were a little bit like him."

"*What?*"

"He's the kindest man I ever knew, and the honestest. I didn't even know there were that kind of men. He's kind, and he's square, and he's sweet."

"This beats me," Monte Jarrad said, the wind knocked out of him.

"There's one thing I can say for you, that nobody can say for him. When you start to do a thing, the thing gets done."

"Thanks," he said softly.

"I only wish to God—"

"You wish what?" Monte asked strangely.

"I wish that wasn't all." Her voice was lifeless now. "I wish there was one other living thing to be said in your favor, when you stand in front of your God."

Monte Jarrad was white from lips to eyes. "So he done what he claimed he done," he said.

She shrugged; the remark had no meaning for her. She started to turn away from him, then looked back suddenly; and now her eyes raked him with surprise, and a new comprehension.

"Monte—you're wearing his stuff!"

Jarrad answered without compromise. "Well—he's wearing mine."

They stood silent, and their eyes held.

"Monte—*you were going to kill him!* You were going to kill him, and leave him to be buried as yourself!"

He would have lied to her if he had felt like it; perhaps even if he had thought of it. But he had fought his way up and down his section of the world so long that he had half forgot the use of lies.

"Cherry," he said, "if I never meant to kill him before, I'd sure lay in to kill him now!"

"To save yourself," she said, her throat constricted. "After all the chances I made him take— You were going to gun him down and go free—"

"Only thing I'm sorry for," Monte said with his teeth in the way, "is I didn't get to it long ago!"

She was looking at him as if she had never seen him before, or anything like him, in all her life. But Monte

Jarrad wasn't watching her now. He had begun to listen again; and suddenly he turned, and half ran to the other side of the house, where a window opened down-mountain. He swung outward the batten shutter which served instead of glass.

Far off, in the direction of Payneville, a long dust was rising. The dust marked the masked line of the twisting road, and when you knew where the road was you could glimpse part of it, a mile off through the scrub oak.

The down-country road was full of riders.

A faint, quivery edge came into Cherry's voice, but it stayed flat and low. "It's time for you to run."

"I'll ride when I'm ready," Monte Jarrad said, "That don't mean I'm ready yet."

He turned toward the back of the house, toward the barn.

🐾 25 🐾

George Fury lay on a couple of bales of hay which ranged along the barn's front wall. The first horizontal sunshine was leveling over Holiday Ridge; it struck through the cracks in the unbattened wall, and laid golden lines of light across George Fury, but his face was in shadow. The early air was crystal clear, dustless for once, even where the light came through, but those thin panelike slices of light confused the eye. First sight did not tell Melody much except that George lay inhumanly still.

"George?" he said uncertainly.

He got no answer, nothing but a ghastly quiet. He hesitated through a moment of dread before he went forward. Lightly he lifted George's eyelid with his thumb.

"Git your damn thumb out of my eye," George said.

"I was only—" He let it trail off.

"Only what?"

"Well, I was studyin' to see if you was daid."

"Well, I ain't damn it!" said George. He sounded a little more like himself. "I be damn if I aim to stand fer this!"

There were black stains of dry blood on George's shirt. Melody dropped to his knees beside George, and unbuttoned the shirt carefully. George was cleanly bandaged about the body, but fresh blood was still seeping through. Melody was stunned as he saw how hard and dangerously George was hit. It was inconceivable that the man had traveled here from the adobe hide-out, no matter what help he might have had.

Melody's hands shook so that he gave up buttoning the shirt again. He started to stand up, but his knees had turned so weak that he had to put this off, too. What he mainly felt was astonishment, and a plain inability to believe.

"For four long years," he complained shakily, "there ain't no way to get a vacation from you. Breakfast time—you're there. Dinner time—you're on hand. Middle of the night—there you be. And now the first time we come to a real clutch of trouble, where's you? Down flat, with all fours in the air, by God!"

"My hand come stiff," George mumbled shamefacedly. "It's them wet joints I picked up last winter in Californy. Rain, rain, soak, drizzle, drazzle, pour—that state's under a leak in the roof."

"Hesh, now." Melody took another look at the bandages, wondering where and how George could have come by them in the open hills. He couldn't make out, at first. Then he discovered a small string of cheap, pathetically ordinary lace, and he knew the bandages were something Cherry had worn. He hadn't the faintest idea what kind of underclothes a girl would wear under a cowhand riding rig, but here they were, torn in bandage strips.

Melody couldn't believe this, at first. He wasn't used to seeing women go out of their way for anybody, much, unless maybe some no-good like Monte Jarrad. When it dawned on him that Cherry had really done her best to help George, he was strangely affected; all the rest of the stiffening went out of him for a minute. He had to stop and blow his nose, even.

"If only I'd of had time to soak my hooks in hot suds," George said with difficulty, "and worked a little liniment in—"

"Never mind, now, George."

"Well, I blame the climate of Californy!"

"This here's going to be worse than the time you lost my saddle in the poker game at Yampai. Hearing you explain a thousand times how come, was ten times worse than the loss of the saddle . . ."

He discovered now George's burned hand, that had laid in the coals of Monte's fire. He caught up a half-used can of axle grease, treated the burn with it, then looked around him vaguely for a moment, in search of a bandage. There wasn't anything, of course. He jerked off his neck scarf, the one he had got for coming in seventeenth at Cheyenne; and unhesitatingly tore it into strips.

George was trying to say something again. Every time he stopped talking he had a hard time getting started again, as if his voice was rusty.

"If—if anything turns out funny here—" he hesitated.

Melody knew what he meant. "Don't try to make out," he said crossly, "that you're worse off than you be."

"If," George repeated. "I wish to hell you'd do one thing."

"Whut's that?"

"Give up the broncs, Melody."

"Whut?"

"You can't stomp broncs. The average mustang starts to laugh when he sees you coming. Mighty soon you'll get slung on your head again, and come up even sillier than you be. There ain't room fer it, Melody. I want you should quit 'em."

"How'll I git a job?"

"Give up the whole cowhand business. It's triflin'. Try to amount to something for a change. It'll anyways be something new . . ."

This last came so feebly that it frightened Melody. "I—I'll think about it. George, was it Monte Jarrad?"

George grunted an affirmative. "If it wasn't fer the climate of Californy—"

"Hesh, now. Expect me to harken to sech drivel the whole day?"

He was watching the house now, through a broken board; his ear had caught Monte's quick step on the gallery, and the ring of Monte's spurs. He had already heard the hoof-trample of distant riders, and made a try at counting them. Whoever they might be, Melody couldn't think of anything to do about them, with George down like he was.

Monte Jarrad moved with the stiff caution his wound imposed, but his step was sure as he pointed himself toward the barn. Cherry came trotting out of the house after him, and overtook him at the gallery step. She caught Monte's arm, and he half turned to look at her for a moment over his shoulder. Cherry tried to speak to him rapidly, urgently, but she stuttered, and lost her words. Monte Jarrad shook off her hands, and came on toward the barn.

Cherry stared after him from the edge of the gallery, baffled, uncertain, and more frightened than Melody had ever seen her. She hesitated while Monte walked seven strides. Then suddenly she called out across the fifty yards which separated barn and house, and her tone was frantic.

"*Melody!* Melody, look out!"

Monte Jarrad whirled upon her so savagely that for a split instant Melody thought he was going to fire on her. Melody started to yell, which, after all, was about all he was equipped for, just then. But Monte Jarrad immediately swung back to face the barn again, and his six-gun had jumped into his hand. He stood with heels planted apart, and his face was frenzied.

"Come out of there!" he shouted. "Come out and make a fight of it!"

"Take *my* gun," George Fury said, his voice amazingly strong and loud. "Take my gun from m'belt, and drill him down! . . ."

Even with Monte Jarrad standing out in front of him, it seemed strange to Melody that George should ever ask another man to take his gun.

George had no gun. His gun was where it had fallen from his hand as he went down, up there in the hills.

Monte Jarrad stood weaving his head this way and that, trying to see through the cracks in the barn wall a hundred feet away from him. Then he started toward the barn again, moving warily and uncertainly, not sure of what he was up against now.

Without hurry, almost with resignation, Melody moved close to the door, and pressed against the wall. He couldn't do anything but try to jump Monte, if Monte showed in the door. There was a hay-hook stuck into a timber, but Melody passed it up. A hay-hook can't grab a gun barrel, even as well as a man's hand.

Then Monte Jarrad stopped again, and pivoted on one heel in a swift jerk, to face a different way. He seemed satisfied now that no gun was in the barn, for he was willing to turn away from it. The distant muffle of hoofs was closer, all of it, but it had split up, and now came from two ways. Some of the approaching horses—it sounded like three or more—were coming in full stretch, very near, much nearer than should have been expected yet.

That last quick movement must have got to Monte, for his left hand went to his side. He listened hard for a moment or two; he started for the barn again, but couldn't make up his mind, and again stopped to listen, judging how much time was left to him. It wasn't enough. Jarrad turned back to the house at a trot, holding his side as he ran.

Almost immediately after that—Monte had hardly reached the gallery—four riders broke over the crest at the drop where the excuse for a road plunged downward into the brush. They were strung out a little, but obviously hanging together. Fever Crick de Longpre was in front on one of his runt mustangs; he was whipping up side and side with his rope-end, like an Indian, and the blown cayuse was running uphill like a scrambling cat. Avery de Longpre was close on his flank; his bigger horse kept trying to pass, but the swinging rope made him flinch back.

After these two, Lee Gledhill came pounding up over the hump, standing in his stirrups to sweep the lay-out with ten times keener a scouting eye than the two ahead of him had used. And last came a rider Melody had never seen before.

This last one loomed up over the break of the drop on a strapping big grey. He rode crosswise of the saddle, hung by one knee, so that he could watch the long slopes of broken country behind him over the tail of his horse. The grey horse, obviously bred a long way out of the Poisonberry country, was travel worn as gaunt as a stand of pole-cactus, suitable for building a fence.

Melody's horse, Harry Henshaw, tied to the gallery now, reared and tried to stampede as the cavalcade came roaring in. But he settled back as the riders set up to a stop, the sliding hind hoofs of the ponies ripping up the dust.

Monte Jarrad was waiting for them on the edge of the

gallery. Lee Gledhill grinned and waved to Monte as he pulled up, and Jarrad responded, without the grin. Everybody piled out of the saddle now, the stranger last and most reluctantly. Fever Crick and Lee Gledhill began talking urgently to Monte, both at once. Their very intensity seemed to press their voices low and breathy; Melody couldn't get anything they said. He got it, though, when Monte Jarrad snapped at Fever Crick to shut up; and Fever Crick did so, flinching back as if he had been clipped with a quirt.

Shortly after that there was a general half-movement toward the horses, and the man Melody did not know promptly mounted again. But Monte Jarrad stood where he was, speaking slowly and bitterly, in a low voice; and when he stopped to spit, contemptuously, the mounted man reluctantly got down from the grey horse. He was a stocky man, very broad in the shoulders, and chunky in the face; as plain as anything in the world, he felt helpless and unsafe afoot, like a horse-Indian.

Lee Gledhill was trying to argue with Monte, hard and quick; Melody knew Lee's face was going sniff-sneer. Avery kept swinging this way and that, unhappily trying to watch in all directions. And all this time that unbroken gabble of hoofs kept coming from the down-mountain road, stronger and closer as each minute dragged out. It grew in strength endlessly, long after it seemingly could come no nearer without the riders appearing. Its soft unrhythmic thrum could be felt in the ground, sensed in the tremble of the wind, as much as it could be heard. Harry Henshaw let go a long, pealing whinny.

And still the five men stood and deadlocked over a

decision which any moment could blow itself up like a powder keg.

It took care of itself now. The short metallic whang of a bullet, exactly like the breaking of a guitar string, ended in the rattling echo of a rifle's voice. The head of the grey horse jerked up, and it screamed. Then it sagged to its knees slowly, and rolled onto its side with a thump. Only its head did not go down. It lay there looking bewildered, as if resting.

Avery de Longpre and Lee Gledhill tied their horses then. They did it in close to nothing and a fifth, and took cover in the house, joining Monte Jarrad who had moved inside, without hurry, in the same moment the bullet struck. Fever Crick first dropped his reins entirely and bolted for the kitchen. Then he was shamed by sight of the others securing their horses, and made a wild spraddle-legged dash at his cayuse, stampeding it past hope. It went crashing down the mountain, its head held high to one side, to keep from tripping on the trailing reins. Fever Crick scrambled for cover, tripped on the edge of the gallery, and sprawled headlong through the kitchen door.

The stranger was the last one in. He appeared to be utterly stunned. He moved half way to the house, then turned back to the down pony, and kept faltering helplessly back and forth, without reaching either one, until Lee Gledhill came out and dragged him in.

No other long-range shot followed the first one immediately.

Now Cherry de Longpre came out of the house, walking steadily and wearily, as if nothing were happening. Monte Jarrad called after her a sharp command that she stay in. She gave some short answer that Melody could not hear; but as he commanded her again, furiously, she spoke over her shoulder to him, and this time everyone heard what she said.

Her tone was soft, and nearly lifeless except that it shook a little; but the words were clear. "Damn you," she said. "Damn you, and damn you. I'll go where I please; and you'll burn in hell before you stop me."

She picked up the carbine that Monte had pitched into the dirt, and started toward the barn. But then she hesitated. The grey horse was trying to get up. She went to it, and bent over for a moment to look at it. Then she plugged a shell into the chamber, and put the muzzle to the pony's skull. The gaunt head, at waist-level, looked half as long as she was tall. Cherry turned her face away as she fired, and the heavy neck flailed down straight in the dust.

Cherry untied Harry Henshaw, and led the gelding toward the barn. Harry Henshaw pulled back, limiting himself to a dragging walk, but the girl came on trotting and tugging, as fast as she could haul him. She was crying, but trying to stop it, as she came on into the barn. She wiped tears from her cheeks with the back of her hand, and snuffled, so that for a moment or two she looked like a little girl not more than six years old.

Melody said, "I'm sorry, Cherry."

"For what?" she whimpered, crossly.

She had him, there. "Well—jest in a general way, I guess. . . ."

"Nearly forty riders are on the road," she told him,

crisply now. "Lester Cotton's pulled them together. Some of these are good men. They'll close in to finish this business once and for all, and this time they'll do it. For God's sake get on this horse and bust him out of here!"

Melody Jones rolled his eyes at George, embarrassed, and did nothing. Cherry thrust the reins into his hands.

"Will you come to life," she begged him. "If you can show enough sense, just this once in your life, to cut out the back way, and not trip up, or ride in the wrong direction, or some other silly fool mistake—there's still a *little* chance."

Melody looked at the reins in his hands curiously, as if he didn't know what they were for; then laid them on the edge of a two-by-four, like something meant to keep on a shelf.

"Heck," he said. "This here's monotonous."

"She's right," George Fury said from where he lay. "You can't do no more damage here."

"Harry Henshaw ain't hardly equal to—"

"Damn Harry Henshaw! Git!" Sweat was standing out on George Fury's forehead, while at the same time his teeth showed signs of chattering. Physical weakness was only part of that. The rest of it was the nervous sense of being trapped helpless here by his wound, while hell-to-pay broke all around him. But as Melody still stood, wordless, George closed his eyes and subsided, washing his hands of further obligation to the impossible.

Cherry de Longpre stared hard at Melody for several moments more, her face blanked by that bafflement he was able to inflict upon her. "Now you look here, you complete fool—" she began, but he interrupted her.

He reached out and closed her jaw for her by lifting her chin with his fingers. "Gal," he said, in a tone she had never heard him use, "I'm right sure I've heard a plenty from you. So be still, before I turn you across that saddle and spank you pink as an apple."

She jerked her chin away from his hand, and stared incredulously. He was licking shut a cigarette he had been rolling with his other hand, and he watched her across it steadily. Cherry opened her mouth two or three times; but she shut it again and obeyed him.

She went to George now, and helped him drink from the gourd dipper. Once or twice she glanced at Melody furtively; and when she spoke again her words were quiet and rapid. "That other rider is Virgil Browning. He's one of Monte's wild bunch, like Lee Gledhill. Monte never rode south at all. After we left, Pa and Avery came in, and Lee signalled up Virg—Virg was laying low in the brush, somewhere. They went down to scout the town, and mighty near ran square into the posse. But they rode hard and got loose."

"So *now* what is their theory?" Melody asked her. "They *insist* on tangling with the Cottons? Or don't they aim to be discommoded by jest thirty-forty men?"

"They wanted Monte to ride. He wouldn't do it. He says he isn't fit to ride a horse race; he's right. He hopes to stand them off until dark. Then one hard effort will get him clear. He can lose them, and take it easy after that, in the dark."

"Most likely you told him he better run, and he was too stubborn to be bossed."

She shot him a glance of surprise. Melody Jones wasn't expected to see through anything like that.

"He cain't ever take it easy," Melody said, "not while he lives. Don't he know he's going to be hunted, and deer-tracked, and laid for, every mile he ever sees again?"

Cherry shook her head a little, and she was looking at him queerly. "He isn't afraid of being followed any more. Because he hopes—he means—that when he's gone from here you'll be found here—dead—in his clothes that you're standing in, and in his name—even with his carbine in your hands. . . . Don't you know that, even yet?" She said this clearly, facing it because she couldn't get away from it any more.

"Reckon I knowed that," Melody said sheepishly. "Reckon I jest forgot."

"You *forgot?* Supposed to die, and *forgot?*"

Melody shrugged. He didn't see anything so odd about it.

Now Avery and Fever Crick de Longpre made a dash from the house to the barn. No one fired at them. They brought with them the rest of the saddled horses, so that their rush sounded like a cavalry charge.

Cherry said to Avery, "Quitting him now, or thrown out?" No rancor was in that; it simply represented the kind of expectations Cherry had in regard to her men folks, after knowing them all her life.

Avery took no offense. "We got to hold the barn. We can stand 'em off a decent piece, if they don't git in the barn."

When the ponies had been tied up, and some of the

hay bales shifted to protect them a little from random bullets, a short harsh argument followed between Cherry and her brother. Cherry believed Melody should be armed, and Avery inclined toward knocking Melody on the head and tying him up. The subject of this debate took no part in it; he smoked, and watched the discussion with an impartiality that infuriated Cherry. But she won, and Melody was given a six-gun. After that George wanted a weapon, which no one could spare him, since he couldn't use it; and this ended by Cherry laying the carbine beside him. His hand rested on it slackly, but he seemed comforted.

Immediately after that the first of the posse came into sight. Just before they appeared Avery said, "Watch it—watch it—" a kind of a strangled cry such as might come from a man in mid-air; and there was a moment of utter silence among the defenders. Cherry whispered, "Here it is. . . ."

❧ 26 ❧

Two riders—one of them Lester Cotton—appeared at two hundred yards on the so-called road, coming up over the break of the slope. The horses came over the hump at a walk, their stride unhurried, but given a look of power and vigor by the strong climbing thrust of their quarters. The long shot which had crippled the grey must have been outside of Lester Cotton's plan; he was going ahead with his first plan anyway, taking a chance of riding boldly in for a close-quarters arrest.

But now a rifle banged from the house, and Lester

Cotton's horse came down heavily, dead before it was still. Apparently it had tossed its head in the nick of the wrong instant, intercepting a bullet intended for a center drill on its rider. Lester Cotton pitched himself backwards down the slope out of sight, untouched. The other pony whirled and plunged back the way it had come, with a violent switch of the tail testifying to swift spurring.

After that there was a strange long pause in the action, an interlude while nothing seemed to happen. No attempt of any kind was made at parley; Lester Cotton already had his answer, and he knew it. But presently the people within the lay-out began to pick up signs of what was happening. A vast amount of movement was going on out there, ominously quiet and most of it unseen. But far up the slope behind the barn a crouching man, running on foot with his rifle in his hands, ran from one bit of brush cover to another, briefly glimpsed. Two guns from the house spoke almost together, and both too late.

A few minutes after that a jack rabbit, tall as a chair and flat-built as a cardboard mule, bolted from the brush in an entirely different quarter. It came spring bounding directly through the Busted Nose, and as it passed between house and barn a pointless shot from the kitchen sent its dead carcass rolling end over end. That would be Monte Jarrad expressing, in his own characteristic manner, his irritation and resentment toward the whole thing.

Fever Crick spotted a scatter of dust behind high buckbrush, fired blind through the cover, and was promptly cussed out by his son for wasting a cartridge. A little covey of mountain quail fled skittering down the hill between the stems of the growth, their curly-plumed top-knots raked forward over their short bills. They ran like little old ladies holding their skirts up and scampering. Suddenly they rocketed into the air on an angle, and went whirring out across the valley—a thing they never would have done if they hadn't toddled directly into something else that scared them.

A stone the size of a man's head rolled bounding down a declivity to the south, and Avery paused in his criticism of Fever Crick's folly long enough to bang a silly shot at the empty-looking place where the boulder came from.

And a little after that the gunfire began, tentative and probing, from the slopes. A howling ricochet, making ten times the noise of a straight-flying bullet, caromed from a rock short of the barn and tore a whole strip of three or four shakes off the rotten roof. Wood dust and punky splinters came spinning and drifting down into the interior. Some of the tied horses, tensed by the increasing smell of powder, tested the stretch of their necks against the tie ropes, squalled unhappily, and stuttered their feet.

A feather of smoke showed from a lonely bush that looked like a sucker mark; but four bullets that immediately clipped twigs from it all ricocheted from the cleft boulder behind. Within the barn a pony was bleeding from a bullet-broken ear, though no one had seen it struck.

Then in a swiftly rising increase of fire those quick feathers of gunsmoke began to sprout everywhere—north, south, down-mountain and up-slope—long-range, middle-range, and point-blank, all converging into the flimsy walls of house and barn. The shadows within were lively with jumping splinters, and the smell of powder filled the whole breeze. The attackers had no organization, and little plan; but each of them out there was effective in his own way, full of individual resource. The people in the Busted Nose were suddenly the center of an echoing, roaring swirl of fire-attack.

"Get down," Melody ordered Cherry. "Get down, I said!"

She was trying to get a look at the ear of the hurt pony, and she flicked Melody a glance so near contempt that go-to-hell was unnecessary. Melody reached for her, caught her shoulder, and spilled her over a hay bale into a slot between two others. Melody watched hopefully to see if a bullet wouldn't buzz through the spot where she had stood. It didn't, though.

"That's the second time you've done that!" Cherry started to scramble up furiously, but she caught his eye upon her, and was stopped. After a moment she settled back, and for the time being stayed where she was, her eyes bewildered upon his back as he turned away.

Avery and Fever Crick were sliding at a running crouch from one wall to another, trying to keep up a semblance of fire on all sides; they desperately feared a rush, and didn't know on which side to expect it, except that whichever way they were turned they felt the threat was at their backs. Between shots they hauled frantically at the hay bales which were their protection against lead. The sleazy walls of the barn hid their movements, but nothing else. They kept trying to shore up the gaps and angles where the bullets were splattering through, but there weren't quite enough bales to afford a double tier all around, and it had them crazy.

Avery, trying to haul a bale to plug one gap, had his coat-tails clipped by a shot that came through the place from which he had taken it; and when he frantically mauled it back where it was before, a slug of lead from still another direction went through the top of his hat from the side. The rake of gunfire was lacing in brutally, this side, that side, crossways, lengthways, *all* sides, with the deadly quartering and spreading of the attack.

"Hard to see why the bastards aren't shooting each other," Fever Crick whimpered.

"Where would be the sense?" Avery snarled at him, firing. "If you think them cagey devils don't know where their shots go, stick your damn head up oncet, and show 'em a *real* ricoskip!"

"That's a fine way to talk to your father!"

The iron pail which stood by George Fury let out a metallic howl, and began to squirt water both sides. Melody propped it on a slant to save the rest of the water. Every minute now new vulnerabilities were being discovered by those probing, searching, all-covering guns. One cluster of rocks three hundred yards above the barn seemed alive with gunners, pouring in a plunging fire that crackled through the walls and thudded into the hay bales.

"They's about seven fellers in that rock nest alone," Avery panted.

"One feller," Melody thought. "He's restless on account of them ant heaps up there, that's all."

A ricochet from the downhill side snarled through the

wall, ripping out a piece of knot-wood beside Melody. He casually put his eye to the new knothole, and peered back the way the bullet had come. It was enough to make a man think, to see what those buzz-fly bullets could do to solid wood. He put his gun muzzle to a crack, belt-high, and, still looking through the bullet rip, made three unevenly spaced spouts of earth jump up from the crest of the slope.

Behind him Cherry asked in a small voice, "Did you get him?"

"Get him? What for I want to get him? I was jest studyin' to make his aim nervous. I ain't got nothing against some feller out there, without I even know who he be. . . ."

He flattened to the hay bales to look slantwise through the broad door. He saw an undersized figure on a mustang horse break from cover far-off, making a dash for a different rift of brush. The rider put the cayuse in a long winging leap across a coulee. In all the hellish rattle that was going on you couldn't tell which gun got him, except it seemed to be from the house. The pony went slack in mid-jump, and struck the opposite lip of the coulee in a heap. The rider fell clear and rolled bouncing down the precipitous drop, spread-eagled, and grabbing at roots to check himself. Then he also went slack before he stopped, and lay loosely where he came to rest.

Cherry gasped, close to Melody's ear. She was leaning on his shoulder, but until then he hadn't known it. She whispered, "That was Homer Cotton. . . ."

George's mind was wandering now. He said, "I don't mind rain. I love rain, like any cowman. But in Californy your life ain't safe a minute, without you got a cockeyed rowboat on your back. . . ."

Along about then a strange inhuman cry sounded in the house; it trailed off in a quaver, and was not repeated. They learned afterward that the luckless Virgil Browning was struck in the jaw, shattering half his face, by a slug that caromed off a stove lid to find him.

"A feller can't see how they live, there in the house," Melody said, "without no hay bales like we got."

"Maybe they ain't hungry yet," George said faintly.

"They'll bank the mattresses against the walls," Cherry said. Her voice was dull and shaky. "They'll use pieces of the stove, and floor planking, and anything that will check a bullet. But they can't stop them all."

Melody sat down near George, his back against a bale. He idly rolled a cigarette. "It beats me," he said. "I ain't got the faintest idee why for we're doing this."

"The fellers outside want to get in," George said. He spoke huskily and faintly, but with a slow distinctness, as if speaking to a child. "The fellers inside want to keep 'em out. Catch on?"

"That don't account for what *I'm* doing here," Melody said.

"You're here to git rich. That's the reason you give, anyway, when you drug us into this. Remember?" His voice died away to almost nothing. "Leave me know when you think we're rich enough, so's we can git the hell out of here. . . ."

A little after that the first extended concentration of fire began to die down. The attackers were getting cagey, tired of pouring their fire blind into the thin walls, without any apparent lessening of the weaker but still dangerous fire power within. They settled down to an intermittent sniping at marks which wishful thinking suggested.

"We ain't accomplished nothing," Avery said glumly. "Not a single God damn thing."

This wasn't so. One determined rush would have laid the outfit flat. But the defense had achieved so spirited an effect, that the Cottons' men never believed, either then or ever, how extremely few were holding the Busted Nose through those hours. No rush was tried.

"Lester Cotton's wearing a deputy's badge," Cherry said. "I saw it on his shirt."

"Naturally it ain't on the seat of his pants," Avery said irritably.

Lester Cotton's badge meant something. The ring of gun-smoke had taken to itself the guise of all the law there was. The people here could have held more hope if they had been a thousand times outnumbered in an Apache raid.

Avery and Fever Crick had time now to tally their remaining ammunition, and went through the inevitable surprise at how much they had used up. Still, they were doing pretty well; if they were prudent they could make it last a few hours yet—perhaps even until dark. Melody began throwing down and hog-tying the horses, taking Harry Henshaw first. This involved considerable uproar and thrashing around, but when it was done the ponies were pretty safe for the first time.

By the time he was finished the posse seemed to have shaken down into a steady siege, fit to last a week without taxing anybody except the people inside. Some smoke columns from cooking fires began to rise from various points. They could hear more people arriving out there out of sight, some of them in wagons; there were distant shouts as newcomers hailed each other. It was a wonder where all the people came from, as the news spread. The hills out of gun-range were filling up with no-goods and hangers-on, attending for the sake of the excitement and the barbecue. Probably there would be political speeches out there, before they were through.

This went on for a long time. Sometimes a quarter of an hour would pass, with no shot fired. But the snipers were still alert: their few shots were accurate as pencil dots. After a while one of them pasted Fever Crick.

The bullet caught him slantwise just above the wrist. It was mostly spent, and ran erratically up his arm for eight or nine inches just under the skin; no especial damage was accomplished by it. Later he would tell about his remarkable casualty a thousand times, until it became his most used possession. But just now he took it that he was much worse than killed. He moaned piteously and continuously, and from then on demanded the kind of attention deserved by a man who was virtually dying; and made of it an excuse to gulp most of their water up.

There wasn't going to be any more water in here when what they had was gone. There wasn't going to be any food either, or anything else, until this thing should get itself over with.

Melody sat on the ground near George with his back against a bale and watched Cherry fuss over her father. "I thought I told you to stay down," he said.

She obeyed him without any question this time. She came and sat on the ground close beside him, looking subdued.

George said dimly, "If it only wasn't for the climate of Californy—"

"He blames everything on he got wet oncet, and shrunk his joints, or something," Melody explained this to Cherry. "He says California ain't a state at all—it's a dang fish tank. George, I swear to God, I'll buy you some liniment. Now shut up."

Melody had got hold of a knife and a piece of manzanita root, which he was carving into a mestook. It appeared to represent some kind of a fish face, but with a long nose, three legs, and wings. When Cherry saw that he appeared to be absorbed in his carving, she leaned against his shoulder, gradually, as if she hoped she would not be noticed.

"You see them shiny specks of dust," Melody said to her, "dancing around in the air where the sun comes in? The feller don't live that can tell you how come that is. It cain't be the sunshine causes it, because there's more of that outside, and you don't see any specks out there. But if you come back in a hundred years, then gold specks will still be dancing around in here, if the barn stands up that long."

"Oh?" Cherry said.

"Uh-huh, that's right."

"This place will burn tonight," Cherry said. Her voice was dead level and depressed, but with that same uncertainty under it. "This is the Rowntree fight all over again."

"If there had been a Rowntree fight," Melody amended.

"I guess I forgot that for a minute."

Melody stopped carving on his mestook. He was thinking of old Mrs. Rowntree, who *might* have laid her head down on her rifle, in the exact spot Cherry had showed him. He could picture that, just as plainly as if it had ever happened. And he could picture something else, that hadn't happened yet: He could see Cherry's head laid quiet on a bale of moldy hay, with the wavering fire-light reflected on her spread-out hair.

"George," Melody said, "I ain't a-going to be able to git it done. I've went to work and fell down again. I kind of thought I would. But I had to try."

"Try what?" Cherry asked.

"He taken and set out to bust up Monte's wild bunch," George said. "He said he wanted to be somebody."

Cherry stared at Melody.

"I reckon it was right silly," Melody said. "I see now that no such thing could be. But that wasn't why I rode Monte's saddle into Payneville."

"Then why—"

Melody looked at her mournfully, but without self-consciousness. "You was all tangled up in Monte's devilments," he said to her. "I could see there wasn't no way to talk sense into your haid, gals being like they be. So, it seemed like the only way to get you out was just to bust up the whole thing."

"Is that why you rode down to Payneville, when you knew you ought to go over the hill?"

"Whut did you think it was? Oh, I see. You thought it

was the thousand dullers. . . . Well, it won't matter much, no more. The wild bunch is gitting busted, all right. But you're still in the middle of it, bad as bad can be. And there ain't much left to do about it, seemingly."

"I give up," George said.

His words trailed off in such a blur that Cherry and Melody looked at each other. Cherry got her feet under her and moved to George's side, but without straightening up. She laid a hand on his forehead and looked uncertain; then placed her lips to his temple to see if there was fever there. Melody felt again that disarming surprise, that a woman should take pains over some old man whom she hardly knew.

Then he saw that George wasn't even aware that she was there. With Cherry's face close by for contrast, George looked so grey that he seemed half out of the world. It came to Melody that what he was already looking at was partial death. He had not been convinced, before, that George Fury was actually going to die. But he knew, then, what he was going to do—what he had to do, without even much choice in the matter, as he saw it.

❧ 27 ❧

Melody Jones stood up, exposing himself to a random shot through the walls as he had forbidden Cherry to do, and he threw his mestook out into the yard. They saw it bounce a little and roll to a stop, balanced on its three legs; and almost instantly a bullet took it, blasting it to flinders.

"That would be old man Miles Cotton," Cherry said.

"He's the only one that wastes shots on purpose."

Fever Crick was whining for water again, and Cherry took it to him. "Why does this happen to a man like me," he whimpered, "that would have fit 'em to a standstill? Why can't they hit a no-good punk like that Jones, that ain't worth his room to nobody?"

For once Cherry answered him in a tone that would have cut the hide off a mule.

"He'll be hit soon enough," she said, "and when he is, you'll be flabbergasted—because you'll get a look at a man who can act a little different from a squaw papoose!"

She took the water away from him before he was finished with it, and left him staring blankly at her back. She crossed to George Fury; he hadn't asked for water, but she poured the last of it into him. The water revived George a little, and he saw that she was watching Melody sidelong, and unhappily. Melody had found himself a piece of oak planking, and had retreated with it to the farthest corner he could find, to work on it with his knife.

There was quiet now for some little time. The widespread, tremendously overmanned posse was getting ready to try something else, but those within could not judge what it would be. Melody finished his job of carving on the plank, and he signaled Cherry to come to him.

"This is for later," he said, showing her the plank, "if anything goes wrong."

Even when she had looked at it, she did not understand what it was, at first.

"It's a tombstone, kind of," Melody said sheepishly,

"in case it's needed, after while."

Carved deeply into the oak were the words:

> I BE DAMN IF I AIM
> TO STAND FOR THIS.
> GEORGE FURY.

"All of his life he's harped on that one string," Melody explained. "I know this is the way he'd feel about it, if he realized he was being buried."

" 'Damn if I aim to stand—' " Cherry read; and burst into tears.

"This time he's right," Melody said, "for this one time. By God, they gone too far! We cain't stand for it. Not even from Monte." He turned the slab face down.

"But—but Monte—"

He shook his head. "From Monte least of all." He walked across and counted George Fury's pulse; then he propped up George's head with a swathe of hay, and turned George's face toward a crack in the wall.

"What are you doing that for?"

"He—he might want to see."

"See?" She was turning panicky. "See what?"

"Jest a kind of—thing—here. . . ."

Methodically Melody checked the loading of his gun, and when this was done he stared at her steadily for a disconcertingly long time.

"Look," Melody said to her. "This one time, listen to me. You're pretty, and you're sweet. This God-forsaken country ain't ever seen anything so sweet as you be, in the worst day you ever had. Don't you never doubt yourself no more. Because anybody would love you, always, any time. Don't you ever forget that, any more." He grinned. "You don't have to lean on no pistol-punk, like him. That's ridic'lous."

He turned away from her, and walked to the door of the barn. He stood there a moment in the sunlight, almost in the open.

"Where you going?" Avery demanded. "What you up to now?"

"Nothing," Melody said. "Nothing you can hinder, son."

"Come back here!" Avery was sharp on the prod, unsure of what was happening, but aware that something was about to bust. "Git back, I say! You ain't boss in here!"

Avery came across the barn at a crouching run, direct and concentrated, like a hunting dog. When Melody paid no attention to him, and did not check, Avery grabbed him by the belt and jerked him backwards.

Melody turned without seeming to hurry. Almost casually he took Avery by the neck scarf, and swung his gun high. "Excuse me," he said, and tapped Avery over the ear with the gun-butt in his fist. Avery came down with a whop, so hard that a puff of dust went up. Melody stood over him for a moment to see if he would get up, but Avery did not move.

An unholy, formless lack of expression came across Cherry's face. She said, "George . . ."

George Fury spoke in a voice of command. "Melody . . . Melody."

Melody stepped out into the open, gun in hand,

exposed to the house and to the hills. He raised his voice as drivers shout to lift mules. *"You, Monte! Monte Jarrad!"*

There was a moment of dead silence; the attackers held paralyzed, taken by surprise. Then one bullet flew over, lisping "Thweet!" as it passed overhead; but it went very high, as if the gun had been struck up. Some voices out there were heard yelling to hold fire.

What was happening in the posse was peculiar and confused. Many thought that some of their own men had somehow taken the barn, and from there were attacking the house. A few thought that a fight had broken out among the defenders; and, between these two schools of thought, the besiegers were shouted into holding their fire.

Melody yelled again, calling Monte's name, and started walking toward the house.

Monte Jarrad opened the door of the kitchen, and stood in its frame. His face could not be seen clearly, there in the shadow, but he was moving very slowly, like a man in a fever dream.

Behind Melody Cherry screamed, "No, no, no. . . ."

Melody called out, "Take care of yourself, Monte!"

Monte's gun came up; but instead of firing he half lowered it again. His left hand moved over and seemed to feel of the gun, as if something had gone wrong there, and he didn't know what it was; but his astounded eyes did not leave Melody.

Melody fired, without effect. He knew where his shot went. Even without seeing the splinters jump from the door jamb, he knew it wasn't any good. He was concentrating everything he had on putting a shot where he wanted it; but he never had had any way of doing that, and he had no way now. He walked closer.

Instantly after Melody's first shot Monte fired; he fired from belt-level, and he leaned into it, as if trying to put his weight behind the starting of the bullet. His whole body curved to it, with the effort of will that was behind the lead. Melody faltered, but he did not go down. He came ahead, walking steadily.

Monte Jarrad stared as if he had gone out of his mind. His gun drooped downward, a thin curl of smoke still trailing from the muzzle; he actually looked as if he were going to drop it.

Melody fired again, and missed clean.

A clear blaze of fury broke up the blank astonishment of Monte's face. He fired three times, crazily, as fast as he could drop the hammer. Melody jerked a little and swayed, but kept his feet. He fired again, and his shot split the edge of the broken screen door.

Something had happened to Monte Jarrad, and he knew it now, without knowing what it was. All his life he had been a natural marksman, but the West was full of those. What had made him a more dangerous fighter than other men was that he was cold; no part of him knew how to waste itself feeling anything whatever, when he fought. But he was not cold now. Something had happened to him. It had started when this man, for whom he had never found anything but contempt, stood unarmed in front of him in the kitchen, talking to him as no one had ever talked to Monte before. This wasn't Monte, firing from the door, but a different proposition, torn in two by enough crazy anger to poison a bull train.

Melody saw that, and he didn't understand it, but he knew his chance. He knew he had a fraction of a second of time now, for he was standing in front of Monte Jarrad, and he was not dead. He fired, and put a bullet through the top of the door.

"Dear God," he whispered, and it was a prayer. "Dear God, dear God in heaven. . . ." He put a shot into the kitchen, past Monte Jarrad.

Monte had one cartridge left, and he sent it now; and Melody was hit again, this time hard. He half spun, and dropped his weapon; but he didn't fall down. He caught himself, and stood for a moment on spread legs. It was only when he tried to catch up his gun out of the dust that he came down on his hands and knees. He groped about on all fours, and found his gun. Somehow he got up, stumbled forward two steps more, and cocked the gun.

A shot sounded behind him, and in the same instant a bullet said "Cousin!" directly in his ear.

Monte Jarrad flailed forward onto the gallery, all joints gone loose, as if everything was cut down at once.

Melody could not believe it at first. When he had got it through his head he backed off watchfully, his heels dragging in the dirt. Lee Gledhill was still in action in the house; but Lee did not take him under fire.

George Fury was prone in the barn door, collapsed from a crawling position, the carbine in the dust by his hand.

Melody said, "George, for God's sake, how many times I got to tell you—" He let it go, speech being considerable effort, and George being three-quarters out and not listening. Fever Crick was standing around stunned and useless, and Avery was just coming to his senses, but somehow Cherry and Melody got George Fury back into shelter.

"That's the first time," Melody said vaguely, "I ever knew George to fire left-handed. . . ."

Cherry spoke breathlessly, as if with panic. "Left— left—" She turned steady and cool. "Anyone who can shoot with one hand can shoot with the other. A whim, no doubt."

"Never heard no such darn thing," Melody said fuzzily.

The girl caught the carbine up, as if she were rescuing something alive. "You—you imagine it." Suddenly she dropped the carbine in the dirt, covered her face, and sat down. Melody stepped toward her, lurching a little; he reached out a hand, and touched her hair.

"Don't touch me," she said, and Melody took his hand away. "Don't ever touch me!"

Melody Jones stepped back, looking befuddled. He swayed a little, and sat down slowly, his back against a bale.

"Heck," he said.

A little after that, Lee Gledhill walked out and surrendered, Lester Cotton taking over.

❧ 28 ❧

With Monte Jarrad out of business, and the shooting died out some, and the horse-frazzling quieted down, the silvery Poisonberry rolled on, ever on, to Syrup Creek, its tarnished reaches badly in need of a polish. Its sluggish shallows almost seemed to shuffle up a dust where it slowly wound its bends, so near it came to being no river at all, in dry season. And on its banks Payneville dozed again in its accustomed befuddled sprawl, like a Mex-Piute brave sleeping it off in the open sun.

But at the heart of Payneville rose an unceasing tireless gabble, in the name of investigation, while everybody and his brother questioned Melvin Jones, alias Melody Jones—and forced him to answer, too, on pain of unhopeful consequences—for three long everlasting weeks. . . .

They turned him loose at last, and he rode out to the Busted Nose morosely, nursing a grouch for almost the first time in his life. He still had one arm in splints; and he was bandaged in places, under his clothes.

George Fury was still out there, for the reason that there wasn't any way to move him. He was still flat on his back, and getting blanket-sore around the shoulder blades, but he was on the mend all right, to judge by his conversation.

"So you finally sobered up," were his first words to Melody.

"They only just now cut me loose," Melody said glumly. "And you already knowed that, without I said it."

"What all went on down there? How many counts was you accused on, and how did you lie clear?"

"They brung a open verdict. That's the legal way of putting that they ended up confused, kind of."

"I know that much, you nump! But what *happened?*"

"Listen, George," Melody said wearily, "my ears is wore thin. I cain't stand to hear all that stuff over again, not even in my own voice. You can go down and read the damn records some time. Or else send down some pack mules, and git 'em hauled up here. Allow for a short ton."

"It beats me," George said. "I never see such a town for kicking away their opportunity. I'd of swore they'd hang you. What did they say when they unloosed you?"

"They said, 'Goodbye.' "

George gave it up then. He glared at Melody for a while. "But the reward—you anyway got the reward?"

"Whut reward?"

George Fury whimpered inarticulately.

"Oh, the thousand dullers," Melody remembered. "Thet. Well, they give it to me."

"Why in hell didn't yew say so?"

"Well, George, you see, I give it back."

"Wha— Why, yew befewzled—"

"I jest didn't figure it was coming to me, George. You can go git it yourself, when you're abler. I'm sick of them jiggers."

It was some time before George could speak. He turned his face to the wall, chewed his mustache, and prayed for the strength to get up and kill Melody. He was under control, though, when he turned back.

"After I turned back the thousand dullers," Melody said, "they come up with a bill for my board. O' course I couldn't pay it. So they held me in the jail three days more, on a charge of vacancy. Or something like that."

"I had hopes for you, for a while," George said. "You looked pretty good around here, once, for a couple of minutes. When first you let yourself get sucked in here, on the theory you could collect the reward—git holt of the toughest killer since Billy the Kid—whup his whole gang, prob'ly—take him single-handed, seemingly—I knowed you was crazy. But I admit there was a minute here when you near had me fooled. I come mighty near thinkin' you knowed what you was up to, there, once . . . ."

Melody was interested. "When was this?"

"When you walked out and fit it out with him—and by God shot him down!"

"Who? Me?"

"How you ever done it—that part they's no answer to," George said. "It'll mystify me in my grave, by Gard."

"Only I never," Melody said somberly.

"Never what?"

"I never shot him, George."

"I see," George said, with bitter irony. "You never killed him. He fainted, and struck his head. The bullet you put through him never had nothing to do with it!"

Melody looked at George very queerly. "I kind of thought to ask you a question, George. But this answers it, I guess. Maybe I already knew the answer. Only, I did kind of hope— You *sure* you didn't shoot him, George? Because you crawled to the door, you know. You crawled to the door, and you—"

"Crawled to the door," George mimicked him angrily. "I don't crawl for nobody, you hear? I stood up and walked like a human bean! Only I tripped. It knocked the wind out of me, or somethin', and I dropped her. Don't you even know when you *shoot* a feller?"

"I—I don't feel good," Melody said. "Of course, I really knowed; but—I guess I still kind of hoped—"

"What the *hell's* the matter with yew?"

Melody looked at him with pity. "The shot come from behind me. I even heard the lead. I reckon the next silliness, I'm supposed to think she went off when you dropped her, and hit dead center by the guidance o' God. Fine carbine, you had, with its own eyes and everything. I never hear sech—" He stopped. "Now whut's the matter?"

A new queer light had come into George's face. "Avery!" he said.

"Whut?"

"It comes back to me now. As I fell down, somebody taken and grabbed the carbine up. Avery must of—" He checked abruptly, and looked even stranger. "Avery was knocked out," he said weakly, watching Melody.

They looked at each other quite a while. Melody's face had reached a low of depression such as George had never seen in it before. It made him look older; almost, George thought, as if he had sense.

"Don't look like that," George said at last. "You otter be glad. You otter be proud of her. If it was me, I'd take it for the best good news I ever see come to you yet. The only good news," he corrected.

"I throw in," Melody said.

"What?"

"You cain't blame her. She knowed him long before

she ever knowed me."

It took a long time for that to soak in upon George, so that he realized what Melody meant. Even after all his long miles with Melody, he found it hard to believe this final thing.

"I otter git up and whup yew." George's voice was low, but it shook. "I give yew up. Git out of my sight! I don't want to ever see yew no more. Melody, I mean it."

"All right, George."

Melody got together such of his few things as were still rattling around the ranch house. He could not find at all some of the things he thought he remembered having had, such as one-half pair of spurs, and his horsehair tie rope. He finally found his other saddle blanket, though, rolled up under George Fury's head. "Please, George, kin I have that?" When George smoked and ignored him he lifted George's head by the hair, and took the blanket anyway, while George refused to notice.

When he had puttered all he could, he went to look Cherry up. He couldn't tell whether Cherry had been avoiding him or only waiting for him to stop avoiding her. But he knew she was in her room now, and he went and knocked on the door. She told him to come in.

Cherry was brushing her hair, just as he had seen her do the night she had found him asleep in her bed. She glanced over her shoulder at him, and said, "Hi." And there was a considerable silence while Melody stood awkwardly in the door and nothing happened.

His wandering eye noticed a random piece of blue ribbon, tossed aside so that it trailed over the end of the wash stand at the end of the bed, by the lamp. He had never seen it before, and didn't know whether she wore it in her hair, or what, but it was crumpled, so that he knew it had been worn. When he had looked at the ribbon for a minute he became aware, without any process of thought, that he was going to steal it.

"It beats me," Melody said, "where that hanged horse has got to, so sudden. One minute he's foraging hay in the barn, like he was moved in to stay, and next minute he ain't any place, and don't even answer my whistle."

"Did he ever?"

"Well, no," Melody admitted. He crossed aimlessly, and sat down on her bed. "He never *actually* done so, yet; but it always seemed like he was fixing to. It's kind of backsetting, in a way."

She didn't answer that, and wasn't looking at him, so Melody casually moved his hand to cover the end of the bit of ribbon he wanted, and began to reel it in with his fingers.

"That there call-whistle I use," he said sadly, "is the most come-hither whistle I can develop. I've give all kind of thought to it. It does seem like *any* critter ought to answer that whistle, if he's fixing to answer anything."

"You don't say."

"Whut? Oh. Yes'm. A feller would sure think so. But I reckon I have to give up."

She stopped brushing her hair, and sat looking at the hair brush in a dejected sort of way, as if it had failed her.

"I don't see why you need him, right away," she said at last.

"I got to get a job. Most likely I got to travel some, to get it—don't seem like I'm popular around here, no more. But I got to get some money to send back to George. He'll need it, until he can work."

"He might never, you know."

"Well, then, he'll need the money all the worse."

"You know," Cherry said, not looking at him, "the country around here would be a wonderful place to start a little cattle stand. It's thin, but there's plenty of it. The Cottons only want the valley bottom. And it isn't the country's fault that Fever Crick wastes all his time running wild horses."

"I—I often thought of that."

He had thought of it, but not on purpose. Saddle-weary men think of that kind of thing when they are bedded down in a soaking prairie rain, or when they sight a homestead cabin, far off in a cold dusk, or when they look at lights across a dark valley, but can't go toward them because they have to circle and listen to ten thousand homesick moos. But if they have sense, they kick the settling-down ideas out of their heads, because they know that hardly a one of them ever gets it done.

"In a few years," Cherry said gravely, "a couple of people could have about anything, if they weren't afraid of work."

"Sure."

She was silent, and waited for what he would say.

The ribbon he was reeling into his pocket was caught on something, but he was afraid to look around to see what it was. He tried to free it with twitchy jerks.

"I guess I got to be going now," he said.

The ribbon came free into his hand. Instantly there was a shattering crash as her lamp came down. The pink china shade, with the little gilt flowers on it, which he had thought was so pretty, broke up in about a million pieces, and so did the chimney, and the glass base broke in half. Kerosene raised a quick reek as it puddled across the floor and began to drip away through the cracks.

From the lean-to at the other side of the house came George Fury's faint yell: "Cherry, if yew missed him with ut, hit him agin!"

"Heck," Melody said. He sat looking at the broken lamp, and the ribbon in his hand, and turning turkey red.

Cherry seemed to notice the ribbon more than the lamp. "You can have that, if you want it," she said. "You don't need to steal things from me. Couldn't you ask?"

Wordless, Melody wadded up the ribbon and crammed it into his pocket. Then, becoming aware of what he was doing, he hastily pulled it out again, snapped it straight, and dropped it on the bed.

"I swear to God," he said honestly, "I don't know how come I done that." He stood up. "I'll send you another lamp," he said, "out of my first pay."

"You're really on your way," she said, as if she didn't believe it.

"Whut?"

She subsided, looking more discouraged than he had ever seen her. "Let it go. . . . I suppose you'll let George know where he can find you?"

"We ain't speakin'."

"But you said—"

"I'll support him while he needs it. I'll do jest that one thing more. But beyond that we're done. George wants it that way, Cherry. I reckon so do I."

She looked at him a long time then, disconcertingly, while he stood turning his hat round and round in his hands. He didn't know exactly how to get out of there, now that he had no more to say.

"I think," Cherry said surprisingly, "you're the hardest man I've ever known."

"Who? Me?"

"You're hard like a rock drill, or a bronc. You're so hard you don't even know you're hard."

"Oh, well, shucks, now—"

"How on earth did you manage to break with George?"

Melody shifted uncomfortably, deeply embarrassed. He would have said he didn't know, except that George would be staying on there.

"Well," Melody said, "he—he—I guess I got to tell you something, Cherry. . . . George remembers, now. He remembers who—who picked that carbine up, and shot it, when—when I was fighting Monte."

Cherry winced as if a quirt had sung in her face, but steadied instantly. She considered for a long moment, with her eyes averted.

"I did," she said at last.

"Yup, sure," Melody said. "We know that, now."

Cherry talked swiftly, in a panic. "Can't he see—can't anybody see—I had to try to—I couldn't help—"

"Cherry," he said slowly, "you ain't got any better friend than George."

"But you just said you quarreled because—"

He met her almost frantically glassy stare with steady eyes. "George is a sentimental old guy. He don't see things very clear, any more."

Every trace of expression in Cherry's face was crossed off.

"It's—it's *you* who hates me for that?"

"Nobody hates you, Cherry."

She dropped her chin, and turned her face away from him.

"I want you to know something," Melody said. "If a feller gets a bullet pasted at him, it's liable to be his own damn fault. Even if it comes from the last place he would rightfully expect it to come from."

She only looked at him.

"Don't feel like that," Melody said. "It ain't fair or right for a man to expect too much of people. If a feller gets to thinking there's some one person he can trust, that's a chance he's taking. And if later she feels called on to take a shot at him, he cain't blame nobody but his-self if he's surprised."

This was so far from anything Cherry had looked forward to, or planned, that at first she could not speak. Her eyelids winked fast as she stared hard at the hairbrush.

"Your horse . . ." she said at last.

"Whut?"

"Your horse is out of sight in the coulee, just beyond the barn."

"Now, how in time did he get there?"

"I put him there," she said.

"You did? Whut for?"

"Because I wanted to talk to you. But—I don't any more."

Melody shrugged. "People around here sure act

queer," he said. "It must be something in the water, like George says. I noticed Harry Henshaw was kind of— Of course, that could be something he et."

He turned away; and she didn't stop him as he wandered to the door. But he hesitated, feeling unhappy, and incomplete.

"George is funny," he said. "Facts *hurt* George. He cain't bring hisself to stand for 'em. There ain't a man in the world wouldn't give the last drop of his blood for a gal that done for him whut you tried to do for Monte. But maybe you'd better let George think whut he wants. He's daid set that you was shootin' *at* Monte."

He paused. Then, as she stared at him, he said, diffidently, "Some way it makes him mad to have me realize that you was only trying to kill *me*."

Cherry dropped the hairbrush, but it landed on its bristles, without sound; and Melody did not see it, because he was getting out of there now, at his own slow pace.

He picked up his saddle, and his bedroll, and a few things he had forgot to wrap in, but could hang from the fork. And he carried this scant lifetime acquirement out to the coulee beyond the barn, where he found Harry Henshaw as Cherry had promised.

He laid his stuff down on the lip of the coulee, sat down on his bedroll, and studied Harry Henshaw. He wasn't in any hurry.

His right hand was mechanically picking cactus spines off his chaps. He noticed this now, and for a moment watched the automatic, idle activity of his fingers. Then he made his hand stop that, and relax. He remembered, without wishing or trying, the things he had said to

Cherry. He could see how God-righteous, how sickening silly he had sounded, if by any chance he had been talking to a girl who had *not* tried to kill him, but had shot to save his life.

"Aw, no," he said. The egotism of the idea flattened him. "Aw, no; she never."

He whistled to Harry Henshaw, the seductive whistle he had practiced so long. The horse didn't notice, seemingly. The awfullest thought in the world was haunting Melody.

"Someday," he said to himself, "you'll be an old man, past use for nothin'. And suppose then word comes in, some way, so's we know then that George was right. Suppose we find out, some way, she really shot at Monte. *Then* you'll set there plucking cactus spines. You'll set there a long time. . . ."

He stood halfway up, hitching his chap belt, but sat down again. "She would of give me some sign," he suggested to himself uncertainly. "She would of said something. She would of told me." He reached down for his soogans.

But he never picked them up. He stopped in his tracks, shocked out of motion by the impression that Harry Henshaw, ignorer of whistles, had turned and whistled at him. Then, as he stared at the dozing pony, Cherry spoke behind him.

"No wonder he doesn't come," she said.

He jumped, and spun around. "Whut? Oh. It's you."

"Yes," Cherry said. "That whistle can't be any good. You don't even answer to it yourself."

"Who? Me?" Melody was utterly befuddled, now.

"Cherry, I swear, it seems like he *otter* come. I thunk a fur piece, figuring up that whistle. That there is the most come-hither whistle a man can think up, I do believe."

"Is it?" Cherry looked him square in the eye, and whistled it at him.

The doggonedest thing of all happened then. Harry Henshaw came up and stood nearby, looking self-conscious.

Center Point Publishing
600 Brooks Road • PO Box 1
Thorndike ME 04986-0001 USA

(207) 568-3717

US & Canada:
1 800 929-9108